DEAD
BALL

Barry Cork

DEAD BALL

CHARLES SCRIBNER'S SONS
New York

Charles Scribner's Sons
Macmillan Publishing Company
866 Third Avenue, New York, NY 10022

Library of Congress Cataloging-in-Publication Data
Cork, Barry.
    Dead ball.
    I. Title.
PR6053.0687D4   1989   823'.914   88-30567
ISBN 0-684-19044-3

10 9 8 7 6 5 4 3 2 1

Printed in the United States of America

For Margaret

CHAPTER 1

If the Committee considers that for any reason the course is not in playable condition . . . it may order a suspension of play . . .

Rule 33 (d)

I never had much luck with leave. The mere fact that my time was my own always seemed to upset the general order of things, not just for myself but for everyone else as well. If the weather wasn't foul there were strikes at ports and airline terminals, and if it was good I had hay fever. This time I'd done no more than promise myself some golf, and that morning, looking out of the big window in the clubhouse bar it really looked as though I was going to get it. The early rain had done little more than lay the dust and now the morning had that new-washed look with only the odd patch of cloud pushing its way across the sky. A tractor with the gang mower thumped its way across the nearest fairway and the groundsman's latest assistant raked over a bunker in preparation for the first hacker of the day. No wind and not a trolley-track on the dew. God was well and truly in business up there in the great Pro's shop in the sky.

Charles said, 'Coffee's up.'

He was right, I could hear the Cona making reassuring glugging noises at the end of the bar. We both knew it wasted time but we liked a cup before we teed off. Freddy, the steward, went over to pour but the phone rang and he went back to his little butler's pantry to answer it. I heard him say, 'Harlington Golf Club,' and then, 'Just a minute,' and my heart sank.

'It's for you, sir.'

He didn't have to say that because I'd guessed it already. Seek not to know for whom the phone rings, it rings for thee. This time the voice inside the plastic said, 'Inspector Straun?'

'Yes, Oakes. What's the trouble?' I could always recognize my desk sergeant's voice and found it rather irritating that he never knew mine. Or perhaps he did but thought it polite to ask.

'The Chief Constable was trying to get hold of you, sir. Left a message. He'd be glad if you'd go to the Royal West Wessex right away. The secretary will be expecting you.'

Colonel Giles Linforth, the CC, was a deity somewhat out of my class in the Force and I wondered why I should have been so honoured.

'You let it be known that I was on leave, I suppose?'

Sergeant Oakes was a dour man but I sensed his distant smile. 'Yes, sir. He said that as they play golf at the West Wessex you probably wouldn't count it as a duty.' When I didn't say anything he added, 'I think he was making a joke, sir.'

'Thank you, Sergeant Oakes,' I said, 'I'm glad you told me.'

I suppose it was by way of being fair comment. I'd played a lot of golf in my early twenties, well enough to get into the Open as an amateur on one never to be forgotten occasion and still be playing on the penultimate day. Had a few things turned out differently in my personal relationships I think I might have taken a chance and turned professional, but they didn't and I ended up as a policeman instead, by no means a bad life, save for now and again. But just the same I wondered exactly what kind of embarrassment could have befallen the Royal West Wessex that they should have called in Giles Linforth and that he, in his turn, should have summoned me. He was, of course, a member of that august institution. That would explain a lot.

I made my apologies to Charles and drove over to West Thorning, conscious that my leave was beginning to run true to form. But it wasn't all bad. The road ahead was clear, the trees had a good late summer look to them and I managed to convince myself that even if I was going to miss my game today the chances were that I'd be all right tomorrow. A white Porsche came up behind me and passed at startling speed, but I watched him go benignly. Someone would pick him up sooner or later and it didn't have to be an Inspector on leave. I turned left at the end of the Ridgeway, following the 'RWW Golf Club' signposts which today were accompanied by a green and yellow arrow that bore the words, 'Tamworth Classic' and the Greek *tau* that was the company's logo. Tamworth Electronics were now in golf promotion and their sign was big in the land.

I saw their sign over the Club's entrance when I got there, and a good many places besides, while the big space next to the practice ground was already littered with the component parts of the marquees that in another week would become a tented village of the shops, bars, banks and telephone terminals that these days are part and parcel of the major golf tournaments. I reflected that, thanks largely to television coverage, modern golf is very big business indeed and I was glad that the Club had landed this particular shindig because I suspected that, old and respected though it undoubtedly was, it rather desperately needed the money.

'Inspector Straun?' Awaiting me in the car park was a tall, dark-haired, competent-looking girl with hazel eyes who seemed used to putting strangers at ease.

'Yes,' I said, 'but what makes you so sure?'

She smiled faintly. 'I was told to look out for a Maserati. My name's Polly Appleby, by the way. Mr Thurston's expecting you on the ninth green.'

'I'll get over there, then.' Policemen, especially golfing policemen, tend to know everyone in a rural community. Not being a member of his circle, I was not what one would describe as matey with Alan Thurston, but I liked him well enough, a good secretary in the classic tradition of well-weathered empire builder. Alan had spent most of his service life in the Middle East and had the slightly dehydrated look that sometimes goes with that kind of climate, but that was as far as the ex-colonial image went because he was flexible enough and by repute a remarkably good organizer.

The Appleby girl said in parting, 'Mr Kempton will probably be here after lunch.' And, presumably to save me the obvious question, 'He's Tamworth's Media Director.'

'Do I want to see him?'

She said enigmatically, 'I don't know. He might want to see you.'

Might he now? I did my best to look as though I'd make my mind up about that later and went on past the clubhouse towards the ninth green. Non-member I might be, but I knew the place well enough and it was startling to find its usual immaculate order reduced to a shambles as a scaffolding company laboured to put up spectators' stands. Electricity cables snaked everywhere and the air was full of the steady crash of metal as endless construction pipes were heaved off the backs of lorries and I guessed that within a day or two there would be TV gantries as well, towering over the lot. It was no sight to cheer the old guard but it brought the money in and these days that was what mattered.

''Morning, Angus—good of you to come.' Alan Thurston in one of those extraordinary checked jackets that some people can get away with, all vents and a sort of skirt.

'I wouldn't have disappointed you,' I assured him. 'Not with the Chief Constable leaning on me, I wouldn't.'

He cleared his throat, a trick that came with the cavalry jacket. 'Sorry about that, but Linforth—' He broke off, presumably taking in my clothes. 'You were coming here anyway?'

I said no, it was to have been nine o'clock off at Harlington, actually.

'Well, I'm damn sorry, Angus, but there you are. Have a look at that green over there.'

There was a Telecom van in the way, so I walked round it and looked down at the wide eighteenth, steep banked on three sides and known as 'Wembley' by members, some of whom criticized it as being too easy an ending to what otherwise was quite a tricky hole. Mind you, if you could go through the green you'd probably go through the bar window as well, so you can't have everything.

'Not that one,' Thurston was saying, 'you know where the ninth is.'

For the moment I'd forgotten. At the Royal West Wessex the turn was about yards short of the final hole, hidden by the raised first tee. It was a small, square green that, through some mystery of natural drainage, had never flooded during wet weather and even in the hottest summer had never been known to go brown. We walked over the first tee and looked down.

'Bloody hell!' I said.

Someone had taken a plough, or something very like it, and cut a large Tamworth *tau*, like a rough italic 'T', from side to side across the sacred surface of the ninth green.

'Exactly.' Thurston thrust his hands deep into the pockets of that ridiculous jacket and jingled keys. 'We've five days before the first round. It's not exactly what one would wish for, is it?'

I ignored the understatement. 'What does Hoskins say about it?' I asked. 'Can he do anything?' Sam Hoskins was head greenkeeper and had been with the Club man and boy, one of those.

Thurston said moodily, 'Oh, he'll be able to make it *look* all right. He's had a sacrificial green behind his sheds for the last couple of years so he'll splice in new turf well enough. Have to shift the pin, of course, and whether the new stuff will stand up to all those feet pounding about on it's another matter. No time to bed down, y'see.' He looked at me for the first time with his rather fierce blue eyes. 'Look, Angus, this is appalling but we can cope—just. But if the same thing happens again we'll be done for.'

I stared down at that ghastly travesty of the Tamworth company logo, a torn brown scar against flawless green, and tried to imagine the financial implications of calling off a major sporting event. What with television rights, a hundred thousand spectators at ten pounds a head, the rental from commercial concessions and God knows how many other less obvious spin-offs, it was no wonder that clubs with championship class courses fought hard and bitterly for the right to stage the big name matches. The West Wessex had been lucky this year, and if the Tamworth Classic went off well the event was likely to prove a useful financial shot in the arm. On the other hand, a positively frightening amount of money had to be laid out before any came in. Call off the tournament and you could just about call in the broker's men.

'Leave it to me,' I told him. 'I'll see what I can find out.'

'Could you organize some sort of police guard?' Thurston gestured towards the vandalized green. 'There are another seventeen of those. What we need is a twenty-four-hour patrol.'

'Well—' I said without any particular enthusiasm. I could see Thurston's point, but policemen come expensive these days and I didn't feel this was quite the moment to break the news that if he wanted that kind of protection the Club could very well find itself landed with the overtime bill.

'Have you any idea who might have done this?' Thurston had got around to the question I'd been expecting from the start. 'Some sort of madman, I suppose. One of those long-haired—'

I said gently, 'I really think it would be better if I looked around before I said anything.'

'Of course, my dear chap. Do your best. Damned swine—'

Well, I couldn't blame him and on the whole he was taking it very well. 'By the way,' I said, 'there was a Miss Appleby who met me in the car park. Part of your staff?'

'Good God, no!' Retired Africa hand, looking quite shocked. 'She looks after Tamworth's public relations, I believe. Until some fellow called Kempton gets down, she seems to handle most things for them.'

She seemed the kind of person I needed, so I went into the clubhouse and ran Ms Appleby to earth, sitting at a card table in a corner of the dining-room.

'I'm supposed to be having a small tent, only it hasn't come yet.' She didn't seem surprised to see me.

'Look,' I said, 'I need your help. Presumably you've been looking after your company's mail since you've been here?'

'Yes, I have.'

'Anything abusive, threatening—that kind of thing?'

12

She shook her head. 'Nothing at all.' Her eyes widened suddenly. 'Well—oh no, it couldn't be—'

'What couldn't be?'

'Well, I did get one dotty letter from some kind of feminist group accusing Tamworth of encouraging male athletes at the expense of females or something. One gets a fair number of protest letters these days and I'm afraid I just threw it away.'

I said, 'That's all right. You don't remember what the group called itself, by any chance? The letter-heading?'

'I think it was another Greek letter of some sort, rather like our own.' She frowned, concentrating. 'I can't honestly remember which one. Gamma? Pi?'

'Epsilon?'

She looked up quickly. 'Yes, it was! But why epsilon, for goodness sake?'

'You may well ask,' I agreed. 'E for Eve, I suppose. I don't imagine it's anything very profound.'

She flicked me a quick smile, nothing to it and not even consciously disarming, but nice to see on an unpromising morning just the same. 'I gather you know them.'

'Yes,' I confessed, 'we have met. It looks as though it's time we did it again.'

April Tonge lived in an olde worlde cottage at a village called Langham, about ten miles away, and I took myself there without any undue hanging about. Miss Tonge's contribution to the battle of the sexes had come to my attention once or twice before, but neither she nor her group of fellow enthusiasts had ever done much more than cause the odd obstruction. True, they sometimes picketed the local rugger club but there, God knows, they usually got as much as they gave. In fairness, they had never tried their hand at hacking up golf greens before, but there's a first time for everything, including murder.

'It's Inspector Straun, isn't it?' In front of her old hay loft when I arrived, doing something vague with a broom. She was a faded, blonde woman in her fifties, with a weakness for flowered dresses and straw hats that should have been cheerful but somehow contrived to be rather sad. She had pale blue, rather fanatical eyes, but up till now I had not thought of her as any dottier than most of her kind.

'Yes, that's right,' I said and looked around. Seeing it again after quite a time, Rose Cottage was bigger than I'd remembered, with a modern metal barn close against one side, and while I was looking a girl came out of it and pushed the door closed behind her. She appeared to be in her early twenties, wearing a blue checked shirt and jeans, which was to be expected. Coffee-coloured skin, black hair, huge eyes, which wasn't. Egyptian—Greek—it has hard to say. I took my eyes off her and went back to where I'd started. 'Miss Tonge, I wonder if I might have a word with you?'

'You may say anything you like in front of my friend.'

Her voice was curiously light, almost like a child's. 'In fact, I insist on a witness. In any case, I wish to protest against your being here. Surely I am entitled to be questioned by a woman officer?'

'No,' I said, 'you're not. And who said anything about questioning?'

Someone moved behind me, a second girl, English this time and rather spotty, dressed in something long and drab. Different again from the dark girl and more my idea of the kind of weirdo that April Tonge gathered about her at Rose Cottage. Incidentally, judging from a roughly painted notice on the gate it wasn't Rose Cottage any more. Epsilon House it was now. Well really.

'You can stand over there and keep quiet,' I said to Spotty. Then, 'I must ask you, madam, if you have any knowledge of an act of wilful damage at the Royal West Wessex Golf Club that occurred last night?' My formal bit which impressed some, but not others.

She sort of simpered, enormously pleased with herself. 'That whole ridiculous tournament is totally male orientated. If someone has thought fit to make a protest the organizers have only themselves to blame.'

'Quite so,' I agreed, 'but that doesn't answer my question.'

14

Those pale, slightly deranged eyes looking up into mine were curiously unnerving. 'If you think I have done something wrong, isn't it up to you to prove it?'

I thought of the casual violation of old Sam Hoskins's life work and wished that I hadn't. If a law is broken a policeman shouldn't concern himself over which one it happens to be, but of course they do and I was well aware that I had a personal thing about vandals. Thieving I can take and a certain amount of the more basic violence because man is a predatory animal and we all do things we regret when the blood is hot. But something about the sheer mindless, pointless obscenity of vandalism bothers me. Should a copper hate sin? I don't know, but it helps, I suppose. Anyway, I said, 'Don't play pussy with me, Miss Tonge. Did you or didn't you?'

'I refuse to answer.' She was pale, just the same. Didn't blame her either, poor silly old bitch, and I wondered what nastiness she'd seen in my eyes. I should have been ashamed of myself but wasn't. 'I'll have a look in that shed,' I told her.

Standing in front of it, the dark girl in jeans said, 'No.'

Her eyes were not at all like April Tonge's, nor were those of Spotty, come to that. Real hatred, wordless and bare, crisping like a flame. Miss Tonge was dotty and a nuisance but when the chips were down I rated her kind as harmless enough. It was hard to see what the silly old bat and her pupils had in common.

I said, 'Stand aside.'

'Do you have a search warrant?'

'No,' I said, 'I do not have a search warrant.' I pushed back the bolt of the big door and hauled it open. At first it seemed that there was little inside apart from a few sacks and a pile of logs, but when my eyes got used to the gloom I could see something that stuck out from behind some stacked apple boxes. It turned out to be the kind of petrol-driven toy plough that stockbrokers keep in their weekend cottages in case their wives feel an urge to return to the soil. I looked at Miss Tonge. 'Going back to the land?'

I wheeled the thing to the back of my car and with some

15

difficulty dropped it sideways into the boot, because it was surprisingly heavy.

Spotty spoke for the first time. 'You've no right to do that!' An expensive voice, but then so many of the really rabid protesters have.

'It will be returned in due course,' I told her.

'But I can't see what possible sort of evidence it can be. I mean, every farmer in the county has a plough!'

I said patiently, 'And every plough has dried earth from the fields on its share.'

April Tonge shrugged her thin shoulders. 'Well, what of it?'

'A golf green is so highly cultivated with carbons and phosphates and heaven knows what, that it's a wonder it doesn't glow in the dark,' I told her. 'That's why I propose giving your little plough a going-over in the lab. If the result is positive—' All at once I felt a sudden revulsion for the whole thing. 'If the result is positive I must warn you that a charge will almost certainly be brought against you.'

'Pig!' said the girl from Roedean suddenly. 'Rotten, fucking PIG!'

As I got behind the wheel I had a last look at the three of them. Spotty mouthing ruderies, poor April fluttering, the dark girl just looking. Nobody in their right mind would have described them as a particularly lovable trio, but I knew which one I wouldn't want to meet in the dark.

CHAPTER 2

An 'outside agency' is an agency not part of the match and includes a referee, marker, an observer or forecaddie.
Definition

I considered giving the office a miss but Harlington was only five miles from Epsilon House and, leave or no leave, I knew I'd have to check in sooner or later. Once there I got the Chief Constable on the phone and made reassuring noises while I filled him in with developments.

'You're quite sure about April?' April? I was surprised that he'd even heard of her but the landed classes are a devious lot.

'Well, sir,' I said cautiously, 'lightning rarely strikes the same place twice.'

'Doesn't it?' He was all for locking her up and throwing away the key.

'Not in my experience.' This being technically my own time, I felt I didn't have to put up with too much, but so as not to show ill feelings I added, 'As she's more or less admitted to last night's lark, she'd really be risking her neck if she tried it again. And in any case we haven't much choice. Not strong enough grounds for holding her, you see.'

'I suppose not.' The voice sounded wistful. 'How's Thurston taking it?'

'He's naturally upset,' I told him, 'but I gather the damage can be made good. Incidentally, he was asking about night-time police patrolling of the course.' What with being all good golf chums together, I could see myself getting well and truly stuck with this one.

'That's not possible, is it?'

'No, sir, it isn't. Quite out of the question.' It wasn't Linforth's decision anyway, but I guessed he wanted to get the facts right in case someone at the Club asked him. I went on, 'McHugh of Traffic was telling me they're having trouble enough getting personnel to cope with spectators' cars as it is—Division would simply laugh at us if we said we needed another couple of dozen men just to walk round a golf course all night.'

'And of course there's no chance from local resources.'

'No, sir, not a hope.' I almost added that there wasn't any point, either. I felt sorry for Alan Thurston, because nobody likes having a golf course chopped up just before an important event, but things could undoubtedly have been worse and it wasn't as though someone had shot the Open champion in the locker room. And in the unlikely event of such a thing happening, I thought bleakly, it was a certainty that an administrative genius like Inspector Straun wouldn't be allowed within miles of the case.

The Chief Constable seemed to have sensed the drift of my thoughts because he suddenly said heartily, 'Well, just keep Thurston happy, there's a good chap. Suggest he gets members to night patrol the greens themselves if he's so sure it's necessary.'

'Yes, sir,' I agreed. 'I'm sure he'd consider that,' and got off the phone with mixed feelings. In principle I was not all that keen on private armies but on this occasion there didn't seem any great harm in letting the public discover what it felt like to produce a task force for themselves, so I rang Thurston and did my stuff. He wasn't exactly overjoyed at the news but there wasn't much he could do about it either, so I promised to drop in on him later to see how things were getting on. Oakes put his head round the door to say it was nearly one and could he get me a sandwich.

'No, damn it,' I told him, 'I didn't take a couple of weeks' leave just so that I could go on eating filthy cheese sandwiches from the canteen.'

'Just as you like, sir.' He was an unruffled lad who had decided to take me under his wing. 'You'll be going home?'

'Don't ring me, Sergeant Oakes, I'll ring you.'

He was right, of course. If I'd gone back to Harlington I could probably have picked up a game, but the good early morning feel had gone and anyway I was now committed to going back to the West Wessex later. Right again, Sergeant Oakes, home it shall be.

It wasn't home as it had once been, but I was getting into the habit of telling myself that it was really a good deal better. After the divorce we'd got rid of the house and split what was left after paying back the mortgage. Angela and Sam had gone to live with her mother in Dorset and I'd bought the smallest flat out of the four that had been carved out of a miniature manor house situated a bare four miles from the nick at a hamlet called Staples Cross. As I swung the Maserati's sleek nose through the gates I got a sudden vista of the grey stone house standing there with its background of oaks, the half-circle of sand-coloured drive and the lilac drooping in front of the toy orangery, I felt grateful for the fact that I'd paid for my bit of it. I also thought with satisfaction that Angela would have hated it. I missed Sam, though.

The postman had called while I'd been out and I carried his offerings into the kitchen while I made myself an omelette. There were a couple of envelopes assuring me that I had won a valuable prize, my telephone bill and a letter from a girl called Laurie Wilson announcing her intention to visit an elderly client in the Harlington area. As she despaired of my ability to reach London, perhaps she could kill two clients with one stone and see me too? No excuses, please, as there were some urgent literary items she wanted to discuss. The date she gave was later in the week.

I was conscious of being pressurized, but there seemed little I could do about it, Laurie Wilson being my literary agent. Only a few weeks earlier I'd have laughed at the idea that the part-time author of a single book—even an unexpectedly successful one—had need of a professional representative. But my publisher had thought otherwise.

'My dear chap, you don't want to fool around with royalties and paperback rights and foreign sales and all that sort of thing. It's just paper work and dreadfully dull.'

I'd said that I was very good at paper work, and that there were times when it seemed I'd never done anything else.

'Then it's high time you had a change.' He'd obviously met the likes of me before. 'Besides, we publishers *prefer* to deal with agents. Look, I'm going to put you in touch with a nice girl called Laurie Wilson. She's a partner in T. J. Cozens and she'll make sure that people like me don't put one over on people like you.'

'All right, if you think it's a good idea.'

Lots of boyish smile. 'I absolutely insist.'

So I'd gone along to Miss Wilson of T. J. Cozens and in spite of myself I'd been impressed. If she was representative of her breed, literary agents appeared to be young, highly attractive and comprehensively knowledgeable in a world I was going to have to live with. Taken all round, I'd decided that the learning process was going to be rather more enjoyable than I'd supposed, although standing there with her letter in my hand I wished she could have chosen a different week to go visiting. I made a note to ring Miss Wilson during the afternoon, which wasn't strictly necessary because I wasn't likely to forget.

My omelette was a good deal better than Angela would have made but I dumped it in the bin half finished and went over to the window-seat that overlooked the dozen or so oaks that lined the drive to the entrance gate. Ramases appeared from somewhere and jumped on my lap. Like all Abyssinians, he was a cat who communicated by chirruping and he made what sounded like a complimentary comment as he stared with pale golden eyes at the Maserati in the shadow of the lilac tree.

'You're right,' I told him, 'worth every penny.'

My bank manager had been visibly upset when I'd blown most of the first quick wash of royalties on four wheels and an engine instead of investing in one of his unit trusts.

'Money makes money, Mr Straun. Capital sums are usually regarded as investment potential, you know.'

I'd known all right. I'd thought of the time I'd spent with the Force, doing a job I didn't like. I'd hung on to it because of Sam and Angela and the mortgage, and even though the latter wasn't so much of a problem any more there was still a family to support. Maybe if this second book went as well as the first, I'd take a chance at resigning from the Force and write full time. Meanwhile the Maserati was well worth the staggering bills the local agents seemed to send in every other month.

'It's just a crutch to your ego, Angus—an extra penis, and a damned expensive one at that!'

Thus Sammy Wilshire at the Club, shortly after I'd got the thing. Well, Sammy was a shrink by profession so he probably knew, but so far as I was concerned that thing down there on the drive was the best fun I'd known in years. Good enough to make me forget sometimes that according to the doctors Angus Straun would have to remain a thirty-six-year-old desk-bound copper till the end of his days.

I wondered what to do with the afternoon. I knew I could go back to Harlington, but by this time Charles would have finished a round with someone else and gone back to the solicitor's office where by rights he should have been anyway. Not that Charles was indispensable, because at this time of year there was nearly always someone at a loose end and glad of a partner. But my eye caught sight of the desk and typewriter over in the corner and I dropped Ramases and stood up. A desk being a desk, I wondered briefly if writing for a living would prove much of an improvement on the Force after all. I ran my finger over the ancient crossbow I'd hung on the wall to remind me that I was supposed to be a writer deeply rooted in the past or whatever it was the critics had said. The crossbow had never gripped my imagination as the longbow had done but this was a lovely weapon and still lethal, the quiver of nine-inch bolts probably still capable of drilling a couple of inches of wood. For a moment I thought of taking it outside and trying it out but reminded myself that writers had to write before they could play. I wound a sheet of paper into the roller of the typewriter and prepared to be creative.

Taken all round, I'd have done better to stick to golf because after two hours I'd not produced more than a couple of hundred words. I fooled around for a bit longer, then reminded myself that I'd promised to make a final call at the West Wessex before the day was over. I gave Ramases his Gourmet Dinner and abandoned the literary life until tomorrow. Did Tolstoy feel relief when he knocked off in the middle of *War and Peace*? I didn't know. I did know he didn't have to do it for the money.

It was about six o'clock before I got back to the Club, at what on an ordinary evening would have been a kind of between time, a lull that bridged the departure of the afternoon players and the arrival of the 'snatch a sandwich and get a round in while the light lasts' brigade. As I'd expected, the Tamworth Classic had changed all that, and the car park was three-quarters full with a haphazard mix of cars and vans, some of the stuffier members looking somewhat askance at the peasants who were getting in their way with scaffold piping and assorted bits of tent. Even Raikes, the bar steward, seemed to have entered into the spirit of the thing and was leaving his rather extrovert cross-country Yamaha bike alongside the secretarial Rover, which I suspected West Wessex members would not have considered quite the thing. Raikes was a somewhat over-weight thirty-five, apparently something of a fixture because I'd played the course as a guest for a number of years and he'd been around for certainly as long as I could remember. All the same, I'd never pictured him as a Rally Cross competitor, but I was in no position to judge people by their transport. God knows, I'd have looked pretty odd driving in the Mille Miglia.

Raikes caught my eye and gave me a jaunty grin.

''Evening, Inspector!'

I inclined my head gravely. ''Evening, Raikes.' I was never 'Inspector' in my club or anyone else's, as well he knew. Cocky little sod. I skirted the clubhouse and pushed open the door of the secretary's office, wondering aloud how it was that tradition decreed club bars should always be managed by stewards who were either overtly obsequious or tiresomely familiar. Why not employ girls for a change? Well, why not?

'Because members would feel inhibited, you ass,' Alan Thurston said. 'I mean, they'd have to watch their language if there was a woman behind the bar.'

I said, 'You mean they fine each other for swearing in the Coach and Horses?'

'No, but this isn't a pub.' Alan was still at his desk, looking very much the man at the centre of things. I guessed that he must have been there for the past twelve hours or so but he still looked well pressed and competent. As an afterthought he added, 'Anyway, the lady members wouldn't like it. Not that they'll be all that enthusiastic about their husbands patrolling the course all night either, come to that.'

'You'll just have to tell them that they come cheaper than policemen.' Jim Tollier of Manning 'D' had put in his own suggestion over the phone that morning. 'They could always put militant pickets on the holes, then they'd get us on the rates!' but I decided against passing it on.

Thurston was doodling matchstick men on his notepad. 'I've managed to round up a dozen members for tonight. If they patrol in pairs they should be able to look after three holes apiece.'

Three four-hundred-yard holes worked out at roughly three-quarters of a mile, which struck me as a long way to run if you happened to be standing on the first green at the moment when someone started to dig up the third. Except, of course, that Thurston would have allowed for some of the holes running parallel with each other. I began to understand how it was that with people like him we had managed to run an empire. I said, 'I hope they're not carrying twelve-bores or anything like that. You may not be able to afford our services but strong-arm stuff is supposed to be the prerogative of the police.'

He gave me a chilly empire builder's smile. 'You have my word that there isn't a firearm among the lot of them. You might find the odd eight iron here and there, but being golfers to a man—'

'Well, just so long as they remember the law allows a reasonable amount of violence in defence of the person,' I reminded him. 'If they catch anyone fooling around with the greens, your chaps are not to beat hell out of him before handing him over.'

'They understand.' Thurston thumbed tobacco into his Sanders of the River pipe. 'Damn it, Angus, they're chaps you've known for years. You don't have to get officious on us.'

'You don't have to have me at all, if you feel I'm prejudiced in any way,' I told him. 'Only if you're going to object, get on with it and let me carry on with my leave.'

'Didn't mean you were prejudiced.' Thurston fiddled with a paperclip. 'Sorry about your leave. Didn't know you were having some time off.'

Somebody went past the window saying, 'There was this chap on his way home from St Andrews. He hadn't hit a decent ball all week and when his train was in the middle

23

of the Forth Bridge he opened the window and chucked his clubs out—bang down into the Firth of Clyde—'

I said, 'Coming home from St Andrews you don't go over the Clyde.'

'Depends where you live, I suppose.' Thurston looked as though he was trying to remember the map of Scotland. 'I gather you haven't any idea who was responsible for that business last night?'

'Suspicions, but no proof.'

'Your lips are sealed, I suppose?' He could only have got that from a book, but I couldn't imagine which one.

'I'm afraid so.' Poor sad April had as good as admitted it was one of her lunatic brood who'd done the damage, but I didn't want to go into that. 'Look,' I said, 'I'm virtually certain that what happened last night was just an isolated occurrence. I've spoken to the suspects and they know there's a charge in the offing. In the circumstances they'd never contemplate a second go.'

'You may be right.' Thurston didn't sound convinced. 'Anyway, I've laid on the troops for tonight. Hang about a while and you can inspect them if you like.' He added, 'By the way, I've arranged an honorary membership for you during the Classic.'

I had a sensation of being leaned on but it was in a nice way. 'That's extraordinarily kind of you.'

Thurston grinned. 'Well, it makes sure you buy your share at the bar. And it may encourage you to be around.'

I said truthfully, 'I'd hoped to be around, anyway. It's not often one gets a major tournament on one's doorstep.'

'That's true.' Thurston looked at me curiously. 'None of my business, Angus, but why aren't you a member anyway? You must know more people here than you do at Harlington.'

In a way that was the trouble. Originally I'd joined Harlington because it was cheap and people went there to play golf rather than prop up the bar. Now I could afford it, the West Wessex still struck me as being rather heavily social, and whether one likes it or not there are certain difficulties about being a policeman off duty. We may not get the downright hostility offered to income tax officials but it's disconcerting to discover how many apparently God-fearing and honest citizens look vaguely uncomfortable when they look round and find you standing next to them at a bar.

'You know how it is,' I said, 'one gets used to a place and I don't get much time for social life.' I couldn't very well plead poverty with that ruddy car standing outside.

Thurston nodded. 'I know. Might do you good to have a change, though. Anyway, come along and have a drink while you're here. Ambrose Hall was asking after you earlier —I gather you're old friends.'

'We were at school together.'

'And old opponents, of course.'

'On and off.' I followed him out of his office and through the clubhouse into the bar, a journey which explained why members of lesser clubs always felt like poor relations. The main building had been put up just prior to the First World War and it had gone up, as the saying goes, regardless of cost. The last seventy-five years had served to bring in an enormous amount of silver, a good many quite respectable paintings and the panelling from a particularly wealthy member's yacht.

'Angus, my dear fellow.' He'd put on a bit of weight, had Ambrose, but his eyes were still very bright blue and the rather tousled fair hair still gave him the air of boyish charm that had so captivated people when he'd won the Open seven or eight years ago. He was a television personality now, one of the great commentators of the game and probably a very wealthy man. But I remembered beating him in the third round of the Amateur a few years before that, so I didn't feel too cast down.

'Hello, Ambrose, it's good to see you,' I said, and it truly was. He loved being rich and famous and unless he'd changed considerably the chances were that he'd patronize me till I wanted to kick his teeth in, but I liked the man none the less. I added for good measure, 'I saw in the papers you were covering the Classic for ITV.'

'Someone's got to pay for my fun.' Ambrose grinned expansively. 'What are you drinking?'

'Bitters and soda.' It was only a week since yet another senior policeman had gone off the road smashed out of his mind and we were getting a bit sensitive about the whole thing.

'Soda and bitters and a pink gin for Mr Secretary, please, Raikes.' Some people would have been unable to resist a comment but there was none forthcoming, which was a plus to Ambrose. He turned back to me. 'You're looking well, Angus. How's the arm?'

'It's fine.' Well, as fine as it would ever be, considering that I couldn't shift it through much more than ninety degrees, but I wished he'd left it alone because I thought about it often enough without being reminded. Surprising after all this time how exactly I could remember how that balaclava-masked figure had looked as he'd jumped away from the bank counter, the sawn-off shotgun swinging to meet me and the shock of the point blank load of No. 6 shot that had thrown me half way back to the door and programmed me for a desk job from then on. But none of that was Ambrose's fault, so I added, 'I can't say it's left me with much of a swing.'

'What do you play to these days?'

'Six.'

He nodded. 'About my mark—it's our age, laddie, you don't want to let it get you down.' He put a hand on my shoulder and led me up to the bar. 'Come and meet some of the boys.'

The boys had been standing with their backs to us, drinking quietly among themselves, but they turned round and made social noises as though they were trained seals. Ambrose had that effect on people. To those who didn't know otherwise, it could have been easy to dismiss this as an instance of three show-business professionals reacting on cue to a master of the media, but these three were not dependent on Ambrose Hall or anyone else. Half of me listened to the introductions, but they weren't really necessary—anyone who knew a golf club from a hockey stick would have recognized these people.

'Don Shroeder—Bill Sadiq—Omi Kawasaki—' Ambrose was saying. Then, to the obvious veteran of the three, 'You won't remember that far back, but in my last year as an amateur Angus here knocked me out in the second round—'

Shroeder said amiably, 'Too right, I remember. Like I remember Vardon and gutty balls and hickory shafts. When you get to my age you've seen *everything*.'

He was one of those lean, sandy-haired, leathery Australians from the outback, a laconic, amiable millionaire who'd been a favourite of the circuits for more than twenty years, and in his case the public seemed to have got it right because it was extraordinarily difficult not to like him on sight—or his companions, for that matter. Bill Sadiq was a slim, good-looking young African who'd been born the son of a taxi-driver in Kariba. Sadiq senior had been killed in some kind of civil disturbance, leaving his son with no money but, of all things, a huge talent for golf, which he had taken to the United States, where people appreciated such things. It was widely forecast that if anyone toppled Don Shroeder, short of shooting him, it would be Sadiq. The Japanese, a champion in the East, turned out to be an affable kind of chap too, as slick and crease-resistant as a stackable sound system.

We drank and talked about this and that until finally Ambrose announced that he was going to spend twenty minutes on the putting green. I didn't have the same compulsion and was rather enjoying listening to Shroeder describing the pitfalls of piloting one's own jet across the Atlantic for the first time. And why did Ambrose have to polish up his short game in order to do a TV commentary? Well, I hadn't seen him since heaven knows when so I hung around while he found the necessary tools from somewhere and I joined him pushing balls about the green. There was no one else about, which, considering the amount of work still to be done, was hardly surprising.

'What did you think of our high flyer from the Third World?' Ambrose asked as he lined up a ball.

I said I'd been rather impressed by his American accent.

'He's been working hard at it—he's a hungry lad.' There are hungry golf players just as there are hungry fighters, and the really competitive ones go on being hungry even when they've got a million in the bank. Ambrose sank a long putt and followed it up with two more. He said, 'Bill's the most efficient golfing machine to appear for a generation, with the temperament to go with it. Four years ago he was a caddie at a beach club course in Kariba, and this year he's made the best part of half a million dollars.'

'And now he can't wait to collect this jackpot as well.' Well, that was what it was all about and better than playing for a couple of new balls, after all.

'I don't know about that.' Ambrose tapped a ball and stared after it fixedly, as though he expected it to change its course and colour. 'He's won his last four tournaments against Don and there's talk of him making the grand slam. But Don's record in this country is fantastic. He knows all the championship courses like the back of his hand and he's lucky here into the bargain. Between you and me, if this event was one that got rained off, I don't think Bill Sadiq would weep any particularly bitter tears.'

'And, of course, Don Shroeder knows this.'

Ambrose raised his eyes to mine. 'I expect so. But my guess is that he'd be glad of an out too. He's thinking of retiring and he wouldn't be human if he didn't want to go out on a win. On the other hand, his back's giving him hell and he's so doped on painkillers that you can see the poor devil sweating when he swings.'

I said, 'Come off it, Ambrose. You can't tell me that if he ducks out of this one the finance company are going to repossess the jet.'

'Hardly,' Ambrose agreed. 'But you know how it is—he won his first big ones over here and I think he'd like to end up here still looking good.'

If I had a quarter of Shroeder's money I knew I'd be quite happy watching the Tamworth on TV, but of course that was why he was a millionaire and I still hadn't paid last year's income tax. And besides, the Australian had been king of the forest for a long time and nobody likes to be pushed aside by some snotty-nosed kid young enough to be his own son. I sank three seven-footers in a row and felt better. 'What about the rest?' I asked. 'Is this going to be strictly a two-horse race or do we expect something from Mr Rising Sun?'

'Or Japan's answer to Lee Trevino.' Ambrose nodded towards the window through which the three players were still grouped round the end of the bar. Bill Sadiq's drink was expanding into brightly coloured balloons that were rising from his glass to pop like soap bubbles or drifting away on currents of warm air. When they reached the ceiling they exploded with a slight *plop*. Omi Kawasaki was watching them with delight and lots of teeth. 'Practical jokes,' Ambrose observed. 'Jokes with everything. *Japanese* jokes with everything. He must be a wonderful chap to have at a party.'

'So I see,' I said.

'You're a member here, I take it?'

'Only honorary.'

'That lark with the green really seems to have given everyone the shakes.' Ambrose kicked his balls together so that they fell into a neat rectangle. 'Still, if you've got the Chief Constable as a member, I suppose they're entitled to an Inspector free.'

'I suppose so.' It wasn't the way I'd have put it, but then I wasn't in the communications business. I went on, 'You know about protests. Now they've had their moment, there won't be any more trouble.'

He stopped in mid stroke. 'From what I hear on the old war drums, this place isn't doing so well it can afford a fiasco with the Tamworth. And there'd be no shortage of vultures to pick over the bones.'

Well, I'd heard a few drums myself, come to that. The Royal West Wessex was an expensive club to run and membership had been falling off to such an extent that the unthinkable had happened and there was no longer a waiting list, prospective members either being put off by high membership fees or simply preferring the new-style country club that was doing thriving business a few miles down the road. 'Vultures?' I said.

'Correct.' Ambrose left a twenty-foot putt just short of the hole and then sank a second shot off it, billiards fashion. 'You must know of a dozen chaps who'd be delighted if this place went up for grabs.'

I looked over his shoulder at a couple of members who were rather pointedly ignoring each other as they chatted with their own friends near the clubhouse entrance. I recognized one as George Dewing, a local contractor and builder, and the other a young councillor named Clive Whitton. A policeman's face shouldn't give anything away, but I suppose Ambrose spent a lot of time interviewing people.

He said mildly, 'Well?'

'As a matter of fact I've spotted two who would fit your argument.'

'Who are they? You don't have to tell me their names.'

I hadn't been going to. 'One's a local builder who'd probably love to cover the course with desirable executive residences.'

'And?'

'The other's a very left-wing county councillor who'd fairly jump at the chance of giving seventy acres of prime land back to the people.'

Ambrose grinned. 'I'm sure you're right. How did your Marxist friend get himself elected to the West Wessex, anyway?'

How indeed? 'You know how it is,' I told him. 'Nobody is going to blackball anyone these days unless they've done something slightly worse than murder. And even then they'd probably be invited to apply again.'

Ambrose putted from three feet and missed. 'It's getting late.' He knocked his balls together and began to gather them up. 'Come inside and I'll buy you dinner.'

Policemen have a built-in resistance to accepting hospitality but I was on leave, and anyway, Ambrose and I had gone to school together, that deep and significant bond. What was even more to the point was that the West Wessex really did serve a very good meal in contrast to the microwave and chips which was all my own club would have had on offer. Besides, food is not all that corrupting for policemen, any more than flowers are for ladies, so I nodded. 'All right, Ambrose, so you shall.'

It had been a long time since I'd spent an evening with the great man and I think I'd forgotten what company he could be. Whereas I had just dabbled on the fringe of the golf scene and cleared out of it early, he had plunged on triumphantly. When he got bored with the jet-setting life-style—or perhaps when Norma, his wife, had—he had got out while still very near the top and devoted himself to the media with which he had always been at home. Success comes easily to some.

But I enjoyed my evening. My host was naturally a good talker and the anecdotes he recounted were of a world I still hankered after from time to time. What was more, he was the kind of person who made the most of what the gods had bestowed—he enjoyed it thoroughly and you had the feeling that it hadn't exactly taken him by surprise. When we said good night he hadn't asked me about my wife and I hadn't mentioned his, but his rather soulful eyes studied me for a few seconds as we parted. 'Angus, I think that did you good.'

'It did,' I admitted. It had been a damn good meal.

'I didn't mean the meal,' Ambrose said. 'For a couple of hours you forgot about being a policeman.'

'I suppose I did.' It was true, though.

'Well, stop fretting about vandals and the like. Nobody's going to blow this bloody place up.'

He was right, of course, and I should have admitted it all along instead of fretting like an old woman, but then that was what came of being locked up in an office since God knows when. The best of luck to you, Ambrose, my good mentor, and thank you.

I went out and stood by the first tee, looking out along the fairway. It was almost dark and the first stars were out in a clear sky, the old moon a silver crescent. There were still lights on here and there among the huge marquees of the tented village and people milling around the car park,

31

but I guessed that would go on for a good time yet. I went to my own car and bumped into Alan Thurston, who had the PRO girl, Polly Appleby, in tow.

'Angus, you go home by way of Fenfield, don't you?'

I said yes, surprised that he knew.

'Could you give Miss Appleby here a lift? She's staying at the Bell and her car's playing up.'

'Of course.' And to the engaging Miss Appleby, 'Hop in.'

Alan nodded back along the way I'd come. 'Been inspecting the vigilantes?'

I shook my head. To tell the truth, I'd forgotten all about Thurston's private army.

'They went off as soon as it got dark.' He seemed to sense that I thought his members' patrol was a waste of time but he went on doggedly, 'I thought you might like to have a look at them.'

It would have been more honest to say that I didn't particularly want to go wandering round a golf course at ten o'clock at night just to see a kind of Dad's Army doing sentry go, but being entirely honest to one's friends is a perilous business and, craven lackey that I was, I kept reminding myself that sooner or later the Chief Constable was going to ask me how they'd looked. 'I'll stop at the Fenfield crossroads on the way home,' I told him, 'I can nip across to the sixth from there.'

'You could probably see how they're covering the fourteenth, too.' Thurston looked pleased. He knew as well as I did that there was a public footpath from the crossroads that cut across both fairways.

I said unkindly, 'You're sure you don't want to come along, too?'

'Oh, I've already seen them off—don't want to make it look as though I'm checking up.' Thurston patted that one back with a flick of his wrist. ''Night, Angus! Miss Appleby!'

'Good night.' I got behind the wheel, conscious that I'd lost that one. Oh well. Fortunately the meal I'd eaten with Ambrose had tended to take the rough edges off the day and I drove to the Fenfield crossroads in a generally relaxed frame of mind. The West Wessex was unlike a lot of the old seaside links courses where you marched more or less straight out for nine holes and then turned round and came back again, the back half side by side with the out. The road to Fenfield didn't run parallel with the Club's boundary, so the crossroads were rather further than one might have expected, but even so it was only minutes before I had the Maserati parked beside a break in the hedge and the sign that said 'Public Footpath'.

I apologized to my passenger. 'I did promise to have a quick look.'

'Of course.' She opened her door. 'I'll come with you if you like.'

Through the hedge then and into the clean smell of fairway already dampened by early dew. You get a curious light in open country when there's little or no moon because the only illumination is the open sky which throws up the tops of trees but leaves pitch black shadows lower down. I've forgotten who designed the West Wessex but whoever it was had a great liking for Scottish pine, which he used as a divider between the two halves. Standing in the middle of the sixth fairway was like standing in a spotlight on some vast stage, with just an impenetrable nothingness on the far side of the footlights. Odd how unexpectedly eerie quite familiar places can be if you sneak up on them at the wrong time. At that moment even mundane things such as the odd unreplaced divot and the quite irrelevant knowledge that this 426-yard hole was a very difficult Par 4 didn't make it any the more homely.

'I saw you having dinner with Ambrose Hall.' My companion retrieved the divot and replaced it, gently treading it in. A well-brought-up girl.

'Yes. Do you know him?'

She shook her head. 'Only since meeting him down here. Is it true that he tried to get into the West Wessex and they blackballed him?'

Police training or not, that stopped me in my tracks all right. 'For God's sake!' I said, 'where did you hear that?'

'Somewhere around the Club. I can't remember who, exactly.'

My client repeated the slander in good faith, m'lud. Unfortunately she cannot remember the source of her information. What extraordinary creatures women were.

'Well, it's not a story I'd spread around, if I were you. True or not.' Really, it was hard to believe. Except that . . . 'Look,' I said, 'you must have got it muddled somewhere. It's not customary for professionals to be members of clubs —except as honorary ones sometimes, when they're about a hundred.'

'I think it was when he was an amateur.' Polly Appleby considered. 'But you're right. Best forget it.'

Like hell I'd forget it. Still. 'We'd better find Thurston's Rangers,' I said. I looked round for them but there wasn't a soul in sight. If the system was working at all there should have been two members patrolling this hole and the next, so we started to walk up the ghostly fairway towards the distant green. It was really quite extraordinarily unpleasant because at that point the fairway was only about fifty yards wide and the unbroken shadows on either side of us seemed full of eyes. I began to appreciate why ladies living alone tended to look under the bed before getting into it themselves, although my lack of ease didn't seem to have communicated itself to my companion. Polly Appleby was walking unconcernedly at my side, humming, and I could have sworn it was not out of bravado.

We walked a couple of hundred yards to the green but it was deserted when we got there, perhaps not surprisingly as I subsequently confirmed that I'd chosen the wrong direction and at that moment the men we were looking for were four hundred and twenty-six yards away on the sixth tee. As it was, I realized what had happened quickly enough, and I was standing admiring the cut of the deserted green when from somewhere beyond it a bike engine barked raucously into life.

I felt slightly sick. Motorcycles and their accompanying moronic teenagers are the bane of a good many golf clubs, the idea of leaving deep tyre scars across close mown greens apparently being irresistible. I grabbed Polly Appleby and pushed her towards the nearest trees. 'Over there! Run!'

She looked at me blankly, surprised and then resentful. No April Tonge, but she knew her rights. She said, 'Now look—'

'Run, damn you!'

She ran.

The sixth green was a small plateau not unlike a boxing ring and I suddenly realized that although I couldn't see the rider because he was in shadow, the chances were that neither could he see me. The exhaust blared louder and there came a faint yelp as the clutch came in and the back tyre gripped. What the devil was I to do? Perhaps it was an obliging devil who touched my foot, because I looked down and saw that I was standing on the sand rake that should have been alongside the nearby bunker. I picked it up and charged up the bank and across the green.

A man pitted empty-handed against a maniac on a motorcycle has frankly very little chance, whereas a chap with a rake is in possession of a very handy weapon, riders having an understandable reluctance to have people jamming broom handles and suchlike through their spokes.

For a split second I saw the machine approaching me head on, its rider a vague, helmeted shape. I must have given him quite a shock, vandal-worthy greens not normally being defended by men whirling long rakes. At any rate he swerved just short of the green, the bike's wheels hurling up turf as the rubber tore into the ground. The unknown rider kicked his mount straight and headed for the tree-lined road at the same moment that I reached his side of the green and fell headlong into the bunker I had forgotten was there.

I lay in the sand looking up at the stars as the bike's engine receded into the distance, fixing things in my mind so that I shouldn't have doubts later. The rider's crash helmet had been some dark colour, blue or black, his face hidden behind one of those plastic masks like some latter-day Samurai. The machine itself had carried no number plates, but its forks had been unusually long and the exhaust pipe had run high across the frame and ended cocked up in the air. It was the sort of machine that was used for cross-country rally work, and I remembered where I'd seen one just like it only a few hours before.

CHAPTER 3

An observer is one who is appointed by the Committee to assist a referee to decide questions of fact . . .
                                                                    Definition

Taking sherry with the Chief Constable at eleven o'clock in the morning was not part of my day to day routine, but the sherry was good and the view from the terrace of his niceish Jacobean manor house was even better. I guessed that I did not get this kind of treatment for nothing and in that, at least, I was right.

Colonel Giles Linforth was no run of the mill Chief Constable but a character who had made the transition from army to police with a certain elegance. Meeting him, one realized he could be a product only of the British Army, an organization that likes its showcase products to look exactly alike, a kind of élitist quality control. Non-commissioned, they come off the production line as guardsmen, the officer model designed to weather into a dapper, blue-eyed, pink-cheeked product with thick, silver and slightly wavy hair. The Chief Constable was a particularly fine example, who wore his out-of-uniform tweeds as though they had never been vulgarly new and would certainly never become disreputably old. He may have looked like something out of an old Ealing comedy but I did not underestimate my master. Like most of his kind, he was a good deal brighter than he looked.

'So this Miss Tonge of yours has admitted to cutting up the green?' He was standing leaning against the balustrade while I was sitting in a chair, an arrangement that in theory gave him some kind of psychological advantage. I didn't miss the bit about 'my' Miss Tonge either.

'Not to cutting up the green personally,' I told him, 'but

36

yes, she reported to the station of her own accord and said that members of her organization were responsible.'

'As a feminine protest against a male-dominated sport and so on?'

'Briefly—yes.'

'And what will she get?'

What would the magistrates give her was more to the point. A pat on the head, costs and a scathing comment or two on the police in all probability. 'I don't suppose she'll even be charged.'

It was up to the Club, of course, but I was hoping Alan Thurston would take my advice, so I added, 'I understand she's undertaken to pay for the cost of repair. Taking her to court would only give her free publicity at our expense and there's every likelihood the Bench wouldn't convict.'

The Chief Constable poured me some more sherry, probably to cover the fact that he was thinking. 'Would it be worth the Club's while to take out an injunction to scotch any chance of her doing the same thing again?'

'I'm afraid you can't take out an injunction to prevent someone committing an offence.' I tried to make it sound as though I was reminding rather than telling him, but I'm poor at these things. I went on hurriedly, 'Only against an alleged offence that will eventually be tried by process of law. Of course you *could* make her good behaviour a condition of bail or a suspended sentence or something like that, but then we'd have to have her in court. As a matter of fact, sir,' I ended heartily, 'I'm pretty certain she'll behave herself. She's nice enough apart from this feminist thing.'

My audience grunted. 'Well, I suppose that's something. But I can't see that there's any connection between a clutch of potty women and some young fool on a motorcycle. You know for yourself that youngsters drive them over any impossible bit of country these days. They see these trials on television and reckon it's all right to try their hand at any bit of local country—golf courses included.'

I said, 'Yes, sir. But why did my chap last night make straight for the green? It wasn't any sort of a rally cross route but it *was* where he could do the most damage.'

'It was dark—there was precious little moon.' Linforth was reasoning in much the same way as I had myself while sitting in that bunker, so I couldn't exactly blame him. On the other hand, I didn't consider he was right, either. He gave up his advantaged position and dropped down in a cane chair beside me. 'Damn it, Angus, I don't suppose the wretched boy knew where he was.'

I was wary of the Angus bit, but I wasn't ready to back out yet. 'If he was lost in the dark,' I pointed out, 'he could have switched his light on.'

Linforth looked up quickly. 'You said he had no number plate?'

'I'm quite certain he hadn't.'

'Then the chances are he hadn't a light, either. Those machines don't, you know. They're just competition things.'

Well, how many kids were there who kept one bike for rally work and another for the road? I drank my sherry and kept my mouth shut, but the CC wouldn't let it go.

'You genuinely think there's some connection between Miss Tonge and your would-be vandal?'

'I can't think of any logical reason why there should be,' I admitted, 'but how close a connection do we need? We both know that if some lunatic blew up St Paul's tonight someone else would be having a go at Westminster Abbey by tomorrow. Miss Tonge and her friends could simply have stirred up a number of people who had dormant inclinations to wreck golf courses.' I paused to let that sink in. 'On the other hand, last night's effort might have been pure coincidence.'

The Colonel produced a large handkerchief and blew his nose loudly. 'Damned hay fever.' We all have our little ways. 'Angus, I'm well aware that you're on leave, and that you're only helping on this unofficially.' Eyebrows were being raised at me. 'Do you want to be shot of this whole thing?'

Well, there it was if I wanted it, and I could get on with the book in peace. On the other hand, I liked watching golf tournaments and I could always write at night. Or the early morning. And who was it who'd been trying to get shot of administration?

'I shouldn't worry about the leave,' I told him, 'I'm happy to help.'

My master smiled and nodded as though he hadn't known what I was going to say all along. 'Good,' he said. 'Much better this way, you know, and there's a limit to the team we can field. What have we got deployed on this little outing to date?'

'Thirty on crowd control. But then most of the work is done by volunteer marshals. Forty-two on traffic, if you include controls.' If he wanted figures he'd come to the right place.

'Well, if we've provided that little lot we hardly want to find an investigating team as well. Besides, it's a club, after all. Better if there's someone keeping an eye on things who knows the form.' Linforth stood up. I stood up. 'All right then, Angus, leave it to you.'

On cue, the telephone rang in the room behind us.

I said, 'That's fine, sir. I'll be off.'

He wagged his hand at me to hang about while he took the call. When he came back he was whistling soundlessly. 'That was Thurston. He's just had an anonymous note.' He waited for me to say, 'What's in it?'

I said it.

'Short and to the point. If the Club wants the tournament to go ahead it'll cost five thousand pounds.'

Alan Thurston was pawing the thing over in his office in company with a shaggy-haired and rather earnest chap in a very heavy striped blue suit who I guessed—correctly— to be Arthur Kempton of Tamworth Electronics. I picked up Exhibit A and tried to look as though it was the kind of thing I saw every day of the week. It consisted of a sheet of plain, cheap lined paper with letters cut out of some magazine or other.

IF YOU WANT THE TAMWORTH TO GO
AHEAD IT WILL COST YOU £5000
STAY BY YOUR PHONE

I dropped it back on the desk. 'How did it come?'

'Elsie Briggs picked it off the mat when she came in.' Elsie was his assistant, a formidable lady of no known age who probably remembered James Braid. He tossed a plain envelope across. 'It came in that—delivered early this morning, I imagine. You can see it's not been posted. No stamp.'

Well, it hadn't an address either but I didn't want to make myself unpopular. 'You'd better do as this joker says and stay by the phone,' I told him. I slipped the message into my pocket, and this seemed to bring Tamworth's sponsorship king to life.

'I imagine whoever phones will give instructions how to pay the money?' He sounded as though he'd taken charge of a lot of finance meetings in his time.

I nodded. 'Probably. It's what happens in most crime stories, which is where most of these people get their ideas.'

'Right.' Arthur Kempton was clearly about to make one of his decisions. 'I think it would be best if I made Tamworth's position in this quite clear. We pay. We're not risking further trouble for the sake of just five thousand pounds.'

That startled me a bit and it probably showed. Policemen who have a lot to do with the public get a special kind of face that registers no more than a certain scepticism, but it was a knack I'd never perfected because Kempton raised a nicely manicured hand just to show who was running the meeting. 'I can guess what you're going to say, Inspector, but I've met this sort of thing before, and believe me, it's money well spent.'

He didn't seem to be joking, either, but I wanted to make sure. 'That's very interesting,' I told him. 'When was that?'

'Well, I don't know that I'm prepared to name names and places, but you probably know that this isn't the first sporting event that Tamworth has sponsored—not by any means.'

'That's true,' I agreed. 'Last year there was a motor race at Brands Hatch, a Badminton Championship, the All England Gliding Race and the Power Boat Regatta.'

He regarded me coldly. 'As I said, we have sponsored sporting events before.'

'Which one?'

'Which one did we sponsor? I thought I made myself clear. All of them.'

'At which event did you receive a demand for money?'

'I—'

'And try not to be tiresome, sir.'

We exchanged glances of mutual dislike but he decided not to make a thing of it. 'Very well, Inspector, since you insist, we were threatened with a bomb in the pits area at Brands Hatch. With all that high octane fuel about the possibilities were horrendous.' He paused, looking like a man who had made a decision and was pleased it had been the right one. He went on, 'The appearance money that has to be paid to the modern Grand Prix driver is pretty frightening, too. Putting the race off was out of the question —it was just easier to pay up.'

'They wanted five thousand that time too?'

Kempton nodded. 'Yes. And I suggest you remember that not only racing drivers get appearance money—golfers expect it, too. Quite a number appearing in this tournament rate thirty thousand for their trouble, so alongside that kind of expenditure, five thousand is peanuts.'

'It is,' I agreed. 'One wonders why you're not being asked for more.'

Alan Thurston stopped staring at the ceiling and said, 'If you ask me, it's because whoever sent this note knows perfectly well that he's being pretty modest in his demands, and that you'll probably pay up and keep quiet about it. A bigger sum and you'd go to the police.' He turned and looked in my direction. 'Agreed?'

'Agreed. Only this time you *have* gone to the police.'

Kempton looked mildly disapproving. 'I understand Thurston here contacted your Chief Constable on an un-official basis because he happens to be a member of this Club. But, of course, the decision as to whether this demand is paid or not lies with Tamworth. And I assure you that I intend to pay.'

What he meant was that Tamworth would pay, but I suppose it's the gesture that counts and it seemed a pity to spoil it. 'I'm afraid,' I told him, 'you can't very well do that.'

He kept the kind of look he probably kept for stroppy shareholders. 'And exactly why can't I, Inspector?'

'It could be construed as compounding a felony.'

'It could be, but I don't think it would.'

It never ceased to astonish me how the public at large fall over themselves to criticize the police yet actively dislike cooperating with them. Really, it's no wonder crime's a growth industry. 'If the worst came to the worst,' I said, 'we should have to do you for obstructing the police in the performance of their duty. And I assure you there aren't many ways round *that*.'

'Like Section 40 of the Army Act. *Conduct to the prejudice of good order and military discipline*,' Thurston said appreciatively. 'Covers everything from barrack damages to buggery. Can't beat it.'

Kempton thought that one over. To give him his due, he didn't take very long to run the proposition through the computer and come up with the right answer. He said, 'All right. What do you suggest we do?'

'Always supposing this isn't a hoax, there'll be a phone call to tell you where to leave the money.'

'And if there is?'

'The chances are that you'll be asked to follow instructions. You follow them and we do the rest.' Well, someone would do the rest. I had a working knowledge as to how these things were arranged, but I doubted very much if I'd be allowed to have a hand in this one.

CHAPTER 4

The ball a player uses should conform in specification set
forth in Appendix 111 on maximum weight, minimum
size, spherical symmetry and initial velocity when
tested . . .   *Rule 5–1*

'You mean they won't let you join in the fun?' Laurie Wilson
sat in my window-seat and scratched Ramases's left ear.
With her free hand she took the glass I offered her. 'Why
not, for heaven's sake?'

'I'd be poaching on CID's territory.' I tried to sound as
though I didn't mind. 'Besides, picking up a villain when
he's just collected a drop is pretty specialized—you've got
to let him get his hands on the money and actually go
through the motions of going off with it if you're going to
make the charge stick. After that, of course, you've got to
make sure he doesn't get away.'

'Do they ever?' Laurie sampled the gin, her eyes studying
me over the top of her glass. She wore those huge round
spectacles that make even good-looking girls appear some
kind of insect. Her hair had been layered so that it had
a curious, colour-flecked appearance that was not unlike
Ramases's coat, and her skin had a tan so flawless that it
might even have been real. She was wearing a pale yellow
linen suit that was as crisp and cool as the rest of her and,
bug-eyed or not, it was all a total success.

'Do they get away?' I thought that one out and decided
on the truth. 'Well, yes. Sometimes.' There had, in
fact, been some pretty monumental cock-ups over the years
but it hardly seemed fair to enlarge on other people's misfortunes.

'You're not exactly forthcoming, are you?' Laurie
frowned. 'You're the only policeman I know so you might
at least tell a girl the good bits. Where's your baddie
collecting his loot, for a start?'

'A rubbish basket in the picnic area on the main road, just short of Winton.'

'Isn't that rather obvious? Blackmailers and kidnappers seem to spend half their lives fishing fortunes out of rubbish baskets. In books, anyway.' She was looking superior, as though she'd read the end of the book and knew all about the butler's private life. 'I suppose the police hide behind the trees?'

'Well, it's a bit fancier than that,' I assured her. As a matter of fact, Hawkins had shown me the communications plan earlier that morning, pushing model cars around a table-top. There would not be a vehicle in sight when our man collected the money, but there wouldn't be a road that wasn't effectively blocked either. Short of turning himself into a bird there was no way he was going to escape. I'd said I wanted to go along for the ride but Hawkins wasn't having any.

'What happens if it turns out to be someone who knows you? One of the members? He'd have to be pretty thick not to smell a rat once he'd spotted his old pal Angus driving a milk float.'

So far as I knew, nobody was planning to drive a milk float on this particular operation but I knew better than to push an argument I clearly wasn't going to win.

Laurie finished her drink and sighed. 'All right, keep your official secrets. But since you've got an in, I can't understand why you don't write crime stuff. It stands to reason you must know more about it than you do about poisoning and intrigue in the twelfth century.'

'I don't, that's the trouble.' Ramases was beginning to claw at her skirt, a sign that he wasn't getting his share of attention, so I picked him up and carried him through into the kitchen in the hope that raw liver would take his mind off other things. The refrigerator door was open again and I cursed the local electricity board and all its works. Didn't it have anyone on its payroll who could fix a magnetic catch? Not that it made all that much difference to Ramases if it worked or not—he seemed able to open virtually any door with one flick of a practised paw.

'You wicked bastard.' It needed only a glance to show that he'd been there before me. An ordinary cat would have hauled the cold salmon on to the floor, smashing the dish while so doing. Not so Ramases, who had contrived to consume three-quarters of the fish *in situ*. Behind me there was a rustle and a tiny slam as something passed swiftly through the cat door. He was no fool, was Ramases. Just the same, he'd put paid to my pretensions to lunch, which meant that we'd have to go out instead.

'Isn't that odd, I had a feeling that you were going to show off your cooking,' Laurie commented as I took her down to the car. 'Just shows how wrong a girl can be.'

'The cat ate it,' I told her.

'So it *was* salmon he was breathing all over me! I thought it must be some kind of cat food exotica!' She was laughing but at least with a certain degree of sympathy. 'Look, we don't have to go out. You can always fix us an omelette—'

I can't remember exactly what I said to that. I know I was suddenly angry with myself and with the day without knowing why. I suppose at heart I resented the way Hawkins had quietly pushed me back where I belonged and that fiasco with the salmon hadn't exactly restored my self-esteem. Certainly I wasn't in the mood to fool around with omelettes, so I said so and drove us to the Gate House instead.

There was no need to apologize because Laurie was doing all right by the change of plan, the Gate House being the kind of riverside pub that more properly belonged to the more expensive reaches of the Thames. I'm not an enthusiast for the expense account rendezvous but I knew that even if it was overpriced the food was good. I think she guessed as much when we came in sight of the packed car park.

'Angus, we'll never get in! Half the county must be in there ahead of us.'

'With the amount of fiddling that goes on in the catering business,' I told her, 'a policeman can get a table anywhere.' It was true, too.

I rang through to the station just in case they should want me and then went to find the head waiter. The place was crowded all right, but we got a table next to the windows

45

overlooking the river. The menu was about the size of a national daily but we settled for vichyssoise and cold duck. The white Mâcon they brought was cool but not cold, and I poured it myself into the heavy cut glasses and waited to see if this agent of mine would take hers in both hands and then look at me over the rim.

'I meant to ask you the first time we met: how did you come to write *The Captive?*' She was holding the glass in one hand when she finally drank and when she smiled approval it was what the wine deserved. 'Come to that, how did you come by a character like Armand?'

I liked the 'come by'. Clearly there was to be no nonsense about my having invented him and I felt a twinge of respect.

'Armand's my Uncle Fred.'

'Your Uncle Fred has a French twelfth-century lifestyle?'

I considered my relative, long dead, with his dreams and schemes, the wife who was always going to leave him but never did. One of life's losers but in a cockeyed way a kind of winner, too. 'No,' I conceded, 'not twelfth-century—just a lifestyle. The period came later.'

'How much later?'

'I was laid up for a while and someone lent me some books, which was when I got hooked on the period.'

She nodded. 'And the trigger for the story?'

The years I'd wasted at an office desk had triggered the story; people have a point when they talk about escapist fiction. 'I was bored. Seven hundred years ago seemed a lot more attractive than real life.'

Laurie laughed. A good laugh is an excellent thing in a woman and hard to acquire. Hers sounded the real thing. 'Do your policeman friends know?'

'They most certainly do not!' Correction. 'Well, only the Chief Constable.'

'Don't tell me he's a fellow enthusiast for the period?'

'I don't imagine so.' But for all I knew he might well be. Soldiers have unexpected private pursuits, few of them trivial. 'As a matter of fact,' I told her, 'he wanted to know where I'd got the money to pay for my car.'

'I'm not surprised. It's lovely but a bit ostentatious.'

46

I said, 'You don't want to read more into it than there is. I just happen to like that sort of car.'

For a moment she looked as though she might dispute that but changed her mind. 'Well, I can't say I blame you. Now tell me how the revise of the new book's getting on.'

'All right.' I'd discovered I disliked talking about the thing—it was real enough while I was writing it but when I tried to put it into words, everything became oddly artificial. And I hated revising stuff I'd already written.

Laurie seemed to sense that because she simply nodded and didn't press. 'You'll have it all finished by the end of October?'

'I think so. Yes.' According to my publisher's contract, November was the delivery date and I saw no reason why the alterations shouldn't be wrapped up by then. 'I was wondering—'

I broke off because my eye had registered something familiar about the back of a head in a far corner of the room. Polly Appleby, no less. Moreover, there was no problem as to who she was lunching with, because I could see her companion full face: the worker's friend, Councillor Clive Whitton, munching happily on what looked like some pretty élitist smoked salmon.

'You were wondering?' Laurie was prompting. She seemed a girl who was reluctant to let conversations hang about.

I said, 'Sorry—I just recognized someone.'

'Wanted?'

'Not so far as I know.' It seemed a pity to disappoint her, but all the same I was wondering what the local Trot and a capitalist PRO were likely to have in common, apart from the obvious, which would seem quick work for two people who'd only just met. With something of an effort I turned my head away and pushed the happy couple to the back of my mind. 'As a matter of fact,' I said, 'I was going to ask you how it would be if I stopped being a policeman and wrote full time.'

Laurie frowned. 'What do you mean by "how would it be"?'

'Could I earn a living?'

47

'I never advise my clients to give up perfectly good jobs so they can write. If you want to write, do it as a hobby. Much more sensible.' She was suddenly very much my agent, not at all my lunch companion.

'Look,' I said, 'let's be realistic about this. You can't call something a hobby when it produces the major part of one's income.'

'It may have produced the major part last year and it probably will this year,' Laurie agreed, 'but there's no guarantee about next year or the year after that. Moreover it won't earn you a pension. Certainly not an index-linked one.'

Odd how so many people homed in on the index-linked pension. Interesting how important it was. But not to me. And why not to me? I refilled her glass. 'I'm a single man on my own,' I told her, 'I don't have to worry about security and I do happen to enjoy writing.'

'So that's fine. Write.'

'I'm bored stiff with being a policeman.'

She sighed. 'You'd probably be bored stiff with writing if you did it all the time.' I suppose I looked slightly sceptical because she went on, 'Honestly, Angus, you've been incredibly lucky. You wrote a book for fun and you not only sold it but made a great deal of money out of it, too. You've already sold the next one before it's finished and, with any luck, you shouldn't do too badly out of that either. But do try to remember this is not the norm.'

'But I do write saleable books.'

'My dear man, they sell *now*. If you'd offered them a couple of years ago or a couple of years hence, for that matter, they might well have been turned down out of hand. Being a successful writer isn't just a matter of writing a readable book—it's writing it at the moment when publishers happen to want it.'

'You don't have to be so bloody discouraging,' I said.

Her eyes disapproved behind those damned glasses. 'And you don't have to be so childish. I'm supposed to be your literary adviser and I'm advising you, which is what you pay me ten per cent for.'

A waiter came up and said there was a telephone call and would I care to take it in the office? Yes, I would. I made apologetic noises and tried not to look in a hurry in case it might be Hawkins, which it was.

'Got him, Angus. No bother. Thought you'd like to know who it was, though.'

'Jack Raikes.'

'Well—yes.' Sounded a bit flattish, so at least one could occasionally keep one's end up. 'But of course you know him, don't you?'

'Only because he's the steward at the West Wessex. You're holding him, of course. Has he said anything?'

I could imagine Hawkins shaking his head. 'No, he seems a bit down. No form, so far as we know.'

'No,' I said, 'I didn't imagine he would have. All right if I have a word with him later?'

There was a pause, because he didn't like it, but couldn't think of any reason why I couldn't. 'Okay, Angus, that'll be all right.'

'You look like the cat that's had the cream,' Laurie said as I got back to the table. 'Has the posse got its man?'

'As a matter of fact,' I said, 'the posse has. At least, it's got the man who wrote the demand note.'

'Are you allowed to say who it was?'

I told her, because there didn't seem to be any reason why not; after all, it was going to be in the local paper next day.

'And you think that's the end of the trouble?'

'I hope so,' I said. Linforth had asked me the same thing, which seemed to suggest there was an air of doubt about me, but for the life of me I couldn't see what Jack Raikes and April Tonge had in common. A movement caught my eye over in the corner: Polly and her escort were getting up to go, and very matey they looked, too. I was glad the girl had her back to me and they didn't have to pass me on the way out. I looked back to discover that my companion was eyeing me speculatively. 'Yes,' I said, and it was the truth, 'I really do hope so. They've had enough trouble staging this tournament as it is, without all this fooling around on the side.'

The duck arrived and we went back to talking about books. It was only the second time we'd had any time together and I was impressed by her apparently instinctive flair for the commerce of words and the way she'd turned her job into a way of life. It's easy enough to be impressed by another person's expertise in their own field but Laurie Wilson did seem an exceptionally competent young woman and I found myself wondering how young in fact she was. Thirty? More? Less? I heard myself asking, 'What would you like to do with the rest of the afternoon?' Which was something of a surprise because normally I doubt if I'd have even got around to presuming she might be available for the afternoon as well.

A pause but not a long one. 'You could take me along to this golf club that's keeping you so busy. It sounds fun.'

I was surprised but gratified, but fair was fair. 'I'm afraid the tournament hasn't even started yet.'

She said patiently, 'I know—you've been making that clear for the past half-hour. I just want to get the feel of the place.'

'All right.' Strange how irrationally curious women can be. 'We'll get going right away.'

But she'd caught a nuance in my voice I hadn't even known was there. 'I'm glad I've delighted you so much.'

'If I sound less than overjoyed,' I told her, 'it's because I'm beginning to suspect that I have a malign influence on the place.'

But in fact the afternoon before me was a bonus, because I was enjoying the company of this good-looking, amiable woman, even though she did insist on rating my literary effort as no more than a profitable hobby. Nevertheless I was beginning to tire of the West Wessex and its troubles.

Laurie said, 'You overestimate your gift of the evil eye. As a matter of fact, it's very rare—only about three authenticated cases this century. But if you'd rather, I can always go back to my other chap. You're not the only client with problems.'

50

'Who is he, anyway?'

'Mind your own business.' She saw me catch the eye of the waiter. 'I'll get this.'

I suppose I was genuinely startled, cloistered as I had been in B Division all these lost years. 'Don't be ridiculous!' I was huffy and probably sounded it.

A frown, followed by a certain crispness that indicated displeasure. 'You paid last time, I seem to remember.'

That was true, that last and only previous time. But just the same—

Cool fingers touched the back of my hand. 'Angus, you're not really embarrassed at the idea of a woman buying you lunch, are you? It's a working lunch, after all, and I promise to charge it to expenses. It's supposed to be very male chauvinist to get upset—unless you're trying to seduce me or something.'

'Yes,' I said, 'I'm trying to seduce you. Now let me buy the lunch.'

Laurie grinned, schoolgirl ruderies all of a sudden. 'Get stuffed!' She took care of the bill with a gold American Express card, that popular sign of credit worthiness, and then we got into the car and went over to the Club. She was a good deal less businesslike on the way and I got the impression that she was doing her best to make up for the lunch bill business. We parked and I took her over to the tented village that was by now looking like something thought up by a Moghul emperor on a particularly extrovert day.

'I'm impressed.' Laurie stared at the nearest marquees, which must have been two hundred feet long, if an inch. 'What do they *need* them that big for?'

'To sell things in.' Once inside, it was difficult to imagine that one was in a tent at all, because a few acres of matting put paid to the village fête smell of sour grass and warm mud. There were already enough stands up and stocked to provide every golfer in the country with enough clothing and equipment for the next ten years, and hospitality was already being dispensed in formidable quantities. Ambrose Hall detached himself from one of the bars and headed in our direction.

'Congratulations, Angus! I hear—'

'I know,' I said, 'news travels fast.' I introduced him to Laurie to take his mind off things.

'The last Laurie Wilson I knew was a feller.' I saw that I needn't have worried, because Ambrose was already being charming with total concentration. 'Won the Mexican Open in his time, if I remember, and then got himself killed in an air crash or something. Any relation?'

Laurie was smiling. 'When I was a kid I hated having a boy's name, but I grew out of that.' Then she stopped smiling. 'Of course you're right. That Laurie Wilson was my father.'

I could cheerfully have killed Ambrose, but I still had time to envy that travelling computer of a mind that could apparently store away a fact for years, then bring it out at exactly the right time. I'd heard of Laurie Wilson, the golfer, just as he had, but it wasn't such an unusual name that it seemed likely there'd be a connection. A computer my mind was not.

'Do you play golf, too?' Ambrose was putting the boot in with a vengeance. Why had I never asked the girl if she played? Why else had she asked to see the West Wessex in the first place? I realized with mounting despair that I knew virtually nothing about women's golf, and that she could be part of the Curtis Cup team for all I knew.

The moment passed and Laurie was saying, 'I'm afraid I don't.' She was looking at me apologetically. 'Does that make me *persona non grata* in these parts?'

'On the contrary, it makes a nice change,' Ambrose assured her. 'Now you'd better let me show you round— there's no knowing what a policeman might turn up for you. Like a corpse or something.' He took Laurie's arm and led her firmly back into the open air with me, poor fool, following meekly behind. I heard him say, 'We'll go over to the practice ground for a while—there's a toy there that'll amuse you. Amuse Angus, anyway.'

The practice ground was on the far side of the clubhouse, out of sight of the tented village. So far as I could see, there was nobody practising but I spotted a small group around something that looked mechanical but which I couldn't for the moment identify. Even when we joined the group the penny still didn't drop. The thing was beautifully finished in polished steel and stove enamel and appeared to be some kind of pump, electrically driven, judging from the power line running across the grass. There was a pivoted clamp three or four feet above a base plate, but it meant nothing to me until a chap in a neat blue blazer picked up a golf club and slotted it into the clamp, screwing it fast. At the same time I noticed the Dodson sports equipment logo stencilled on its side.

'That's right.' Ambrose agreed with my unspoken thought. 'It's an automatic driver from Dodson's research department.' He patted the machine's blazer-clad guardian on the shoulder rather as though he were a large dog. 'Tell my friends about your little toy, Sam.'

Sam was not one of your new boy technicians, he had the face and mannerisms of the old-time mechanic and he smiled shyly at me. 'Simple, really, sir. Just a tool for the quality control of balls—the company brought it into use when we were developing the Dodson Hyper Flight. Basically, it's a pneumatic pulse that can be fitted with any size golf club and it will hit the ball with any force you want. Under laboratory conditions it enables us to compare the performance of our products against balls made by our competitors, but mostly we use it for checking batch samples.'

I'd heard of such gadgets but this was the first one I'd seen—an engaging little robot. I asked, 'What's it doing out here?'

Sam glanced at Amrbose. 'Well, we're showing it on the Dodson stand, sir, but Mr Hall here wanted to try it out for real, so to speak. He thought some gentleman might like to take Charlie on—for a bit of fun, you understand.'

'Charlie?'

'That's what we call him—it—sir. Among ourselves.'

We all looked at Ambrose expectantly. Finally I said, 'Well, go on. You know you're dying to try.'

He looked round as though he'd lost something. 'As a

matter of fact, I thought we might get a few feet of video of this. My bloke—'

I should have realized that Ambrose wasn't a man to miss a chance of public exposure but I didn't see why we should hang about. 'You'd better see how it works first,' I suggested.

'Maybe you're right, laddie.' He took the point readily enough. Obviously if the pneumatic Charlie was going to make a fool of him, he didn't particularly want it recorded for posterity. Ambrose collected a club and teed a ball up just clear of the machine. 'What do you want me to do?'

'Three balls as far as you can go and as close a group as possible?'

'Look, I'm not risking pulling a muscle swiping from cold.' He waggled his club. 'Three wood. Two hundred yards. Okay?'

'Okay.' Even a couple of hundred yards is a long way to drive just like that, but the ground was firm enough to let the balls run on. I wondered how much golf Ambrose actually played these days.

'Here we go, then.' He was putting on weight and certainly by tour standards wasn't competitive any more, but self-advertising patter notwithstanding, he was still one of the greats. I watched the club head come back lazily, hesitate for a fraction of a second at the top of the backswing in that way that had become Ambrose's hallmark, then the blur of the chrome shaft as it slashed down, the light *crack* as the ball climbed into the sky, fell endlessly and bounced on into the distance. It looked near enough two hundred yards to me, and judging by the appreciative noises from Sam, he thought so too.

'Two to go.' Ambrose took another ball and repeated his performance, landing his second shot what looked like no more than two or three yards from the first. A third went much the same way. Fifteen yards at the most between the three.

'You haven't lost your touch.' I was impressed and it seemed churlish not to admit as much.

Ambrose acknowledged the compliment with the expression of a bishop extending a hand to have his ring kissed —a sort of benevolent acceptance of his due. He put the club down. 'Well, there's no wind to speak of. Let's see what Charlie can do.'

There really wasn't very much to it. Charlie went *chugga chugga* for a bit while he built up pressure, then Sam pressed something and there was a tiny sigh in the moment before the club whipped down and the ball sailed away.

'That's up to mine all right,' Ambrose acknowledged. 'No problem.'

Charlie's second go was no problem either, landing what looked at a distance to be a spot almost alongside the first. The third must have hit a patch of soft ground and rolled away a bit to the left, but even so three feet would have spanned all three balls. It was a staggeringly impressive performance, and one could imagine that indoors, or over ground that was perfectly even, the balls would have been almost touching.

'I often wondered what it would be like to play against a machine,' Ambrose remarked, 'and now I know.' To give him his due, he managed to concede defeat with good grace, but then a machine is a machine after all and everyone knows that they're getting increasingly clever. As if to drive that particular point home, he added, 'There's no way anyone could win against that thing—it's like doing calculations against a computer.'

'Come off it, sport, it ain't as bad as that!' I imagined that Don Shroeder had come down for a quiet practice session because he had his caddie with him carrying his clubs and a bag of balls. He looked at Ambrose. 'You trying to outdrive this thing here?'

'No. Just trying to see who can get the better group at two hundred yards.'

'Hell, you won't ever win doing that.' The Australian looked amused. He also looked rich and fit and approachable—anyone could see what had made Don Shroeder one of the all-time popular heroes. Privately, I also thought he looked tired, but then that was hardly surprising for a man in his forties meeting the tour schedule ten months of the year. But he walked up to the machine light-footed enough and slapped it affectionately. 'Tried a few balls against one of these at St Augusta some years back.' He looked reminiscent. 'Iron Oscar, they called him.'

'How did you get on?'

'Lost out to start with, till I got the hang of it. Beat the damn thing in the end.'

Ambrose frowned. 'You actually beat it?'

Shroeder grinned. 'Too bloody true! It had its own way on the long shots but I could see it wasn't so good when it had to pull its punches. No short game.' He looked at Sam. 'How about taking that wood away and giving it a nine iron instead?'

Sam nodded. 'Anything you say, Mr Shroeder.' He unclipped the wooden club and slipped a short iron in its place before glancing over his shoulder in query. 'How far?'

'Three balls at a hundred and twenty yards. Okay?' I saw Shroeder hesitate. 'Reckon we'd better play the same balls to make it fair.' He turned to his caddie. 'Give him three of ours, Dex.'

The caddie produced three balls and handed them over. Judging by the logo on the golf bag, Don Shroeder used Penfolds.

'Fair enough.' Sam placed one of the three on the machine's driving platform. 'Right?'

Shroeder nodded. 'Sure. Let her go, mate.'

Sam pressed his button. White light seared our eyeballs and something exploded with a sound like the crack of doom.

CHAPTER 5

The diameter of the ball shall be not less than 1.620 inches. This specification shall be satisfied if under its own weight a ball falls through a 1.620 inches diameter ring gauge in fewer than 25 out of 100 randomly selected positions, the test being carried out at a temperature of 23±1°C.

App.111(b)

The anti-terrorist people don't carry stun grenades from a sense of fun but for the reason that a really big bang at close quarters is an experience that leaves one physically and mentally incapacitated for five or six seconds, which in terms of killing somebody, is quite a long time. The explosion that occurred when Charlie's club head struck Don Shroeder's ball was probably short on grenade standards simply through lack of size, but it was pretty effective just the same. It produced the kind of moment during which one's mind should have been racing or at the very least cursing one's luck, but so far as I was concerned the effect was not unlike a freeze sequence in a film, a seemingly endless crack of sound and an equally endless light as the flash stayed put on a numbed retina. Then the glare died and the sound stopped as the film got going again amid a strong smell of burnt cordite and the hiss of hastily indrawn breaths.

I said, 'Is anyone hurt?'

They looked at me blankly, still too shocked to work out an answer to any kind of question, but rather to my surprise everyone was still on their feet. A golf ball isn't intended to be a grenade but even so it seemed that bits of the casing must have gone somewhere. Sam seemed the worst affected because he'd been nearest the explosion, but even he was only opening and closing his mouth not unlike a perpendicular goldfish. It was Shroeder who brought us back to some kind of reality.

57

'Why, the son of a bitch, he could have killed me!' He sounded more surprised than angry.

I looked past him towards the clubhouse, the tops of the tents poking up behind. Nobody was coming running, the only people I could see were a long way off and not one of them had even turned round. What had they thought all that noise had been about? Really, our passion for minding our own business was incredible—no wonder murder was so popular. 'All right,' I said, 'let's have it. Who could have killed you?'

'That bastard Kawasaki! Our fun-loving neighbourhood Japanese!' If Shroeder had any doubts, he wasn't showing them. Besides, the Australians are a litigious race and you have to be sure of your facts there before you're rude in public. I watched him go over to the machine and run a finger over the striking plate that was stained and blackened by blast. 'For Chrissake! He must be out of his mind!'

He was a bit shaken, but nobody could have said he was all that surprised. 'Look,' I said, 'are you seriously trying to tell me that Omi Kawasaki was responsible for this?'

'Too bloody right I am!' Shroeder grinned unexpectedly. 'I tell you, he's a mad bastard—' He broke off, looking over my shoulder. 'He's over there now. Probably coming over to see the fun.'

As a matter of fact, the pride of the Rising Sun looked more as though he was planning to hit a few golf balls than study the results of an explosion. As usual, he was dressed immaculately in his favourite pale blue, with a white baseball cap tipped over his eyes. His clubs were following him, borne by one of his own countrymen who had somehow contrived to be about twice as tall.

I turned back to Shroeder. 'Suppose you let me in on this. Are you suggesting that this was some kind of practical joke?'

'You saw him in the bar last night, didn't you?'

I'd forgotten, but of course I had. All those balloons pouring out of somebody's drink. But then, balloons weren't grenades.

Kawasaki came abreast of us and sniffed the air. 'Been

cookin', Don san?' His American was as good as it should have been for someone who went to college there. His face was straight but his eyes had the expectant look of the committed life and soul of the party man.

'You crazy sod!' Shroeder exploded. 'You could have killed someone! You and your joke golf balls!'

The Japanese grinned delightedly, teeth half way round his face. 'Pretty good, eh!'

We looked at him. He looked at us. 'Mr Kawasaki,' I said, 'I am a police officer—'

He studied me. He was only about five foot nothing but, my word, he looked bigger. 'It is illegal to play jokes in this country?'

'It's illegal to cause dangerous explosions.'

'Sure, it's illegal in Japan too, but I haven't made any yet. You sayin' I have?'

'I'm saying somebody has. Didn't you hear it?'

He frowned. 'I heard something. That was here?'

'That was the Dodson driving machine hitting one of Don Shroeder's practice balls. Now, I gather you have some joke golf balls—'

He didn't actually say, 'Ah so!' but for a moment I thought he was going to. What he did say was: 'Sure I got joke balls. They come from a place in Kobe. You want to see some?'

Shroeder prodded him in the ribs with the shaft of a nine iron. 'Listen, sport. Did you or did you not unload some into Dex's bag?'

The Japanese nodded cheerfully. 'A coupla boxes this morning. Thought maybe they liven you up a bit, eh?'

'Well, they did that all right.' Either this man's conscience was clear or he was out of his mind. I said, 'Mr Kawasaki, perhaps—'

'Oh, I got them right here. All makes. Mr Australia here plays Penfolds.' Kawasaki said something over his shoulder in Japanese and his caddie fished out a box of balls. Another guttural order and he'd handed one of them to me.

I had to admit that for a joke ball it certainly looked the real thing, even its weight didn't give it away.

'You want to see what happens?' Kawasaki took a ball for himself and placed it on the grass in front of him while the silent caddie handed him an iron.

Don Shroeder took a step backwards. 'We've *seen* what happens, Omi, you madman! I tell you it damn nearly blew the machine to bits!'

'You crazy?' Kawasaki addressed the ball. 'These are joke balls, man. You think they're our answer to Hiroshima or something?' He swung unhurriedly, made contact. The ball exploded with a kind of plop, rather as though someone had smacked a rather soggy paper bag. A small puff of green smoke drifted upwards, followed by a couple of sparks. It could hardly have been more harmless.

'Are they all like this?' I asked. 'You don't have any more powerful ones?'

Kawasaki shook his head. 'Nope. Some maybe have red smoke. The bang just the same.'

I looked at him. Reading oriental faces isn't all that easy because, as someone once pointed out, they all look much alike to us. You don't call a Japanese inscrutable for nothing, and all I could dredge out of those dark eyes was a certain hostility, but then, who likes policemen?

'Look,' I said, 'what went off in the driving machine was nothing at all like the thing you've just shown us, but we can't stand here all afternoon or we'll get ourselves an audience. I suggest we go indoors somewhere.' I imagined that Thurston would have to know sooner or later but I balked at involving him over what still seemed like a joke. Or did it?

Ambrose said, 'I've got a place.'

He had indeed. It turned out to be one of those vast mobile homes so beloved of Grand Prix drivers, office, bed and bath, furnished regardless on top of heaven alone knows how many thousands of pounds' worth of Mercedes chassis. He said something about having been lent it, but I had my doubts.

Shroeder settled himself in a swivel chair and waved me to another one. 'It's all yours, sport, but don't let's be too long about it. I got practice to do.'

60

I looked round at them—Don, Omi Kawasaki, Laurie, Sam, Ambrose and the two caddies. It wasn't exactly a crowd but it was enough. I said, 'I suggest we keep this to ourselves for the present—you can imagine the kind of headlines there'll be if the papers get hold of it.' Most of them nodded, so I went on, 'For a start, we'd better find out how many of the Big Bangs there are, so perhaps Mr Kawasaki can help us there. You *did* put some of your joke balls in Mr Shroeder's bag?'

'Oh sure. Not with his club. I put them in the bag Dexter carries practice balls in.'

'How many?'

'Not know exactly. A dozen or so, I guess. Penfolds.'

I'd overlooked the complication of different makes of ball. 'Suppose Shroeder had been playing with something else. Like Dunlops?'

The Jap shrugged. 'So I give him Dunlops. Firm in Kobe sells all makes. Billiard balls, too.'

My God, I thought, a laugh a minute. I went over to the bag Dexter carried and peered in. Unlike common folk who try to improve their game with the help of cut, discoloured and only fairly round balls, tour players practise with clean, virtually new ones, these being supplied free by their sponsors. The bag must have held upwards of five hundred, every one as alike as the next as modern technology could devise. With maybe a dozen exceptions. I took one off the top layer and studied it cautiously. The writing said *Penfold Ace*, printed over the number used to identify one ball from another. It looked very much like a straightforward golf ball to me.

I turned back to Kawasaki. 'Can *you* tell a funny ball from the real thing?'

'Can do.' Kawasaki took the ball from me and glanced at it intently for a moment. 'Yes. One of mine.'

'How do you tell?'

'So customers are knowing, there is full stop after name. But also one remembers that joke balls are made in two halves stuck together. You know what you are looking for, you see where paint covers join.'

I took the ball back. He was quite right—if you *did* know what you were looking for, it was possible to spot the difference—just.

'I suppose you couldn't have hit on a freak ball—some kind of manufacturing error? An accidental overload of explosive or something?' Even as I made the suggestion it sounded unlikely.

Kawasaki shook his head. 'I have seen made—the charge is a pellet, so girls are not measuring charge themselves. Also there is no room for more than one pellet.'

Which meant that someone had opened the joke balls, substituted an entirely different charge, re-sealed the covers and returned them. Someone who knew of the balls' existence and of Kawasaki's weakness for practical jokes.

Laurie spoke for the first time. 'It made an appalling noise, but it didn't do any real damage. I wonder why?'

'No fragmentation.' It hadn't struck me before, but of course it was true. She was still looking at me so I went on, 'Grenades and suchlike are made to break up and fly around, just as a terrorist's home-made bomb is stuffed with nails or ball-bearings. But, as you say, this was just a bang.'

'I know. But *why?*'

Why indeed? Omi Kawasaki's joke balls made a little pop, the one we'd just exploded made a mighty crack but neither were in the least dangerous. So what was the point of going to a lot of trouble just to make more noise? I gave up, but fragmentation or no fragmentation, I was glad it was Sam's box of tricks that had hit that ball and not me. I tried to imagine what it would feel like to swing at a ball that exploded. Maybe it didn't blow your legs off, but it would be a second or two before you were sure. God, I thought, you wouldn't feel like hitting another ball in a hurry. I caught Shroeder looking at me. 'Suppose,' I said, 'we hadn't been fooling around with that gadget and you'd started practising as you'd intended—'

'It would have been me that hit the ball, I reckon. Some shaker!'

'Enough shake to put you off your game?'

'Too bloody true it'd put me off!'

I thought that one over. 'For how long?'

'Dunno.' Shroeder frowned, concentrating. 'For quite a time, I reckon. You got to imagine looking down at the ball at the top of the backswing. That's the moment of total concentration—total balance. Right?'

'Right.'

'Well, there you go. Every next time you do that you're going to wonder if that little beauty down there is going to blow up too. That maybe the next one *will* blow your legs off. Hell, you'd have to be inhuman not to let it get to you.'

'Yes,' I agreed, 'that's what I thought.' People were beginning to look at watches and I didn't want to outstay my welcome, so I picked up the caddie's bag. 'Perhaps Mr Kawasaki here would identify the balls that were originally his, then I can have someone open them up to see exactly what's been done to them.'

Omi Kawasaki nodded. 'Sure, I do it now.'

'And I suggest we keep this whole business under wraps —we don't want half the competitors getting neurotic about their driving. Oh, and Mr Kawasaki—'

'Yes, Inspector?'

'No more little jokes, please.'

He smiled, showing all those teeth again. 'No more jokes!'

But his eyes weren't smiling. They were as dark and blank and as unreadable as ever.

It was four o'clock by the time I got around to seeing Raikes, and by then I was hardly in the mood to hold his hand. Laurie had picked her car up from the flat and gone back to London. I didn't blame her for that as there had never been any question of her staying, but just the same I couldn't help feeling that I should have been able to give her my undivided attention, which I hadn't.

'Now you're quite sure you'll get that manuscript finished on time.' She'd stood by her open car door studying me from behind those Praying Mantis glasses as though she was checking on whether or not I'd got my sandwiches for school.

'Yes,' I told her, 'quite sure.'

'By October 30th.'

Well, she was my agent and I paid her ten per cent to check this kind of thing. I said, 'Yes, God damn it, by October 30th. You think I can't read?'

'I'm sure you can read. It's just that if you're going to be late, I want to know. Publishers' contracts are as binding as anyone else's, but if you're in trouble I can usually chat them into extending the deadline.' Unexpectedly she'd taken her glasses off and was fiddling with them, the first unsure thing I'd seen her do. 'Angus, don't get yourself too involved in this golf thing. Pass it over to whoever would handle it if you weren't around.'

'But I am around, and I can hardly tell the Chief Constable to get lost,' I said. And, never one to ignore a sitting duck, I added, 'Particularly as it seems I can't support myself any other way.'

A skein of geese flew over the woods, honking and complaining to each other. We watched them till the trees hid them before I spoke. 'It's only a lot of minor nuisances. Sort themselves out in a day or two.'

'Do you really believe that?'

'No, not really.' I'd meant to turn the question aside but I guessed that with this girl I wouldn't have much chance of success. I stopped looking at the sky because the geese had gone and they wouldn't be back till morning. 'Bits and pieces of nonsense all over the place,' I told her. 'Women's libbers, kids on bikes, money with menaces and now exploding golf balls. There should be some kind of link between them, but I can't think what.'

'But surely—the steward?'

'Maybe.'

'Well, take care of yourself, Angus.' I knew the 'maybe' hadn't satisfied her. She'd known I was shutting her up but in any case she had to go. She touched me briefly. 'Ring me and let me know you're all right.'

'By deadline date?'

She ignored that. 'Promise?'

'Yes, of course.' Pompous ass. Why did I always say

64

things the wrong way? I tried to improve on it but the car's window had shut, the starter whined and she was gone. Those sad words: too late.

It seemed a long way from home back to Harlington nick and I was still on leave. I told them to bring Raikes up to the interview room while a WPC fetched me a cup of coffee in a plastic beaker, and by the time he arrived I was sitting at the table waiting for him. He looked at the coffee but I didn't offer him one.

'All right, Raikes,' I said, 'you'd better tell me about it.'

'I've told them once.'

'Well, tell me.'

'I didn't have anything to do with that business of cutting up the green.' With the table between us, Raikes could almost have been back behind his bar. He even had the brisk, confidential manner he used there when he was telling a member how many someone had gone round in that morning. Those watery blue eyes full of phoney intensity. 'Nor the bike business, neither.'

'You mean that if the five thousand hadn't been forthcoming you'd have thought up a bit of damage on your own account?'

'No, of course not,' Raikes said with a touch of asperity.

It was amusing to see how virtuous he could become all of a sudden. 'Then why write that note in the first place?'

He rubbed his chin, presumably fishing around for the right words. Finally, 'Well, I mean, those things had *happened*, hadn't they? Some nutter carving up the green and then that kid on a bike. I mean, it's pretty obvious they were done by two separate people, isn't it?'

'Is it?' I tried to imagine poor April Tonge riding a motorbike cross-country. Possibly Raikes had the same thought, too.

Unabashed, he went on, 'Well, it was to me. On their own they didn't amount to much, but if they'd been done by the same bloke and there was a chance of it happening again—well, that would be different, wouldn't it? Something worth worrying about. And when you think what they're paying out for tents and suchlike up there, five grand's just peanuts. I mean, a firm like Tamworth would pay that out of the petty cash just to avoid the aggro.'

'They might,' I agreed, 'but they didn't.' I drank my coffee and tried to look as though I was enjoying it. Interesting that the attitude of the Tamworth director, Kempton, had been exactly as Raikes had predicted, but then one could well get a special insight into human nature while working behind a bar.

'No, they didn't,' Raikes agreed shrewdly. 'But that might be because you got at them.'

'Possibly.'

He sighed like a man accepting the inevitable. 'What do you reckon I'll get?'

It was an understandable question but the best I could tell him was that it was unlikely to be anything very terrible. According to our records he hadn't been in trouble before, so with luck he might well get away with a suspended sentence, although I wasn't going to tell him that. Instead I went through the whole routine again, but he stuck to his story, claiming this time that he'd got the whole idea from a book. By and large I believed him.

'Look, Inspector, are they going to keep me here?' We'd been at it for an hour and for the first time Raikes was beginning to look worried.

I shook my head and told him he'd be out shortly and he seemed relieved. What Thurston was planning to do about him I had no idea—rogue he might be but this was hardly the time for the Club to lose the services of its head steward. I consoled myself with the thought that at last this was one problem that wasn't likely to be passed on to me.

'Silly bugger,' Hawkins observed when I called in to see him on my way out. He had no more belief in Raikes as an arch villain than I had. 'Probably read about it in a book. Surprising how many of 'em do.'

'His very words,' I told him, 'but I suppose they've got to learn their trade somewhere.'

Hawkins nodded. 'You'd think they'd read up something a bit more ambitious, wouldn't you? Wastes a man's time, all these piddling little offences. Give me a good honest crime—'

I drove home slowly, thinking it over. Hawkins was right, of course—they were indeed piddling little offences, with perfectly straightforward explanations for almost all of them. The ninth green had been dug up to serve April Tonge's feminist cause, the demand for money was the work of a bar steward who had read too many whodunits and it was obvious that neither incident had the slightest connection with the other. The motorcyclist I'd scared off with a rake remained unidentified but I had a feeling he was going to stay that way. After all, half the golf clubs in England got kids riding over their greens and fairways now and again and there was no reason to suppose that the West Wessex would remain sacrosanct for ever. As for the golf ball—

Well, there was no getting away from the fact that the exploding golf ball lark was different and I didn't begin to understand it.

'You don't want to bother about Omi, sport. He's just a little Nip joker.'

Don Shroeder on Kawasaki and probably not far out, because top professional golfers had other things to do than try to blow each other up. But *why* had someone gone to the trouble of altering the charge in those parlour trick balls? Certainly there didn't seem to be the remotest connection with any of the other odd happenings at the West Wessex. But then why did a Club have odd happenings in the first place?

I turned at my home crossroads and swung into the gates and up the drive, cheered by the conviction that, having earned an evening to myself, I was actually going to get it. I calculated that if I wrote ten pages of typescript this evening that would represent two-and-a-half thousand words. Four similar evenings and I'd have ten thousand in the bag. It was the kind of sum I'd done many times before and I knew perfectly well that it never worked out like that, but it was comforting just the same. There was also bacon and eggs in the refrigerator, just so long as my vulture of a cat had left them alone.

I let myself in and went into the living-room, aware of a draught where there shouldn't have been one. Had I left that window open? I shut it and looked round. The room was orderly enough, nobody had done it over and yet I didn't relax because something was different and took me an appreciable time to discover what it was. The wall above my desk was empty. The crossbow had gone.

Aloud, I said, 'Bloody kids!' Crossbows were the latest 'in' thing for the dangerous end of the teenage layabout belt because for some lunatic reason modern versions of the weapon could still be bought without a licence. At a hundred pounds a crack, they were a bit expensive, so my thirteenth-century model was obviously collectable. I decided that there wasn't much I could do about that one until I'd had something to eat, so I went into the kitchen, to be pulled up sharp by the open refrigerator door which only partly obscured half a familiar rabbit-coloured body crouched on the floor.

I said softly, 'Ramases, you're a thieving bastard!' and slammed the door shut. I need not have hurried, because Ramases didn't move. Presently I began to understand why. He wasn't ever going to move again, because someone had taken the largest of my razor-sharp Sabatier kitchen knives and used it to cut off his head.

CHAPTER 6

A 'rub of the green' occurs when a ball in motion is accidentally deflected or stopped by any outside agency.
Definition

I had no desire at all to go to the party but they'd asked me and I couldn't think of any reasonable excuse to say no. It was the West Wessex captain's idea of a thank-you to the various members who'd helped get the tournament organized, and a good idea if you like that kind of thing, which I don't.

'Incidentally, there's a committee meeting before it starts,' Alan had said. 'Afraid you've been co-opted, if that's all right with you. Six o'clock in the committee room.'

'All right.'

'You're not doing anything else?'

No, I'd said, I wasn't planning to do anything else. I'd buried Ramases under the big sycamore where he used to lie in wait for birds, together with a tin of his favourite tuna to see him over whatever Styx cats cross before they reach their new hunting grounds. I'd cleaned the spade and put it away, but it was a windy afternoon and occasionally the cat door flapped as though something was passing through it. By and large I was glad of an excuse to get out.

The meeting was nothing if not predictable, item one on the agenda being the night security patrol, which it was proposed should be discontinued forthwith. Happily the series of annoyances might now be considered at an end, so hardly fair to ask members to give up more of their time, and besides, they'd miss the party. Would Inspector Straun agree that this was in order? I said yes, it was all right by me, feeling a little guilty because it was nice of them to ask. After all, it had been their own patrol, the police having let them down.

'You agree, Inspector, that it's unlikely there'll be any more trouble?'

'Well, I think you've done all you can.' I was trying to sound confident but what I said was true enough. There comes a time when almost any campaign becomes counter-productive simply because people get bored, and nothing could conceal the fact that the top brass at the West Wessex were getting very bored indeed with things that went bump in the night. Perhaps not so much bored as sceptical, and I was not surprised at the speed with which it had been agreed that the patrols should stand down.

'Oh, and another thing.' Alan Thurston prodded his agenda. 'We've had another couple of nonsenses, but if it's all right with everybody I suggest we just accept the fact that we seem to be attracting more than our share of cranks and ignore them. One's a note warning us against going ahead with the Tamworth—no demand for money or anything, just a warning.'

He might have told me, but apparently that wasn't on any more. *Just another couple of nonsenses.* Well, we didn't get our reputation for understatement for nothing. I held out my hand. 'Do you have it with you?'

He passed it over, a single sheet of paper. 'Arrived with the second lot of mail. Posted locally.'

As an art form that kind of message doesn't vary much and this one was very similar to Raikes's offering—letters cut out of newspapers or magazines and stuck down to form the words.

STOP THE TAMWORTH CLASSIC
WHILE THERE IS TIME
THERE IS SO MUCH AT STAKE
PLEASE ACT NOW

The envelope was typewritten on a newish machine with pica type by someone using two fingers, which wasn't going to be of much help in the immediate future. Typewriters are always a potent lead in whodunits, but peering at type bars with microscopes doesn't help much when you've every machine in the country to choose from.

'Obviously some kind of nut,' Alan was saying. 'I mean, one can't be expected to stop everything just because one person cries doom and destruction.'

'He doesn't actually mention that.' I folded the note and put it back in the envelope. '*So much at stake* is subjective, after all. Could mean the English Sabbath.'

Alan grinned. 'I suppose it could. But you must agree it's not very explicit.'

I did agree but it was an odd message, just the same. There's something unnerving about appeals that don't mention money but just sound desperate. But then, for all one knows, being mentally unstable is a pretty desperate business anyway.

'You said a couple of nonsenses. What was the other one?'

'A member of our ground staff found ten gallons of—'

70

Alan consulted his notes but apparently couldn't find what he was looking for.

'Aminotriazole,' someone helped him out, a someone new to me. Small, round, with thinning fair hair and thick glasses. Fiftyish and boffinish, which is a poor description, really, because I've met plenty of boffins who looked like rugger blues—a few who *were* rugger blues, come to that.

'Thank you.' Alan looked relieved. Then to me, 'I don't know if you've met Keith Fletcher, Angus. Our agronomist. He's been kind enough to have a last-minute look at the greens.'

We nodded to each other and I decided that I'd not been far out, because the grass experts who advise golf clubs today are fast becoming a highly specialized scientific élite. Not that there was much of the élitist air about Fletcher, sitting there with very little of the confidence one expects from the usual cocky scientific whizzkid who has inherited the earth and knows it.

'What exactly *is* Aminotriazole?' I asked.

'It's a defoliant.' A soft voice with a hint of Midlands accent that played down the word so that it didn't have quite the impact it might otherwise have done.

I wasn't up on defoliants, knowing roughly that they were the substances sprayed on the forests of Vietnam to get rid of the leaves and that was about all, and said as much.

Fletcher regarded me from behind his glasses, which must have been pretty powerful because they made his eyes look unnaturally large. 'You're right, of course. The Americans used defoliants extensively in order to get rid of troop cover. This stuff isn't quite the same—it's used more against scrub than trees.' Given the chance to talk about his subject, he seemed to assume more of an air of confidence.

It's a constant source of astonishment how people with nothing to hide so often delight in avoiding the point. 'What you're saying,' I probed carefully, 'is that this stuff has no right here. I mean, it wouldn't exactly do the greens any good.' The light touch that turneth away wrath.

He didn't smile. 'Oh, good heavens, no. It would kill the grass immediately. Not only kill it but render the ground completely sterile for years. You'd have to dig everything up and start again from scratch.'

I tried to imagine April Tonge and her girls gaily sloshing defoliant over every green in sight and didn't much like the idea. I suppose my feelings must have shown because Fletcher went on hastily, 'I really don't think you should be too concerned about this. I'm sure the whole thing is just a mistake.'

'I certainly hope you're right.' I did my best to sound as unconcerned as he did, and after all, it was his grass and not mine. Odd, though, that he was taking it so lightly. I asked, 'Whose mistake is it, do you suppose?'

He managed a small smile. 'The manufacturers, I'm relieved to say. I shouldn't have liked to think that I had been personally responsible.'

'Which firm are we talking about?'

'Grestock and Hives.' Fletcher produced the name without hesitation. 'I'd ordered ten gallons of a branded nitrate compound and this stuff arrived instead. The despatch note and invoice came at the same time and that's what both of them specified. It's just the product itself that's wrong.'

One could imagine asking for one kind of fertilizer and getting the wrong brand, but to ask for fertilizer and get defoliant instead seemed to be carrying idiosyncratic British service to an extreme. Presented with a prescription for aspirin, not many chemists regularly serve cyanide. 'Do you suppose,' I suggested, 'that there might have been some confusion over names? Are they similar?'

'Well, they're not dissimilar.' Fletcher thought the matter over and then nodded. 'Come to think of it, not dissimilar at all. I imagine that's how the mistake happened.'

'Let's hope you're right.' But I found it hard to imagine the stores control that could make that kind of mistake possible and I was puzzled by the fact that Fletcher himself seemed to have no such difficulty. Maybe among agronomists this kind of thing was always happening. If so, it probably explained why visiting Americans were always complaining about British greens.

'Well, that seems to have cleared those points up.' Alan

Thurston was putting his notes briskly together. 'Anyway, got anything else before we make for the bar?'

Nobody had, so that was that. I wondered what had brought about the change. After all, it had been only a few days since everyone had been in a blue funk, whereas all of a sudden there was a distinct air of couldn't care less. I watched the committee moving purposefully towards the bar and decided that I'd probably been right in thinking that people simply got bored with trouble.

'What are you drinking?' Alan gathered me up and pushed his way through the amiable crowd of men and women who were relaxing with a good deal of dedication, judging by the way they were pouring alcohol down their throats. As is usual on such occasions, the noise level was pretty deafening and I had to shout to make myself heard.

'Have you known Fletcher long?'

'On and off for five or six years.' Alan was looking over his shoulder, nodding to someone, cheerfully unconcerned. 'We used to use Stamford Bates, like everyone else, but when the old man died we had to find a successor. Fletcher had some kind of loose partnership deal with Bates, so the next time we needed help we asked him to come along.'

'Is he any good?'

'He's damn good, as a matter of fact. In my opinion, he's well up to Bates's standard and doesn't waffle as much.' Alan took another drink off a passing tray. 'You know what agronomists are like—they like to blind simple souls like you and me with science. But Fletcher isn't like that. If you've got a green that's going bald, he'll give you a fifty-page report for your money but he'll also tell you in words of two syllables what's got to be done. Mind you, he's an odd little chap, but I suppose you can't have everything.'

The bar at the West Wessex covers about an acre and it was rapidly filling up. I saw Polly Appleby in a flame-coloured dress busy doing what was presumably her duty with Kempton, introducing him to a rather trendily dressed young Indian who somebody told me was in charge of television coverage, while Ambrose Hall was being amusing to a group who were hanging on to his every word, and

73

what seemed like dozen upon dozen of members and their wives all bent on relaxing after a lot of hard work. I felt vaguely guilty at feeling jaundiced about them because, God knows, they must have given a lot of time and sweat to the tournament in one way or another. I didn't begrudge them their fun but somehow I did resent their light-hearted abandon, even though I couldn't put a name to my own niggling forebodings. Keith Fletcher was standing in a corner by himself, holding a drink and biting the fingernails of his free hand. *Why* was he biting his fingernails? Why not? Maybe he hated his mother or something.

'Let's get you another drink,' Alan shouted in my ear.

I made 'no' gestures and waved a half-full glass. It struck me suddenly that I hadn't seen his wife anywhere. 'Where's Melanie?'

'Couldn't come. Dicky tummy. Some sort of bug going round.'

'Oh,' I said, 'I'm sorry.' I was, too. A nice, noisy woman who was good with restless policemen.

'There's a lot of it about. She'll be all right in a day or two.'

There were a number of things I would like to have talked to him about but it was hardly the place. Someone came up and buttonholed him and so I circulated, which wasn't difficult because there were a lot of people I knew and I had no great desire to go back to the flat and its small ghost. Time passed satisfactorily, and later rather than sooner I found myself spearing slices of turkey at the buffet alongside Polly Appleby. She gave me an amiable grin and somehow managed to indicate the rest of the room with her plate. 'Hello, Inspector. Work or play?'

'I imagine in about the same proportion as yourself.' I led her out of the scrum around the tables to a spot by one of the big windows that overlooked the putting green. By now night had fallen but the moon was up and one could just see the first tee and a hint of the fairway beyond. I said something about it being a nice night.

'You're as bad as that funny little grass wizard—I can't remember his name.'

'Fletcher?'

'That's right.' She nodded up at the starbright sky. 'He kept looking out at the night and saying the same thing. He's something to do with seeds, isn't he?'

'He's an agronomist.' She raised her eyebrows. 'They get called in to advise on how to prepare greens—recommend types of grass. That kind of thing.'

'I thought it was something like that.' Polly munched a piece of turkey reflectively. 'Funny little man.'

'Why so?' She was right, of course, but I wondered what had registered with her.

'He seemed a bit—lost.'

'Shy, perhaps. He didn't look the party type.'

Polly laughed. 'No, that's true. I tried to chat to him earlier on but it didn't get me anywhere. He just wanted to tell me what a nice night it was.'

'Perhaps he was trying to get around to suggesting a walk in the moonlight?'

She shook her head. 'I don't think so. Anway, he doesn't seem to be here now, so I imagine he's gone home.'

I looked round but, as she said, Fletcher seemed to have called it a day, which was more than could be said for a couple of dozen members and guests who were dancing to the music someone had switched on via the public address system. It seemed a good idea. Polly was pleasant to dance with, almost as tall as me in her high heels, but light on her feet withal.

She said, 'You seem a troubled policeman tonight.'

'You could say that.'

'I suppose it would be stupid of me to ask if there's anything I can do?'

'I don't think there is, but it's not stupid, your asking.' How nice people can be sometimes.

We went outside. We weren't the only ones by any means, and for a moment I wished we were. I could hear Ambrose booming away from the other side of the clubhouse and I looked over to see what he was up to. He caught my eye.

'Come on, Angus! Take your lady for a spin!'

He'd got half-a-dozen electric caddie carts lined up like

dodgems and was renting them out at a fiver a time for some charity or other. So far as I knew the carts were used by the TV company during the commentary but the Indian, Patel, seemed to be taking it all in good part. Two of the carts were whining away with a couple apiece aboard, loud cheers from everyone. I hoped for Patel's sake that they came back in one piece, a considerable amount of drink having been drunk.

Polly was saying, 'What fun! I've never been in one of those!'

She was stone cold sober or as near as makes no difference, being one of those favoured souls who get happily high on party spirit rather than the other sort, and I was doing my law-abiding policeman bit. Nevertheless, it would have been churlish to let the lady down. I paid my five pounds, thinking how peaceful and private it would be out there in the moonlight. Cheap at the price.

'Can I drive?'

Of course she could drive. Why not? I settled myself beside her and we set off along the fairway beyond the first green, turned left and headed somewhere of her own contriving. Caddie carts aren't big on performance but to look at Polly you'd have thought she was flat out on a motorway, with her eyes shining with excitement. I envied her sheer capacity to have fun.

'Absolutely great!' She looked at me, laughing. 'Where are we?'

'Heading for the eighth, I think, once we get round those trees.' It was hard to tell in the moonlight, because things looked different.

'We always seem to be exploring this place in the dark.'

Well, it was a second time, certainly. I said truthfully, 'It's a habit I've grown rather fond of.' And then rather more urgently, 'Watch it, you'll have us in that bunker!'

'Whoops!' Polly swerved to avoid the ridge that I guessed concealed deep sandy depths which weren't likely to improve a caddie cart. We missed it by a foot and I looked back. There was a shadow there that didn't look right. Something extra dark that I didn't like at all.

I said, 'Stop!'

Polly must have reckoned that I meant it because she stopped dead. 'Angus, what is it?'

'Stay where you are.'

She stayed. I went over to the bunker and ploughed across it until I was standing looking down at the darker than dark shadow, a small man in a crumpled suit who lay there motionless, face downwards in the soft sand. I wasn't all that surprised. Perhaps some kind of mental alarm bells had been ringing in my ears for some time and I was just beginning to learn how to recognize them.

Behind me, Polly was asking in a small voice, 'Who is it?'

'Keith Fletcher.'

I lifted his head with some difficulty because the dead are heavy and he was dead all right. There was moonlight enough to see that it was undoubtedly our hired grass expert and that from the way his head hung, his neck was broken. I eased him down gently and straightened my back. From the direction of the clubhouse you could hear faint shouts and boisterous laughter, but where we stood it was dark and very quiet. A cloud drifted over the moon and a small wind sprang up. I found myself thinking that they'd be lucky if there wasn't rain before morning.

CHAPTER 7

Except as provided in Rule 8-2, a player may give advice to, or ask advice from, only his partner . . .

Rule 8-1

Mike Oliver, the police surgeon, tipped me the result of the post-mortem by coffee-time the following morning. Death due to fracture of this, that and the other, to wit his neck, and all very routine. Dull, really. Mike, I suspected, dreamed of forensic wonders but he never got the chance, murder being thin on the ground on our patch.

'No sign of any kind of blow?' I asked it more as a

confirmation than anything else, because if there'd been anything like that he wouldn't have been able to wait to tell me.

'Apparently not.'

'Alcohol?' I don't know why I asked that because from what I'd seen, Fletcher was unlikely to have had more than about half a drink all evening.

Mike shook his head. 'Virtually none. At any rate, you can take it he was as sober as a judge when he died.'

Hawkins came in, obviously briefed because he was grinning from ear to ear. ''Orrible murder?' he inquired.

'You would not,' I said, 'wish me to anticipate the coroner's findings?'

'God forbid, but you know as well as I do that it's got to be misadventure. It's no good, Angus, you can forget about solving the year's great murder mystery.'

'I don't want a murder,' I said. Strictly, that wasn't true, because I'd have liked nothing better, but there's such a thing as pride.

'I thought you were supposed to be on leave.'

Hawkins was in a particularly lovable mood this morning, but I ignored it. 'I am, but I presume I'll be called at the inquest.'

'Well, keep the bloody coroner in his place—I'm sick to death of retired quacks playing at being Lord Chief Justice.'

'I'll do my best,' I promised him.

Inquests are odd affairs. Newspapers usually play them down but they must be nerve-racking for those directly concerned. After all, if you've poisoned your lover there isn't even going to *be* a trial if the coroner can be persuaded that the corpse died of a nasty cold. Keith Fletcher's swan song was due to take place within twenty-four hours of his death, which was unusually brisk, and I had hopes that the whole business would be wrapped up pretty smartly, the official concerned being a doctor by the name of Matson, with a reputation for common sense which is rarer among coroners than one might expect.

In the event, my hopes for Matson turned out to be justified and he questioned me briskly and sensibly, not wishing to see things that weren't there but still giving me ample opportunity to be steered if such was my wish.

Did I consider it odd, for instance, that the dead man should have chosen that time of night to walk round a golf course?

I said no, I didn't in view of the circumstances. A great many people had been doing much the same thing, myself included, albeit not on foot.

I watched the coroner's pencil as he jotted or doodled something. 'You have already described the circumstances under which you discovered the deceased, Inspector. But Mr Fletcher had not hired a golf cart. Why did he choose to walk the not inconsiderable distance to the sixth fairway?'

Well, I'd wondered that myself without arriving at any worthwhile conclusion. I said, 'I don't know, sir. It was a pleasant night. It's possible he felt like a breath of air. I suppose he could have wanted to look at the greens.'

'In the middle of the night, Inspector?'

Well, it seemed as likely as driving round in a caddie cart. I said, 'He'd come some considerable way to advise on them, and he seems to have been pretty single-minded with regard to his work. It was not all that dark, so I think it quite possible that he would have gone out to look at the greens.'

'And fallen into a bunker.'

Had he made it a question, it might have sounded more likely than the flat statement. 'Mr Fletcher was familiar with the greens,' I said, 'but he had nothing to do with bunkers. I very much doubt if he knew where any of them were, and if you approach a bunker from its closed side it is sometimes quite easy to miss in daylight, let alone the dark.'

'The closed side, Inspector?'

It was not unlike judges who insist on defining a motor bus, but I did my best to explain. 'The bunkers are presented as hazards to the golfer playing that particular hole, in effect shallow holes, lined with sand. Once you have passed them there is often very little to indicate they are there at all.'

The pencil stopped whatever drawing it had been engaged

upon. Matson was a meek enough looking little chap but when he stared at you he had a certain something. 'Thank you, Inspector. So you are personally satisfied that Mr Fletcher walked accidentally into this bunker and broke his neck.'

'There is nothing—' I paused, resenting entirely his switch to the personal. So far as I was concerned, Fletcher had just gone for a walk, and at this stage of the game nobody was ever going to know his exact motivations. It seemed blindingly obvious that after that he had simply fallen into a hole he hadn't known was there. Blindingly obvious, and yet for some reason I found it extraordinarily difficult to accept. Would a man really break his neck if he fell into a sand-filled bunker? If the thing was deep enough for a man to turn himself upside down, the answer was clearly yes, but the fact was that the one in which Fletcher had been found couldn't have been more than three feet at the most. On the other hand, people managed to break their necks tripping over kerbs and dogs, so the depth of the bunker was obviously neither here nor there.

'Yes, Inspector?'

'Well, sir,' I said, 'there is no evidence to suggest that he did not.'

'By that you mean you are not personally satisfied?'

Personal misgivings have no place in a Coroner's Court and I knew it. Moreover I found it genuinely difficult to put my doubts into words. In a moment Matson was going to stop being sympathetic and suggest that if I had any reason to suppose Fletcher had been murdered it was time I said so, and as I hadn't any reason, the sooner I got off the stand the better.

I said, 'I am personally satisfied that there is no evidence of foul play.'

'I am glad to hear it.' Matson could be a bleak little man when he wanted. 'Thank you, Inspector, you may stand down.'

I stood down. The rest of the business took no more than another ten minutes and Fletcher was duly recorded as having met an accidental death. Really, I hadn't expected anything else, but I was still unhappy about it. Why does one so unreasonably expect other people to go along with one's own ideas, fears, prejudices—call them what you will? I was not even clear in my own mind as to how Keith Fletcher had met his end, and my general mood wasn't helped by the Chief Constable ringing me up and putting in his oar.

'Being a little difficult this morning, weren't we, Angus? If the Coroner is satisfied that there's been no funny business, I don't see it does anyone any good for you to bend over backwards trying to put ideas in his head.'

I said, 'I'm sorry if you feel that way about it, sir. I stated quite definitely that there was no evidence of foul play.'

'Damn it, man, I know you said there wasn't any evidence, but you still managed to give the impression that you suspected there would be if we looked long enough.'

'That was entirely unintentional, sir, I assure you.' I hadn't got a tape-recording of my evidence but I was prepared to believe that what Linforth said was true. Probably I'd used what Angela used to call my 'sanctimonious' voice, by which she meant I occasionally oozed disapproval.

'Do you honestly think Fletcher's death wasn't an accident?'

'As I told the Coroner, sir, there's nothing to suggest that. But, come to that, there's nothing that proves anything else.'

The Chief Constable's voice smacked that one back pretty promptly. 'For God's sake, man, you know as well as I do that we don't have to look for evidence that *proves* accidental death. We assume it unless there is evidence to the contrary.'

'Yes, sir.' The soft answer that turneth away wrath, and I supposed that he had a point.

'Then be a good chap and try not to rock the boat.' A pause. 'I don't want to get officious about this, Angus, but just remember you're on leave, will you?'

Yes, I said, I'd remember. I couldn't very well blame him, because it wasn't as though he was deliberately taking me off a case because it might prove to be socially embarrassing. Linforth was simply saying that if I didn't know what it was that was making me uneasy, I could hardly expect him to feel the same way.

I went home and cooked myself some lunch, deliberating as to whether to take myself off somewhere and forget the whole thing. Only, of course, I knew that I wouldn't. If there was any connection between a vandalized green and a murdered cat, I didn't know what it was. How was an agronomist's broken neck to be linked to an exploding golf ball? I took out the last anonymous message Thornton had received and stared at the stuck-down words for the fiftieth time.

STOP THE TAMWORTH CLASSIC
WHILE THERE IS TIME
THERE IS SO MUCH AT STAKE
PLEASE ACT NOW

The appeal in the message still puzzled me. No demand for money, only an implied threat, if that. And this time one could be pretty sure Raikes had nothing to do with it. I studied the letters carefully. Some had been cut from some publication with a shiny surface, mostly in colour, others seemed to be of a slightly inferior paper, still with a certain amount of gloss, but a good deal thinner, and in black and white. Presumably that meant that some were from covers, others from inside pages. On an impulse I took the sheet of paper into the bathroom and left it floating in the handbasin while I had a cup of coffee. By the time I'd finished the letters had unglued themselves enough to be lifted off, so I dried them carefully and turned them over with an increasing sense of disappointment. It had seemed a bright idea, but obviously the source of the cut-outs wasn't going to be instantly apparent because the coloured letters seemed to have backed on to advertisements or illustrations of some kind, so that in almost all cases the printing consisted of uneven patterns with occasional part words in larger than normal type. The black and white letters were of little more help because again what little printing there was consisted of no more than a couple of words here and there. I don't know what I'd expected—probably something satisfactorily identifiable such as a phrase like 'remove gearbox' or 'turn up hem' that would at least have told me what kind of publication had been used to supply the letters. As it was, the most I could find were odd groups that made up such telling phrases as *less it will, and so it, there's a* and so on. On an impulse I rang up Laurie and said I wanted to see her urgently that afternoon.

'Trouble with the book?'

'It's nothing to do with the book.'

'Well, it should be.'

'Oh, for Christ's sake—' I felt in no mood for verbal pitch and toss—'are you in or aren't you?'

'I'll be in.' Then, 'You don't sound in any state to be loose on the roads in that car. Best come by train.'

All I needed was a mother figure, but for the wrong reasons she was right. Travelling into town by road gave an impression that one was actually doing something, but in fact it was considerably quicker by rail. I left the car at Harlington and took the train.

At the back of my mind I must have had a picture of a literary agent's office as being white rugs and black glass, whereas in fact it could have done with a coat of paint and was almost entirely lined with books which I supposed was what I should have expected. Judging by the pile of folders on the large but battered desk, she was busy but she wasn't going to make a thing about it.

'What is it, Angus?'

I put the pile of individual letters from the message in front of her and explained what I'd done. 'I thought you might know something about printing.'

'So I could identify them?' She picked up an 'E' and inspected it warily. 'I thought the police had forensic laboratories that could identify just about everything.'

I said, 'The police do. The trouble is that it wouldn't be very tactful to try using them just now.'

'Ah.' Laurie took off her glasses. 'I see. Well, you probably need a paper man more than a printer—magazine publishers aren't exactly wildly adventurous when it comes to

83

choosing typefaces. Most of the paper comes from two or three main suppliers too, if it comes to that, but we'll have to start somewhere.'

'You know anyone?'

'I think so. Someone who'll pass you around, anyway.'

The someone turned out to be a cheerful character in his forties who welcomed me in a seedy red brick office near the Isle of Dogs. Somewhere down in the basement a printing press ran with a subdued roar and the air held a curious aroma that I imagined was ink. The name on his door was M. A. Lucas and I felt he was as expert in his field as I was likely to find, but then, other people's crafts are always impressive.

Lucas rubbed letters between his fingers, held them up to the light, sorted them like playing cards. 'Three sources,' he said finally. 'Did you expect more?'

I told him that I hadn't known what to expect, but as there were seventy letters, that didn't seem too bad. 'What are the chances of identifying whatever publications those letters came from?'

'Dunno.' Lucas was scribbling on a pad. 'One lot is cut from a 70 gramme Process Coated paper which looks to me like Silver Blade Art. The second's another Silver Blade, only 60 gramme Multi-Purpose and the third is Huntsman Opaque M.P.—60 gramme again.' He looked up. 'Any objection to someone else coming in on this? Print's not altogether my thing.'

No, I said, I hadn't any objection, and he called in a gnome-like little man in his sixties, wearing an ancient duster coat, who peered at the backs of the letters and muttered the names of typefaces like an incantation. They meant nothing to me but, by the time a third member had been called, they seemed to have forgotten me and were deep in the investigation for its own sake. I sat in the chair they'd given me and stared out over the Thames. Eventually they seemed to arrive at some conclusion and Lucas came back with the letters in his hand. 'We're pretty sure of the printers—only two of them, so you're lucky. M. and T. Crossthwaite and Rainbow Press Services. They're both independents who take on contract stuff from smaller publishers, mostly. I imagine anyone there will tell you which titles these things were cut from.'

'Where do I have to go?'

Lucas produced a folded sheet of paper from his pocket. 'Crossthwaites are in Cardiff and the Rainbow place is somewhere outside Chester.'

'I suppose I'm lucky the bloody places aren't in Penzance and Edinburgh.' I didn't feel like smiling but I made an effort. One can muster almost any kind of expertise, given time, but these boys could hardly have been quicker and I didn't want to give the impression that I expected any more. As it happened, I got more anyway, because Lucas held out the sheaf of paper with a grin. 'We thought you'd probably say that, so I gave my opposite number a ring at both places and got them to give me a list of the titles they publish. I know it's not as good as getting the exact ones but maybe it's better than nothing.'

I took the list, because it was indeed a great deal better than nothing. It read:

CROSSTHWAITES *Weekend Golfer*
Weekend Rally Cross
Weekend Gardener
Weekend Glider

RAINBOW *Big Girls*
The Leather Look
UFO
Black Hole

Lucas tapped Crossthwaites. 'Their *Weekend* magazines are a series, with the same format in each case. The paper and printing are identical, so unless you can settle down with a file of recent issues it doesn't look as though identification is going to be all that easy.'

'What about *Rainbow*?' I asked.

'*Big Girls* and *The Leather Look* go together—usual soft porn stuff. Likewise the science fiction ones. I've scribbled which is which on the back of the letters.'

I wished I could have done something more than just thank him, like giving him a free break-in or something but he didn't seem to think he'd done much. In fact, the last I heard from him was as I was going down the stairs and he was saying he'd wished he'd been able to more.

I rang Laurie from the pay phone at the foot of the stairs. 'Any luck?'

'Yes and no. Helpful chap.'

The voice in the earpiece said, 'I'm just leaving here. You'd better come round to my place and tell me about it. 12 Francis Mews. It's sort of behind the hospital at Hyde Park Corner.'

I doubt if I'd have found it but the cab driver did, a rather well done-over row of flats over garages that had once housed carriages, white-painted tubs full of growing things, with BMWs and suchlike being polished on the cobbles.

'You were quick.' She was standing at the open door of No. 12, wearing slacks now, and a kind of seaman's jersey. She led the way inside. Modern, one or two niceish bits of antiquery, books and foldered manuscripts everywhere. Every girl's dream of home.

'I'm impressed.'

She said calmly, 'No, you're not, you're costing up an S.W.1 mews and wondering how it's paid for.'

'It's the policeman in me. Pay no attention.'

'As a matter of fact, my sister had a long lease and she sold what was left of it to me when she got married.'

'Lucky you.'

'Don't you believe me?'

People always say 'Don't you believe me?' as soon as they've made some highly implausible statement. Maybe they don't expect to be believed. I said, 'Yes, damn it, I believe you. If you go on about it I probably shan't.'

She sighed. 'It's just that one gets so bored with people looking understanding. If I'd got a rich Arab who was paying the rent I'd be quite happy to introduce you—' She petered out, shook her head. 'Sorry. Tell me what you found out.'

I took out the list Lucas had made and gave it to her. 'If

anything, it's a bit too much what I'd expected. At least half the members of the West Wessex must look at the *Weekend Golfer* at some time or other—if they don't buy a copy of their own, someone probably lends them a copy. There must be umpteen back numbers lying around in the bar, come to that.'

'I suppose you could say the same thing about the gardening mag.' Laurie frowned at the list. 'Not as common as golf, maybe, but gardening must be pretty popular where you come from. Whereas Rally Cross—'

'I know,' I agreed, 'a dead cert for Raikes. Only one title won't do.'

'Leather Look?'

'Could be. It would go with Rally Cross, now I come to think of it.' One pondered what proportion of motor cyclists were leather fetishists. Judging by the number of girls who looked as though they were stark naked under their riding gear, probably quite a lot. I said, 'The sex mags could belong to absolutely anybody, and I can't imagine that there are all that number of flying saucer fanatics in the West Wessex. But gliding—'

Laurie fiddled with her glasses. 'Is there a local gliding club?'

I could remember seeing sailplanes soaring silently somewhere, the occasional aluminium transporter blocking the road in front of me like some kind of enormous horse box. 'I think there's one that operates from Sletting,' I said. 'It's an old wartime airfield that's still got one runway in use for light aircraft.'

'You could always ask if they've got any members who play golf—I don't see why they should mind telling you. Do your policeman act and they'll have to tell you, anyway.'

Well, it was better than doing it the other way round. I was beginning to understand how it was this girl made her way in the working world. 'The policeman act isn't very popular at the moment,' I confessed.

'How so?'

I told her. 'Unfortunately there's not a lot of chance to turn the blind eye. Ask anything you care to mention of half-a-dozen members of the public and at least one is going to complain to a higher authority. Maybe you haven't noticed, but the law isn't a respectable profession these days.'

Laurie stared at me indignantly. 'You mean you're going to let that kind of nonsense put you off?'

I said, 'You bet.'

'I think that's perfectly dreadful.'

'You said yourself that I wasn't capable of supporting myself any other way.'

'God, but you're thin-skinned!' Laurie said accusingly.

'If you prick me, I do indeed bleed.' But she deserved an answer, though a bright girl like that should have been able to see it for herself. 'Being a copper is much like being in any of the services—you do what you're told or else, and if anyone starts rocking the boat they're expendable.' Then I added, 'That doesn't mean there can't be a certain amount of blind eye turning. You just don't have to call attention to it.'

Laurie went into the kitchen to fix some drinks. 'I've only got sherry or whisky—which will it be?'

'Whisky will be fine.'

'What sort of blind eye turning did you have in mind?'

Well, how had she known that, for God's sake? I did my best not to look particularly surprised, but I don't imagine it fooled her any. I said, 'I wouldn't mind a look at Fletcher's flat.'

Perhaps that did surprise her, because she looked faintly startled. 'But why Fletcher? You're not seriously suggesting that that funny little man dug up one of his own greens?'

'No, of course not.' Actually odder things had happened but on this occasion I went along with a little honest scepticism. From what I'd seen of Keith Fletcher's dedication to his craft, it was difficult to imagine any circumstances in which he would have intentionally harmed a golf course.

'Then why?'

A good question. The answer wasn't even because I had some sort of a hunch, because I hadn't. 'Nothing much more than curiosity,' I said at last. 'As I said to the Coroner, there's not a shred of evidence to suggest that the poor bloke didn't die accidentally. The chances are that even if someone broke his neck intentionally and dumped him in a bunker—both of which seem highly unlikely—the murderer wouldn't have told him about it beforehand. It's just that we seem to know extraordinarily little about Keith Fletcher. Not married, no close friends—no family of any kind. I'd just like to find out what else there was in his life besides grass.'

'Maybe there wasn't anything.'

'Maybe.' But I didn't believe it. Everyone has something stored away, even if it's not readily accessible. A secretive lot, taken all round. I was secretive too, if it came to that. Why did I have to have all this dragged out of me? Because I'd been busy hiding it from myself, I supposed, which was devious but once again human nature. I said, 'He lived in Chiswick.'

Laurie looked surprised. 'Isn't that an odd place for an agronomist to live?'

'Well,' I said, 'he had to live somewhere. Chiswick is a highly thought of district, unless you think he should have lived beside a golf course.'

'Well, it would have been more likely, somehow. Where do you study grass in Chiswick, for God's sake?'

'Kew Gardens—it's just round the corner.'

Laurie shook her head. 'I think you're barking up the wrong tree. Besides, how do you know the local police haven't been through his things already?'

I knew the answer to that one. 'Because his solicitors were on to us before the post-mortem. They wanted the keys to the flat so that they could take an inventory—apparently Fletcher left everything to some kind of fourteenth cousin who lives in Spain. The cousin has no intention of coming back, because when the solicitors rang her up she said in effect, "Just sell everything and send me the money." So I suppose that's what they'll do.'

'Funny that he bothered to leave it formally to that kind of distant relative. Why not the local cats' home?'

I shook my head. 'Probably reckoned that any kind of

relative was better than none, and if he was that short on relatives, the Spanish cousin would inherit eventually anyway.' Being an only child from something of a line of only children, I was pretty deficient in blood relatives myself. It wasn't something that worried me but it had left me with a certain curiosity as to family relationships, which by and large seemed unpredictable to the point of lunacy.

Laurie looked at me much as I imagined her discouraging a very unpromising author. 'Is this all supposed to mean that you're contemplating a break-in, or whatever it's called?'

'Yes, I am, as a matter of fact. And you know perfectly well that a break-in is exactly what it's called.'

She rested her chin on one hand. 'Do you actually know how to go about it?'

'I've read the books.' Which was about as far as it went, come to that. Plenty of theory but short on experience, but one has to learn some time. I was sensitive just the same.

Laurie took my empty glass and refilled it. 'When does all this happen?' she asked. If she still had doubts about my qualifications as a burglar, she kept them to herself. In fact, if she thought that this was a slightly odd conversation to be taking place between a literary agent and her client, she kept that to herself too.

'Tonight, I suppose.' I did my best to make it sound casual. 'There's no point in coming up again, and one never knows when the solicitors may take it into their heads to start clearing the flat or something.'

She frowned. 'I presume we don't go till it's dark?'

I was startled but I did my best not to show it. 'We?'

Laurie said cheerfully, 'Well, somebody's got to drive the getaway car.'

'Considering the number of books you have to read,' I said, 'I'm surprised you have time for so much television. And the fact that I'm going to make a fool of myself doesn't mean that you're getting in on the act.'

'If you didn't want me in on the act you should have shut up about the whole thing,' Laurie responded. 'And anyway, you *need* a car. Unless you propose taking a taxi and have

90

it wait while you stick a jemmy under the front door or whatever.'

'You'd be making yourself an accessory to an unlawful entry,' I informed her.

Something began to kindle behind the glasses. 'Oh, for goodness sake, Angus, you're a policeman, aren't you? You know perfectly well that even if you got caught red-handed the worst you'd get would be a wigging. Nobody raises a finger to squatters when they let themselves in to other people's property, so why should they fret about you? I'll drive you there and wait for you discreetly round the corner, and that's that.'

There must have been any number of reasons why that wasn't that, but at the time I couldn't think of them. A virtuous woman is above rubies but a bossy one is something else again. We left the mews at eight-thirty in Laurie's Mini and pulled up outside 34a Riverside Grove, Chiswick, twenty-five minutes later. A clean, well-lighted street with plane trees just past their best, cars parked in rows. Here and there the odd householder going about his business trimming the hedge. Not so with 34a, which turned out to be a substantial Edwardian property set back from the road, with a group of four garages newly built at right angles to the drive. It was the kind of place that converts into flats cheaply and well, and I was faintly surprised because somehow it was all rather more comfortable than I had expected.

'Well, that's it,' I said. 'And it won't be dark for a couple of hours. We'd better go and get something to eat and come back.'

Laurie looked doubtful. 'I'm not sure that I'm all that keen on eating.'

'I don't know why not. You said yourself that all you had to do was sit in the car.'

'I suppose you're ravenous.'

'Moderately.' I was rather pleased to discover that this was true. Someone had once taken me to the City Barge on Strand-on-the-Green so I directed my driver there, hoping that the place hadn't closed in the meantime. Fortunately it hadn't and the food was as good as I'd remembered, so that by the time we got back to the flat we were probably both feeling a good deal better.

'Where shall I wait?' Now that we were ready for the off, we weren't quite so chipper, but then, there's a first time for everything. I told Laurie to park a couple of houses along where she'd be just one more of a line of cars, then walked back and up the driveway. There was a light in the top flat which I guessed would be No. 4, but the rest were in darkness. I wondered if the front door would be open or if callers had to announce themselves. I needn't have worried because the door to the hall was open and No. 2 was there waiting for me on the right.

Funny the way people are about security. Not a sign of penny-pinching about the conversion—good paintwork in the hall, decent carpet on the floor. One could tell without taking a second look that the furniture in any one of the flats was at least respectable and at best very good, with videos and cameras, word processors and the other high-cost goodies to which modern man is heir. But the locks on the doors were cheap Yales and I opened No. 2 in ten seconds flat with the help of a credit card.

I'd borrowed a flashlight off Laurie but there was enough light coming from the street lamps to read a newspaper by, so I simply walked round and made the best of it. It wasn't a big flat, just a single bedroom, a living-room and what was presumably meant to be a second bedroom but which Fletcher had fixed up as his office, complete with desk and filing cabinet. I hesitated over it for a moment but I suspected that the files were unlikely to contain anything other than details of the condition of the greens of half the golf clubs in England, and that wasn't exactly what I was looking for. What was it that I was looking for, anyway? Christ, I thought, I didn't know. Here I was, cheerfully breaking the law and the only justification I had for risking my pension was a certain curiosity about a dead man that I had barely met.

A certain curiosity. I went into the bedroom and opened cupboard doors. I remembered Keith Fletcher as a rather boffin-like character and his bedroom seemed to bear that out. Clean, and the clothes in the cupboards were good but most of them wanted a press and the room itself had the oddly unkempt look, the more than untidiness, of the busy single man. Long-term bachelors often show an astonishing orderliness that sometimes touches neurosis—the classic old woman of comedy. Fletcher seemed to have been essentially normal, having apparently lived in a state of scruffy comfort.

I moved into the kitchen but it yielded nothing apart from a well filled freezer that indicated either a total lack of interest in cooking or a genuine passion for junk food, so I shut the door and went into the living-room, trying to make some kind of contact with the man who had lived in it, which wasn't easy. Some people leave their signatures on rooms but it didn't seem to me that Keith Fletcher had been one of them. This place was practical and comfortable, with decent furniture, a big stack audio system, Piper lithos on the walls. Over the fireplace there was a rather good painting of a golf green, one I didn't recognize, but which must have meant something because there was a small brass plate let into the bottom of the frame, suggesting it had been a presentation. There were newspapers on a coffee table, and a couple of magazines. I went over and bent to pick one up, but whatever it was hit me hard under the ear before I got that far. I saw the table coming up at me and tried to get my hands down first, only they didn't seem to move. My face and the table became one, and there was some fairly painless shock before the dark rolled over me and swallowed me up.

CHAPTER 8

The player shall not discontinue play unless he believes there is danger from lightning . . . or some other good reason, such as sudden illness.

Rule 6–8

I suppose I should have been surprised to wake up in a bed but I wasn't because my head felt as though it was being levered apart with a cold chisel, and for someone who felt as terrible as I did a hospital bed was an entirely logical place to be. I opened my eyes and then shut them again hurriedly because they wouldn't focus and the light exploded in my brain like a bomb. Odd, the prevalence of fictional heroes who get slugged, to smile wryly as they wake up concussed, and then bravely soldier on.

Laurie's voice said, 'It's all right, don't try to talk.'

I hadn't the slightest intention of talking, because just thinking was difficult enough, but it was pleasant when something cold was pressed against my head. I opened my eyes rather more cautiously than last time and made out the foot of the bed, an unfamiliar picture on the wall and some rather fancy curtains. Apart from my shoes, it felt as though I was fully dressed but with a duvet thrown over me. I wondered what the hell was going on.

'You're in my bed,' Laurie said from somewhere out of sight range. 'Someone hit you while you were in Mr Fletcher's flat. Do you remember?'

I tried to remember. Remembering was like trying to recall a dream that had seemed real enough at the time but was now no more than a kind of mental echo scrabbling around the edges of one's memory. I got Fletcher out of cold storage and thawed him out. I saw him at the party at the clubhouse, then lying dead in a bunker. From there it was only a matter of a few jabs with the chisel to get myself as far as his flat, the leaden thump of whatever it was across the base of my skull.

'Yes,' I said, 'I remember.'

'Do you remember getting back here?'

'No, I'm damned if I do.' Odd, but that was a complete blank. I tried painfully to dredge around a little but apparently there was nothing on the tape to recall. 'You tell me,' I said.

Laurie came into view round the bottom of the bed and sat on the end of it and I saw that she had taken her glasses off. Maybe she saw better that way. She asked, 'Did you get a chance to see who hit you?'

Under normal circumstances I suppose I'd have shaken

my head but, as things were, I simply said, 'No. He came up behind me and slugged me.'

'I imagine I saw him arrive,' Laurie said. 'At least I saw a car pull up in front of the flats and a man get out. He went inside but I didn't think too much about it—after all, there are other flats and I hoped he was going to one of them. After about ten minutes he came back and drove away.'

'Had you ever seen him before?'

'I didn't recognize him, but it was getting dark and in any case he was quite some way away.'

'Car?'

'A dark-coloured Metro.' Laurie frowned. 'I suppose I should have taken the number but I just didn't think—'

I said, 'There was no reason why you should have done. What happened next?'

'I waited what seemed to be ages, and when you didn't come back I decided that something must have gone wrong. So I thought I'd better have a look.'

She had a nice line in understatement. 'How did you get me up?' I asked with genuine interest because I weigh the best part of a hundred and seventy pounds and there was no way I could see Laurie picking my unconscious body up and tossing it over her shoulder.

'I spoke to you. I think I tried to lift your head up.' She didn't look any too certain, and no wonder. 'Anyway, you mumbled something about being all right and got to your feet. You were pretty shaky but I led you back to the car and brought you back here.' Laurie added reflectively, 'It was rather like hauling a drunk around. Once I got you on the bed you passed out like a light.'

I said, 'You seem to speak from experience.'

'I suppose I do. How do you feel now?'

'Pretty awful.'

'Do you think I should call a doctor?'

'No, I shouldn't imagine so.' All the doctors that I'd ever met would have muttered about concussions and fractures and sent me off for an X-ray before admitting there was nothing much to be done about it outside a fair amount of rest. I said, 'I'd best wait here for a while. What's the time?'

She glanced at her wrist. 'Getting on for four.'

'Jesus!' I was startled enough to try to sit up and changed my mind immediately. I felt cold sweat break out on my face and even run down my chest and for a moment I had the uncomfortable conviction that I was going to be sick. Even in my anguish I found myself thinking that chaps weren't supposed to throw up in ladies' beds and somehow or other I managed to think my insides back into a position of armed neutrality. 'You never said it was that late,' I protested weakly.

'I suppose you weren't in a position to ask.' Laurie mopped at my streaming face sympathetically. 'Look, this isn't getting you anywhere except worse. Why not have a nap for a couple of hours and see how you feel then?'

'All right. You'd better knock off, too.'

She grinned wryly. 'I must admit, it's been a long night.' She kicked off her shoes and without embarrassment lay down beside me on the double bed. With her eyes closed and without her glasses, her face looked young and vulnerable. I wondered how badly she needed the damn things. If I could have moved, I'd have taken them off the bedside table and had a look through them but I wasn't as curious as all that, so I listened to her quiet breathing and stared at the ceiling and tried to sleep. I'd ended up in bed with a girl but it had still been a poor sort of a day.

I caught an early train home, picked up the car and went back to the flat. It had an air of being so empty that if I'd picked it up it wouldn't even have rattled, and I wondered if it was missing Sam or Ramases or just me. It seemed unlikely it would have missed Angela but one never knew. I changed my clothes and studied myself without enthusiasm in the bathroom mirror, which was probably a mistake because my eyes looked as though I was riding a monumental hangover and my complexion was a dirty grey. The lump on the back of my head was about the size of an egg and as tender as a boil, and as I was feeling it cautiously, the phone rang.

'' Morning, Angus. Heard the news?'

Hawkins, cheerful and noisy. I'd half expected him to ask where I'd been but apparently sleeping dogs had been left to lie since yesterday. 'No,' I said obligingly, 'what news?'

'Your friend April Tonge was busy again last night. Had a go at digging up the eighteenth green this time.'

I could have said something like 'You're joking!' but I didn't because Hawkins wasn't given to being funny about things like that. Instead I said, 'Badly?' I was trying to imagine Alan Thurston's reaction to the news.

'Only about a yard or so, luckily. I gather the groundsmen can patch it up again. Lucky you took that plough gadget away from them—they probably didn't find it so easy having to use a spade.'

Well, that was true enough. 'But look,' I said, 'how did they get away with it? There were supposed to be patrols and the eighteenth is slap in front of the clubhouse.'

'God knows.' Hawkins sounded remarkably cheerful about the whole thing, but then, he was doubtless thinking it could all have been a lot worse. His voice went on, 'I imagine they waited for the right moment—it doesn't take long to mess up a bit of grass. And I understand the patrols had been taken off. Still, they must have been scared off by something or they'd have finished the job.'

'Yes.' I'd forgotten about the no patrol bit. 'What makes you so sure it was April Tonge who was responsible, anyway?' I asked.

'Because we went down first thing to pick her up and there wasn't anyone there. Hardly surprising, I suppose. The silly old bat must have guessed we'd be down on her like a load of bricks.'

I found it hard not to laugh. 'What are you going to do? Mount a guard on the place in case she comes back?'

'God, no! I've got enough on my plate without wasting time over our Miss Tonge. I'll get around to her after this bloody tournament is over.'

'Do you want me to do anything?'

Hawkins made appropriate noises down the phone. 'Good

Lord, of course not. You're supposed to be on leave. Just keeping you in the picture.'

'Thanks,' I said, 'I'm grateful.' I was, too. 'I'll call in and have a word if I'm out that way.'

I put the phone down and wondered if I should go out to the West Wessex to see how everyone was taking it, but one didn't have to be clairvoyant to guess that they wouldn't be taking it very well and I was a bit tired of being the whipping boy. But April Tonge really had to be out of her mind thinking she was going to get away with the same nonsense twice in a week. Once he found time, Hawkins was going to throw the book at her. No wonder she'd done a bunk.

After a while I convinced myself that I wasn't going to do anything about it and I went downstairs and sat under a tree with a can of cold beer and Hardy's treatise on the longbow. I enjoy reading about other men's obsessions, and this one could easily have been my own. It's not easy to write about the fourteenth century and ignore the longbow, because even if you have no battle scenes, it's always there, the ultimate argument, Edward the Third's nuclear deterrent. In his day every commoner in the land had a legal obligation to learn the art of that terrible six-foot stick, and yet when Hardy wrote his book there wasn't a single British war bow in existence anywhere in the country. I read about the bow and the men who strung it and the bees made satisfactory noises and there wasn't reason to do anything. But we are a perverse race and I couldn't settle.

I went upstairs and took out the bow I'd been making in my spare time. It was based on Hardy's research, of course, so I couldn't claim to have done more than labourer's work, and even that had taken me a good six months. I balanced the thing in my hand and it felt pretty good, certainly a lot better than my last effort. All it needed was the grip finishing and the arrows ringing and it would be ready for a shoot. I propped it up against the wall, put on my jacket and went back downstairs. As I got into the Maserati I wondered why I hadn't the courage to leave the whole business alone. Maybe Angela had put her finger on it the time she said,

'At least you're not a shit, darling, but then you haven't the guts, have you?'

One of the bad nights, no holds barred and hitting where it hurt most. Strange how marriages survive for years on mutually agreed local rules. But of course she'd been right. The shits of this world are the chaps who trample on everybody but nevertheless act according to their lights. You wouldn't have caught a French copper on leave meddling in someone else's business, but then, I wasn't a French copper so I put my foot down and went round to look for April allee quick one time, just in case God should catch me.

As usual, it seemed a nice place to visit on a sunny morning. I parked in the yard in front of the barn and admired the roses climbing round the door, the dog scratching himself, the paint peeling off the window frames. Put it in any estate agent's window and it would sell in a week, but then April probably couldn't have cared less, most ladies of her persuasion having enough money to support their eccentricities. I went to the door and gave a rap with the wrought-iron ring which a wrought-iron lion held obligingly, waiting without any great expectation of anything happening. As it turned out I was wrong, because the spotty girl from Roedean opened the door.

'Oh,' she said, 'it's you.' She eyed me with a certain wariness, which was understandable, because she hadn't been particularly civil to me on our last meeting and it may have seemed to her that I'd returned to pay off old scores.

'Yes.' I showed her my warrant card just so that she'd register the fact that I was not collecting for charity. 'Is Miss Tonge at home?'

'I'm afraid she's not.' Very civil we were, this time.

'And you are—?'

'My name's Delphine Rosewall.' Moist pale blue eyes looking at me hopefully as though asking if the name was satisfactory. But really, Delphine—

'Do you have any idea when Miss Tonge is likely to be back?' I asked.

Delphine shook her head, but there didn't seem much

fight in her this afternoon and I got the impression that she really didn't know.

'Do you know anything about damage to a second green at the West Wessex Golf Club last night?' Very much the policeman, all I needed was a notebook and pencil.

'N-no.'

'Do you think Miss Tonge knows anything?'

She shook her head rather desperately and I decided against scaring her because for some reason she looked scared enough already. In fact, there was something about the girl's whole manner that puzzled me. Something had brought about a major change in the bolshie brat I'd last met and I'd have given a lot to know just what it was. I summoned up a smile and did my best to put her at ease. 'When *did* you last see her?'

'I—I don't know. This morning. I think she must have gone out shopping.'

'Where were you earlier this morning?'

'I went out for a walk.'

I changed tactics. 'Did Miss Tonge take her car with her when she went shopping?'

Delphine shook her head. 'She hasn't got a car—as a matter of fact, she can't even drive. But there's a bus stop only a few yards up the road and she always takes that.'

'I see.' I wondered how I'd managed to miss such an obvious fact as that. I also wondered if it was true. Reluctantly I decided that it probably was—it had the kind of essentially non-practical individuality that one associated with her. But I didn't believe for one moment that April was shopping. My guess was that her nerve had failed her and she'd run off in a panic somewhere.

'Look, Miss Rosewall,' I said, 'have you got any idea what might have happened to her? People don't just disappear, you know.' In fact, people disappeared all the time but she seemed a girl who needed encouragement. But still, surprising how all that early aggression could virtually vanish overnight. There had to be a reason but for the life of me I couldn't think what it was.

I tried again. 'Perhaps it might be a good idea if I came

inside. We might look around and see if she's left anything that might give us some idea what she's doing. Is your friend in?'

'My friend?'

'Last time I called there was a coloured girl here, too. I didn't get her name.'

'Oh, Selina de Cruz.' Delphine hesitated as though she was about to say something else. It might even have been, 'She's not my friend', but instead it was, 'No, she's not here.'

'You're not telling me that she's disappeared as well,' I said.

'No, she's just out.' A car turned into the yard and I looked over my shoulder, thinking that it might just be April, turned up in a taxi after a stint at the supermarket. But I was wrong, even though one of my missing characters had made it back to base. Selina de Cruz had spotted me in one, and she was staring at me from the passenger seat as though I was something particularly nasty that the cat had brought in and was about to be ordered to take out again. She was wearing a bright red shirt and her dark hair had a patch of the same colour—it could have been a flower, real or plastic, it made little difference because the effect was there all right. I looked to see who was in the back of the taxi with her. At first it wasn't easy because whoever it was was lost in shadow. Then the taxi stopped and Selina's companion got out and I saw it was Africa's contribution to the international golf scene, Bill Sadiq.

I think he recognized me at about the same moment because he raised a hand and smiled.

'Hello.' I nodded to him and walked over. The de Cruz girl didn't move and I wondered what she'd have done had we been alone. I said, 'Good afternoon, Miss de Cruz.'

She hesitated. I suppose it wouldn't have fitted with whatever picture she'd built up of herself for Bill Sadiq if she'd let herself go, so with a bit of an effort she managed what for her must have been a gracious acknowledgement.

'You were looking for me, Inspector?'

I saw Sadiq's expression alter a fraction. I suppose he'd

forgotten that I was a policeman even if he'd taken it in, but there didn't seem to be any hostility there, nothing more than mild surprise.

I said, 'No, I was looking for Miss Tonge. Miss Rosewall here hasn't seen her. Have you?'

No, she said, she hadn't seen her. Her eyes never left my face, hostile and resentful, and I wondered why. Because I'd caught her out coming home with a man?

I could feel Sadiq looking from his companion to me and then back again, as though trying to get the relationship sorted out, but I ignored him and carried on with the girl. Not that it did me any noticeable good. I asked her much the same questions as I'd put to spotty Delphine and I got back much the same answers. Either they'd at some time got themselves together in a very meaningful way or they were speaking the truth, which on the face of it seemed most likely. Selina was a load of trouble in anybody's book but I just couldn't see Delphine conspiring to upset the course of justice with anything approaching efficiency. I gave it up and turned back to Bill Sadiq.

'If you're going back to the course I can give you a lift,' I told him.

He thought it over. I think in his position I'd have told me what I could do with my offer but he'd either been better brought up or he had an aversion to paying for taxis, because in the end he nodded and settled with the driver. He said goodbye to both the girls rather formally and then we went to my car.

'My!' he said, 'kind of fancy for a policeman, isn't it? In the States they just have ordinary sedans.'

'And what do they have in Kariba?' I asked him.

'You got anything against Kariba?' He was a good-looking lad, very dark, but with the kind of bone structure that looks good in bronze. At a guess there must have been some fairly massive Arab settlement in his part of the world at one time because he had that kind of face.

'You mean they're so bad it's racist even to talk about them?' I finished backing and turned out on to the road. I'd rather enjoyed talking to him the last time we'd met, and at his income level there didn't seem much call for tears about his sufferings on behalf of the Third World.

Probably I'd misjudged him because he said quietly, 'They were pretty bad last time I saw them, but that was some while ago.'

'I don't imagine they play much golf there,' I said tentatively.

He grinned, and I felt him relax. 'No, you could say that.' Then, 'You miss your own folks sometimes. Not often.'

'Your family, you mean?'

'There ain't no family,' Sadiq said. 'I meant just folk from where you come from. That's why I spend some time with the lady back there. You know she come from a place no more than fifty miles from where I was born?'

I said, 'I didn't even know she came from Kariba.' I took that in. Should I have known? I decided not, though I supposed I could have asked, though for God's sake she had to come from somewhere. 'How did you come to meet her?' I asked.

'After practice yesterday. I shot a 68 and this girl comes up and asks for my autograph in my own language. It's not the kind of thing that happens often.'

'How would she get to be called de Cruz?' I asked. 'It doesn't sound very African.'

He shrugged his shoulders. 'Kariba was a Portuguese colony way back. You know how it is.'

I didn't but I could guess at a Portuguese great-grandfather or suchlike, which would account for the paler skin.

'So you took her out to lunch?' There was little traffic on the road and what there was didn't get in the way. Sadiq seemed unconcerned at being questioned, but a certain level of sportsman gets used to that.

'You don't see that many Karibans about. And I guess her being good-looking helped.' Although I had my eyes on the road ahead I could sense Sadiq looking at me. 'What's with this April someone who's gone missing? You reckon Selina had something to do with that?'

'No,' I said, 'asking her was just routine.'

He frowned. 'That's what they say in the movies.'

'I know,' I said. 'But Miss Tonge hasn't been missing long enough to worry about it—she's just not at home.' I changed the subject and asked him what he thought of the West Wessex as a course and how the general arrangements compared to what he was used to on the pro tour circuit. I asked him partly to get him off what was a potentially touchy subject, partly because I wanted to know. Players tend to be cagey about almost any facility other than the course itself, because sponsors spread a wide net and nobody wants to criticize something when it may turn out to be owned by the people who are paying you fifty thousand a year.

'I like the people fine.' It could have been the familiar 'you lovely people' line, but he went on to say that the place was barely a course at all by American standards, that the rough was jungle and the fairways little better than footpaths. He was used to the vast, transatlantic parkland courses where rough means grass an inch high and fairways are manicured to something approaching a European green. He added reflectively, 'But I reckon this is the way golf should be. Traditional.'

'Even if it's two different games?'

Sadiq had a big smile and I caught it out of the corner of my eye. 'Hell, it's the same game. If it wasn't we wouldn't have won the Open fourteen times out of the last twenty.'

'We?' So far as I knew, he was still playing as a Kariban national.

'Well, I guess it won't be long.' He hesitated a moment as though wondering if it was his business or mine. 'I'm putting in for US citizenship next year.'

It was where his money came from, so why not? Listening to him, most people would have judged him to be American anyway. I said, 'There must be twenty top-ranking golfers in the States and you're the only one from Kariba. Why make the change?'

Sadiq sighed. 'You know how many golf courses they got back where I come from?'

I did my best to imagine Kariba's social assets, as they might have been in its colonial past. There would have been a decent club at the capital and that would be about its lot. 'One?' I ventured.

'None.' Sadiq grinned in my direction. 'Sure, there used to be a course at the N'Gamba Club, but they haven't played on that since 'eighty-two. I started as a caddie there, then made assistant pro under Mr McAlistair.'

I liked the 'Mr' that still stuck. I asked, 'What happened to him?'

'He got chopped one night for the takings in the club shop. I lit out and went down south, worked as a caddie again at a place near Pretoria. Then someone staked me and I got a chance in the States.'

I wondered just how that chance had come about. Sadiq was a good-looking youngster, so there could have been a woman involved somewhere along the line. I said, 'You don't have to be a citizen to play in North America.'

'No. I just prefer the place. Besides—' he shrugged his shoulders again—'I made me half a million dollars there, and I aim to marry an American girl later this year. God damn it, I *am* American!'

'Fine,' I said, 'I only asked.'

I sensed him push down irritation. 'I tell you this, man. When that girl spoke to me I had to think real hard before I could answer her in Yosa—even when I was with her I found it real hard to speak my own language. You know why?'

'You tell me,' I said. He was going to tell me, in any case.

'Because Yosa ain't my language any more. My language is *American*.'

I said, 'It looks like the Tamworth is going to be Kariba's final big win, then.'

He grinned. 'Could be, just so long as the game's still on. You heard the TV camera men are on strike?'

CHAPTER 9

Except as provided in the Rules, during a stipulated round the player shall not use any artificial device or unusual equipment.

Rule 14–3

I found Ambrose in the bar, drinking with Polly Appleby and he waved me to join them. 'You heard?' he asked as I took a stool.

'Yes,' I said. 'Bill Sadiq just told me. What's it all about?'

He shrugged. 'What's it ever about? More money.'

'Presumably the company will have to pay up,' I said. 'It's going to cost them more to break their contract than it will to pay the brothers off.'

Ambrose said moodily, 'You'd think so. But it seems they've got a new broom sweeping clean at head office—a dour wee Scot called Purdie who hates trade unions like John Knox hated sin. He's said in public that he'd cancel coverage of the Second Coming rather than give in to Union blackmail and so far as he's concerned the Tamworth Classic doesn't rate that high.'

I said, 'That doesn't sound like a Scot.'

Ambrose ordered me a drink. He looked depressed, as well he might, because the Ambroses of this world wither on the vine if they don't get their share of media exposure and the thought of TV cameras lying idle must have worried him no end. He said, 'Purdie plays a mean game of golf himself but I imagine his Puritan soul doesn't altogether approve of the game being exposed to television anyway. So far as he's concerned, the strikers can strike till they rot.'

'Bill Sadiq seemed to think that the whole thing might fall apart,' I ventured.

'Bill Sadiq thinks he's still in the States,' Ambrose said,

misunderstanding me. 'Over there nobody, but *nobody*, would go ahead with a major tournament if there wasn't going to be TV coverage. If there was a strike—which there wouldn't be—they'd simply shift the date. But over here—'

'Over here there are still sponsors,' I said. Looking out of the window of the bar I could see a banner advertising a cigarette firm stretched thirty feet across one of the through-ways of the tented village. Without having to try over-hard, I picked out two drink ads, the logo of a car hire firm and, of course, the Tamworth 'T' that seemed to be just about everywhere else. Tamworth, I guessed aloud, would have to take the lack of TV coverage and make the best of it but I couldn't imagine the fact going down very well with anyone else.

'They're small fry,' Ambrose said confidently. 'They'll kick but they'll take it.' He downed his drink and eased himself off the stool. 'I shall leave you two to discuss world affairs while I dispose of an interview.'

I wondered how many interviews a day Ambrose was in the habit of giving. There must be something extraordinarily satisfactory about being paid for doing what you enjoy most, and even more satisfactory if you're paid as much as he was. We watched him make his way out of the bar and into the ante-room where a group of sports reporters awaited him. The door shut.

Polly said, 'The Ambroses of this world don't need a Union.' She sounded sourer than was her wont.

'I suppose not. But you must admit he works,' I said. 'Isn't a fair day's work for a fair day's pay what it's supposed to be all about?'

'You think what that man makes is fair?' I wondered how long Polly had been at the bar. If it had been long and she'd been drinking alongside Ambrose, it wasn't surprising if her liver was playing up.

I said, 'I suppose anything you can get without actually holding people up to ransom is fair. But holding the firm that employs you to ransom isn't fair by my book. Quite apart from the fact that TV cameramen make more than the Prime Minister and I've never quite been able to see why.'

Polly studied me with what I took to be a certain disenchantment. Seen at close range, her eyes were a curious shade of blue that might just as well have been green. In fact, seen at close range, there were quite a number of points that were equally impressive. I had never been a slave to the statuesque but there was no gainsaying the fact that Polly Appleby was a lot of woman. She said amiably, 'Maybe because they're more use.'

'How's practice gone?' If one subject tends to be a bit touchy, move on to the next. 'I gather Sadiq went round in 68.'

'Shroeder did 69. Several at 70, and everyone says the course is playing well.'

I said, 'So everything looks all right for the first round tomorrow.'

Polly grinned. 'I think the players are going to be all right. There's a certain amount of panic in the village, but then there always is. Most of the contractors will be up all night but the stands will be ready and willing, come the morning.' She hesitated. 'Are you on duty or anything tonight?'

'No,' I said, 'I am not.'

'Remember you gave me a lift the other night because my car was in dock?'

All those caddie carts tearing round the course in the dark. Fletcher's body in the sand at the bottom of the bunker —oh yes, I remembered all right. 'If you're game to risk it again,' I said, 'it's all right with me. I don't fall over a corpse every time I go out.'

'Oh, I thought you'd laid that on for me. But seriously, my car's ready—I just want to pick it up.'

I said, 'No problem. Which garage is it at?'

'Actually it's not *at* a garage. It was supposed to have been left at my hotel but some idiot of a garage hand got it wrong—I've been ages on the phone trying to locate exactly where he did put the thing.'

'And where is it?'

'God knows why, but it's outside your flat.'

Anywhere else, I thought, that would have been a bit of a come on, but not in these parts. I said, 'You must have gone to Wright's Motors at Detting.'

She looked surprised. 'I did. How did you know?'

'Because I used to go there myself before I got the Maserati. They were always bringing cars round to me.'

Polly looked mystified. 'I still don't get the connection.'

'The flats take the name from the place—Staples Cross. Your pub happens to be called the Southern Cross. There's a mechanic at Wright's who's a bit hard of hearing and he's always mixing the names up.' I got off the bar stool. 'Have you eaten?'

She shook her head. 'No.'

I was happy enough at the prospect of her company and I hadn't eaten anything since the previous night. My head had stopped aching and the relief made me feel at least twice as good as I'd been before. I steered her in the direction of an Italian place a couple of miles down the road and we stuffed ourselves with *gnocchi* and *saltimbocca*, washing it down with almost black *Valpolicella*. I don't know how long it had been since Polly Appleby had tasted food, but judging by appearances it must have been about a fortnight.

'I'm a pig about pasta.' She could read thoughts, too, it seemed. 'Lucky it isn't fattening.'

'I thought it was.'

'Lies, all lies.' She was an amiable companion, funny and informative as well. With a bit of prompting she told me a lot of high scandal about the PR trade, naming most of the names and only here and there leaving me to guess. She told me about her breathless childhood, being rushed from school to school in the wake of the never very successful actor who had been her father, and her equally breathless, no-longer-there marriage, that had never managed to get off the ground. She was a good talker, slightly professional with an anecdote perhaps, but she'd had to inherit something from her father so it might as well have been that. She

109

laughed a lot and her marvellous skin glowed with health and candlelight and rough Italian wine. Presently I paid the bill and we went home.

Polly's car, a grey Granada, was parked under the willow tree just across from the entrance, so I put the Maserati in the garage and we went upstairs for a drink. The flat, which had seemed cold and clinically cheerless, lit up a bit at Polly's arrival. Places need a woman to make them come to life, and Polly was a woman all right. She sat in front of the empty hearth and looked up amiably at me while I poured whatever it was she was drinking into her glass, giving the general impression that she knew what I was thinking and didn't mind all that much.

She said, 'This is nice. You policemen do yourselves well.'

'Don't we.' She was wearing some sort of linen jacket with a roll neck sweater underneath, and I found myself involved with the way the line of her jaw merged with the firm column of her throat. For lo, thou art beautiful and fair in my eyes. Well, don't just stand there like a schoolboy, son, do something. I put the bottle back where it belonged and a scatter of squally rain rattled against the windows. I should have grabbed her then, but like a fool I didn't.

Polly stood up. 'Hell! Do you suppose that's going to last?'

'No.' What was I being so uptight about? I made a move to put on a tape but it was too late and we were both aware of a tension between us.

'You don't happen to have any cigarettes, by any chance?'

I didn't want to go on saying 'no' all evening but she was giving me no alternative.

'It doesn't matter,' Polly said, 'I've got a packet in the car.'

'I'll get them for you.' If anything, things were going from bad to worse. Saved by the telephone ringing, which was more than I deserved.

Polly said, 'No, you answer that. I'll go.'

'Thanks.' The rain was still coming down hard and she was going to get wet. 'You'd better put a coat on—there's one by the door.'

As I picked up the phone I watched her pull my raincoat cloakwise over her shoulders, then, on impulse, pull on one of those green felt hats that carry with them a kind of near-Alpine look. She saw me watching her and spread her arms in an expensive gesture. She was the sort of woman who was so overtly female that she looked almost instantly erotic in men's clothing and again I felt the urgent tug of desire before she swirled away. On the phone Laurie was saying, 'I've been trying to get you for the last hour. Where have you *been*?'

I said, 'Don't be so bloody wifely.' But she had other things to do than ring me, after all. Contrite, I filled in. 'I've been investigating a missing person.' And then before she could say the obvious, 'It's not anyone you know.'

'That's all right, then. But I dug around the local newsagents like you said. Fletcher dealt with Martin's in Alma Crescent.'

I nearly said something I'd have regretted about the colour of the newsagent's tie but decided against it. Not one witness in ten can resist throwing in all kinds of irrelevant information and it was rather gratifying to discover that the capable Ms Wilson was no exception. So all I said was, 'Yes?'

'He has a standing order for *UFO* and *Galaxy*. Apart from the *Guardian* and the *Observer*, that is.'

'The devil he did.' I should have sounded as though that was what I'd expected, but there are limits to everything and this was something I hadn't expected. I take it all back, Laurie Wilson, you were right all along. 'Funny,' I said aloud, 'he didn't look like a nut.'

'I don't suppose many of them do,' the telephone suggested. 'The newsagent said I'd be surprised at the number of copies of *UFO* he sells.'

'You should have bought a copy.'

'I did—someone was away on holiday so he had a spare.' Laurie's voice sounded faintly one up, and why not indeed. 'It's surprisingly readable. Plausible, too, in a way. Did you ever read the Adamski book?'

111

'As a matter of fact, I did,' I told her. 'It was a long time ago but I can't remember being impressed.'

'That's what I mean—you only had to read half a dozen pages to wonder if the man was either a fraud or completely round the bend. But *UFO* isn't just full of bad snapshots of dustbin lids and things like that. I'm not saying it's convinced me that the sky's full of little green men, but at least it's literate. You should look at a copy, Angus.'

I had a thought. 'Give me the editor's name and phone number, will you.'

She gave them and I wrote them down. Michael Woods sounded a down to earth kind of name, and a good deal more confidence-inspiring than Adamski, but for all I knew, that was why he chose it. Mike Woods, the people's friend.

'How are you feeling?' Laurie was asking.

'Fine.' Only fine would hardly do for someone who'd sat up with you most of the night after steering a half-daft zombie from Chiswick to Kensington. Next time, I thought, she'll leave you there to rot, if she hasn't slugged you first herself. I enlarged graciously. 'At least, a good deal better than I did this morning. And I never got around to thanking you for what you did.'

I don't know if she laughed or not but at least she sounded amused. 'That's all right. Agents are supposed to look after their clients.'

'Agents are supposed to take ten per cent too, but I don't quite see how you're going to collect it.'

'We can always talk about that later.' A pause. 'Angus —you'd better get that head checked with a doctor. You never know—'

Doctors were a kind of last resort, never to be invoked of one's own free will. 'We can talk about that later, too.'

I put the phone down and looked at the time. Ten o'clock. How long had she been trying to phone me while I indulged myself with erotic thoughts over breaded veal and a background mural of Mount Vesuvius? Doubtless as some kind of penance, my head began to ache again so I stood up and walked across to the open door to see what Polly was doing.

It was better outside with the evening air and the good dank smell of rain on wet earth. A late bird was complaining bitterly over something and a steady drip of water around the eaves reminded me that the leaking gutter that the builder said was fixed hadn't been.

'You there, Polly?'

Answer there was none. It was quite dark outside save for the pools of light splashed from my own windows, because my neighbours were away and if it hadn't been for me the place would have been deserted. There was a faint glow from the Granada's interior, which suggested that the door had opened and the courtesy light had come on, but from where I stood the car seemed empty.

'Polly?'

I went down the steps and had a look, and it was empty all right. The light was on because the door had been pushed shut but not far enough to operate the plunger switch in the frame. I gave the door a push and the lock clicked and the light went out. As if on cue, the wind stirred the branches of the willow behind me and something moved. It was my raincoat blown in the breeze. In the half light of the moon I could see Polly standing with her back against the trunk of the tree watching me, the bottom of my coat flapping round her legs.

'What are you standing there for?' If I sounded irritable, it was because I was no longer in the mood for fooling about. Man is a fickle creature and the best of us lose our sex drive if you hit us on the head hard enough. I liked Polly and I had every hope that sooner or later I'd see a lot more of her but as I stood by her shadowed car, apparently talking to myself, I rather wished she'd go home. 'Look—' I said. Then the penny dropped and, even as I jumped forward, I knew it was too late to make any difference because she must have been dead for several minutes. What puzzled me for a moment was how her body still managed to stand up, and I had to switch on the car lights to find out. It was clear then all right. The crossbow quarrel had driven itself clean through her and was pinning her to the tree.

*

Hawkins got out to Staples Cross rather quicker than I'd expected, together with a sergeant, a photographer, O'Henry, the police doctor and an ambulance into the bargain. There was a good deal of flashgunning and measuring, so it was probably as well I hadn't any neighbours that night. Two o'clock saw the most of it over and Hawkins having one for the road with me in the kitchen.

'You're going to have a busy time with the newspapers,' he said. 'Half of Fleet Street's going to be here tomorrow, doing Robin Hood stories all round you.'

'Just so as they don't caption my picture *Can this Cop be Crossbow Killer?*' I said.

Hawkins looked at me. 'You're not really worried about that, are you?'

'It was my arrow.'

'*Was* it?'

'Unless someone else in these parts has a working fourteenth-century crossbow.'

He helped himself to some more of my whisky. 'You said yourself that the arrows—'

'Quarrels.'

'Quarrels, then.' Hawkins disliked being corrected. 'The quarrels weren't original.'

'No,' I agreed, 'but they were damn well made reproductions and the shaft they took out of Polly Appleby was undoubtedly one of them.'

'Well, even if it was, you'd already reported the thing stolen.' Hawkins was looking at me with what was beginning to look like despair. 'Damn it, Angus, nobody is going to deny that there are deer here, and it's on record that one was wounded by an ordinary arrow only a couple of months ago. Now tonight we've got a dead woman on our hands who's been killed with a missile from a stolen crossbow, and what did we find on the ground just behind her?'

I said obediently, 'You found fresh deer droppings.'

'Well, what more do you want?' Hawkins was a master of the rhetorical question. 'The country's full of young layabouts who like to go about shooting arrows into any poor bloody beast they can find. This one nicked your crossbow and then decided to try it out on one of your deer —or what he thought was yours. By sheer bad luck this girl happens to be around at the time and gets hit instead. Or do you have any other suggestions?'

'No, I can't say I have.'

Hawkins hesitated. 'What you reported about her being here because she had to pick up her car. I suppose that'll stand up?'

'If you mean is it true, the answer's yes,' I said. 'The garage will confirm it.'

'I wouldn't ask, except that someone else is bound to sooner or later. There wasn't—I mean between you and—?'

'No,' I said, 'never laid hands on her.'

Hawkins sighed with relief. 'That's all right, then.' He put his glass down. 'I'd best be doing. Good night, Angus.'

I said, 'Good night, Ted. Nice to know you care.'

He went down the steps and I heard him saying something to one of his men and then the door of his car slammed and I watched its rear lights wink down the drive and out of sight. It was late and I felt like hell but for all that I was reluctant to go to bed, so I got out a torch and went back to the willow where I'd found Polly. The deer droppings were at least ten paces behind the tree and about five feet to its right. Given the relative height of a deer and Polly's heart, I thought that seemed about right, which still left a question as to where the bowman would have stood. How close would a man have to be to drive a quarrel right through a woman's body.

So thicke did thee British arrows fall that they did seem lyke rain—

But that was someone writing about longbow arrows. At Crécy the Genoese loosed at a reputed two hundred paces but, judging by the way the battle went, it seemed unlikely that anything drove in very far. I tried to remember what modern experts had to say on the subject, but I'd never read all that much on the crossbow and the best I could do was some kind of vague recollection that a greased shaft would penetrate three inches of hardwood at fifty paces. How hard was a woman compared with three inches of wood? I didn't know and there didn't seem any immediate chance of finding out, but a hundred paces seemed a fair adjustment. I turned my back on the tree and started walking.

Full ten score paces doth the longbow throw—

Well, maybe it did but again this was a crossbow and if whoever was using it had wanted to take a pot shot at either Hawkins or myself, there had been plenty of time during the last couple of hours. Even so, it was an effort not to hurry things. There was an occasional rustling from the small spinney ahead but I decided that was more deer. Poachers didn't rustle. It was highly unlikely that rustlers did either, so why call them that?

Ninety-eight, ninety-nine, one hundred—

It had brought me to the edge of the spinney, which made sense, so I switched on the torch and looked around. A pair of glowing green eyes stared back at me and a hedgehog hoisted himself up on his suspension like a Citröen and scuttled away. The ground was covered in rough grass and the usual debris of broken twigs, even my own shoes left no noticeable prints. The trees stood fairly close together, which was probably why the branches grew fairly high on the trunks so there was plenty of room to move around. An archer would have had no difficulty in using six foot of longbow, let alone a crossbow, and from where I stood there was a good, uninterrupted view of Polly's car, the willow and the front of the house. It was a good place to hide but that was about all that could be said for it. What was it some old poacher had said to me once?

You've got to get near enough to clout the buggers on the head—

It made sense. Poachers weren't interested in fancy shooting, all they wanted to do was to be certain of making a kill quickly and quietly. But a hundred yards was a hell of a long shot for a poacher, and unnecessary into the bargain since the deer at Staples Cross were half tame. Anyone who wasn't a complete fool would have been able to get within a few yards of them without difficulty.

116

I stood there and reflected on Ted Hawkins's well-intentioned efforts to make me accept his poacher and deer theory, and I still hoped that he'd got it right. If a woman gets shot in the middle of the night, it's cosy if you can convince yourself that some layabout was trying to knock off a deer and managed to kill a girl by mistake, and indeed it would have to be a particularly bloody-minded coroner who'd think any different. But Polly had been as tall as most men. Wearing my coat and hat and in the shadows—and certainly at that distance—she must have looked as much like me as made no difference. Suppose the deer had just happened to be there? Suppose whoever it was had been aiming at the figure under the tree all the time and had simply killed the wrong person?

Well, either way it was a mistake. The one to whom it made no difference at all was Polly Appleby because she'd lost out either way.

I started back to the house. It was a good deal better on the return trip, knowing that there wasn't anyone in the spinney waiting to put an arrow in your back. Polly's Granada stood where she'd left it—Hawkins had simply locked it and taken the keys, presumably he'd decide in the morning what he wanted to do about it. As a vehicle it was every inch a company car, and even with what little light there was, I could make out the scattered Tamworth promotion booklets in the back. There was absolutely no reason to suppose that there would be anything else, but all the same Hawkins shouldn't have taken away the key.

Most modern cars are remarkably easy to enter without the use of a key, which is why seven thousand are nicked in London every year. Granadas are no different, and a cloth-covered spade chisel springs the door half an inch or so without the metal kinking. I collected the necessary tool, inserted a length of wire down the side of the window frame, lifted the catch and let myself in.

The Tamworth stuff seemed to be everywhere—the car was a mobile wastepaper basket. No orderly soul, the late departed. Cigarette packets, maps, receipts for petrol and garage services, a block of plain chocolate, two dusters and a place mat from a Little Chef diner. There was an unfamiliar-looking magazine stuffed down beside the back seat which, to my surprise, turned out to be something called *Socialist Society*. A new offering from the lunatic Left. I turned the pages over and their contents didn't seem to be all that new: the joys of Nicaragua—the thoughts of somebody or other on China—Trotsky rediscovered. There was a double spread on black fundamentalism and a rather stirring feature on Lesbian councillors who were running what was curiously styled a 'workshop'. And there was a quarter-page picture of a group standing round the microphone on a platform that could have been in any town hall in the country.

Odd the things one sees and does not see. There was a caption that told me the meeting had been in Liverpool and it was some kind of Trotskyist action group. The man at the microphone was large and black and very well dressed and his name meant no more to me than those of the others of the group hovering around him. As a party it was a pretty representative cross-section of the hard Left—moneyed, intelligent, and as ruthlessly dedicated to subversion as the IRA and with far less excuse. I was about to turn the page when my eye caught two faces in the background that pulled me up sharp. They had obviously been part of the meeting and at the moment the picture had been taken had apparently been deep in conversation with each other. I guessed that the photographer must have taken two pictures because flash beats most human reactions and both these people had had time to half turn towards the camera with looks of annoyance growing on their faces. The man was my trendy local councillor, Clive Whitton. The woman was unmistakably Polly Appleby.

CHAPTER 10

An 'outside agency' is any agency not part of the match. . .

Definition

By mid-morning of the following day I was lost in darkest Harlington and had to ask a milkman the way to Bostock Avenue.

'Third left, the second on the right, Squire,' he said without hesitation. 'You'll know it by the Pencil Cedar on the corner.'

I said, 'The what?'

'The *Juniperus Virginia*. It's the best one in these parts by a long shot.'

'Thanks for telling me,' I said. 'I'll watch out for it.'

I drove past Elkington Drive, Wilson Road and turned left at Cooper Crescent. The first road on the right had for some unaccountable reason broken free of the list of Harlington councillors past and present and was called The Ridgeway and then I was turning into Bostock Avenue.

It was indistinguishable from all the other roads I'd passed but presumably the people who lived there homed in on it reliably enough. The road was planted with cherry trees and the houses ranged from the small 3 bd. 2 rec. det. through semis to bungalows. They were nearly all immaculate, lovingly gardened and were probably the most mortgageable properties in the country. 'Elton' turned out to be a bungalow with a low, well-trimmed privet hedge, a lot of crazy paving and some white-painted wooden tubs that had probably made a nice show with geraniums earlier in the year. A large man of forty or so was polishing a very shiny Japanese car.

'Mr Harborough?' I asked.

He put his duster down and studied me. He had sandy hair and largish glasses and I put him down as a rep for a firm of educational publishers.

'Yes,' he said, 'my name's Harborough.' His voice was West Yorkshire but a long time ago.

I said, 'Michael Woods said you might fill me in on what's happening round here.'

'Friend of Mike's, are you?'

Well, Mike had been friendly enough. It's a matter of common knowledge that there are very few magazines whose editors, rung up out of the blue by even someone who claims to be a regular reader, are prepared to chat for twenty minutes flat, but Mike Woods had been. I'd told him that I was moving to the Harlington area, which wasn't all that far from the truth and was I likely to find any kindred souls in those parts.

'UFOs or Audio Reconnaissance?' Mike hadn't made it sound like a password, he was just trying to help.

I was glad I listened to Radio 4 while shaving, because they'd had something about radio signals from Outer Space only the other day. I'd said, 'UFOs.'

Woods had said, 'Hang on a bit,' and presumably consulted some kind of card index. Then, 'Bernard Harborough looks like your man.'

'Harborough?'

'That's right. Harborough.' Then, surprisingly wary all of a sudden, 'You're not Press?'

Editorship of *UFO* clearly did not make one a member of the Press. This world was one world and the other worlds were something else again.

'No,' I assured him, 'I'm not Press.'

'We have to be careful, you know. This is the sort of thing that gets all over the front page of the dailies.'

'Of course.'

'Well, I'm sure you don't need me to tell you what's going on.' He'd sounded relieved. 'But contact Harborough as soon as you can, because it looks as though there's something very exciting going on down there.'

'Friend of Mike's, are you?' Harborough was repeating with curiosity but no hostility.

'No,' I said, 'I'm a police officer. But I'm still interested in UFOs.'

120

'Really interested?' He looked at me doubtfully.

'A man was found dead in a bunker on the West Wessex golf course a few nights ago,' I said. 'His name was Keith Fletcher.' Then I added, 'I thought you might have known him.'

Harborough folded up his duster and put it in a shoebox that contained a number of pads of cheesecloth and a couple of tins of liquid car wax. He put the whole lot away on a shelf in the garage before he said, 'You'd better come inside.'

We went into the little front room. It was freshly decorated with some rather attractive modern lithographs on the walls and a vase of well-arranged chrysanthemums in the window.

'My wife's out shopping or we could have a cup of coffee.' It was a statement and not an apology. 'I suppose it's no good offering you a sherry or a beer or something if you're on duty?'

'I'd enjoy a beer,' I told him and saw him relax. It's curious how many people get inhibited by a pious refusal to accept hospitality. I wouldn't drink with a man I knew to be a villain because I know damn well that he'd turn it to his advantage sooner or later, but I wasn't planning on arresting Harborough. I said, 'And in any case, this is hardly a formal investigation. Incidentally, you didn't say if you knew Fletcher or not.'

'I met him a few times.' Harborough handed me a tankard. 'I can't say I *knew* him.'

'You just shared an interest in unidentified flying objects?'

'That's right.' Harborough sipped a glass of sherry. 'If it's not something you can't answer, Inspector, why does it interest you?'

'Curiosity, I suppose.' But it wasn't just curiosity. I wasn't even sure that I knew myself. 'Look,' I said, 'Fletcher seemed a very ordinary sort of chap to be involved with flying saucers. I don't want to sound objectionable, but the number of people who really do believe in them must be pretty limited. Plenty of kids and a certain amount of the lunatic fringe—the kind of people who go in for odd cults or believe that the earth is flat. But serious students—no.'

Harborough said mildly, 'Oh yes. You're absolutely right.

121

Although I'd be interested in your reasons for assuming that Fletcher was an exception—and sane.'

'I knew him. Along with a lot of other clubs, the West Wessex employed him as an adviser. He was the last person I'd have thought would have believed in—' I broke off awkwardly.

'That sort of nonsense?' Harborough hazarded.

'If you like. Yes.' I tried to enlarge a little. 'If a man dies in circumstances that are hard to explain, one wants to know as much about him as possible. We thought we knew the kind of man Keith Fletcher was. Now we're not so sure.'

Harborough said mildly, 'Aren't you being rather subjective about this? If it turned out that the man was a Jehovah's Witness or a Mormon, I don't imagine you'd give it a second thought.'

'No,' I said, 'I wouldn't, unless there was something about his death that seemed to have something to do with one of those religions.'

'So you think that because Fletcher believed in UFOs it had something to do with his death.'

'It's a factor we have to take into account,' I said.

'Even though the Coroner's verdict was accidental death?' Harborough met my glance steadily. 'Naturally I read the report in the paper with interest.'

'Look, Harborough,' I said, 'at the time of the inquest we didn't know about Fletcher taking UFO magazines. And even if we had, I very much doubt if the Coroner would have been in the least interested. I don't even know that *I'm* interested, come to that. It's just an odd fact that has to be tidied up. I can't honestly see any connection between Keith Fletcher's death and flying saucers. Can you? It doesn't seem to make sense to me. Does it to you?'

'Well, it makes sense to me all right.' Harborough stood up and took my tankard away to be refilled. 'So far as I'm concerned, it's perfectly obvious that there's a link between Fletcher's death and the aliens.'

'There is?'

Harborough looked genuinely puzzled. 'But of course! My dear Inspector, it must be as clear to you as it is to me!

Fletcher experienced an encounter. Not just a sighting of a craft but an actual encounter of the third kind.'

Strange how easy it is to slip from reality to fantasy, from a purveyor of encyclopædias to just one more nut. The trouble with the lunatic belt is that it always has a jargon all of its own. 'Wasn't there a film called that?' I said. I had to say something.

'Yes. An early Spielberg.'

'I'm afraid I still don't know what it means.' To some officers patience comes easy, but not to me.

'It is the term for an actual physical meeting between one of us—a human—and an alien.'

'I see.' Meaningless term, but the kind of thing one says in the circumstances. 'And in your opinion it was during such an encounter that Fletcher was killed?'

Harborough nodded. 'Oh yes. How else would you explain it?'

'Well, he could have been killed the way the Coroner suggested,' I said. 'He could simply have fallen into the bunker in the dark and broken his neck.'

'Do you honestly think that is what he did?'

I said, 'Look, Harborough, it's not my job to have opinions. The Coroner ruled that death was accidental and that's that. If you thought Fletcher had been killed by little green men, you should have spoken up while there was still time.'

He said sulkily, 'You don't have to be offensive. Nobody's asking you to believe in anything you don't want to.'

Well, he had a point and in any case I wasn't going to get anywhere by upsetting him. 'It isn't a question of being offensive,' I assured him. 'It's just the probability of the thing. If Fletcher was really killed by something from outer space, how did it happen? Why? And where are the things that killed him now?' Even asking the questions gave one a curious feeling of unreality and I suspected that Laurie would probably have done the job better. Still, coppers are notoriously unimaginative.

Harborough stood up. He was a big man and in that small room he looked impressive. Come to that, he even gave one a feeling that he knew what he was talking about. 'We have no idea how or why Fletcher died,' he told me calmly. 'We have no reason to believe that the ETs—extra-terrestrials—were anything but friendly. Perhaps he showed aggression—there is no accounting how people will react when they are frightened.'

'We?'

'Those of us who were expecting an encounter, of course.'

My friend the arboreal milkman whirred past the window on his electric float. Perhaps he was a part of this mysterious conclave? Were they like Masons, busy exchanging secret signs? How much of this subculture had I been missing all these years?

'Could you enlarge on that?' I asked.

Harborough showed his first signs of irritation. 'I find it hard to enlarge on a simple statement. Those of us who were expecting an encounter had no reason to fear it.'

'How many is "us"?' I asked patiently. 'And what reason did you have for expecting this—this arrival?'

He said petulantly, 'It really is extremely difficult to answer these questions in a manner comprehensible to a layman.'

'Why don't you give it a try?' I suggested.

I think he sighed but at least he wasn't going to be intentionally obstructive. 'Well, you are obviously aware that there are a very considerable number of people who believe that there are high intelligences other than ours. That we are not, in fact, the only inhabited planet and that for some considerable time alien intelligences have been trying to make contact with us.'

'Yes,' I said, 'I've read my science fiction.'

'Suppose for once it isn't science fiction.' Harborough relaxed suddenly and sat down on the edge of his three-seater moquette-covered settee. 'Just suppose it's all true and there are a certain number of people here on this planet Earth who are aware of what is really going on.'

'And what is going on?' I asked.

'Probes have made it clear that a landing was to be attempted at 10.35 p.m. on Tuesday evening.'

'Probes?'

Harborough said, 'Inspector, if you were investigating a fraud at a computer centre and one of your witnesses went into minute details of programming, would you understand what he was talking about?'

'All right,' I said, 'let's say that you had good reason to believe that a landing was imminent. How many of you believed this?'

'Not more than six of us. The observations we had made were at variance with accepted research.' He smiled apologetically. 'You might describe us as the lunatic fringe, if it makes you feel any better.'

'Did this six include Fletcher?' I asked.

Harborough nodded. 'Yes. In fact, one might say that it was his preliminary work that made the accuracy of our calculations possible.'

I wondered how they made their observations. Did they study the stars, translate radio signals or use a medium? I could have asked but I doubted very much if I'd have got an answer I'd have understood. You don't ask a Jehovah's Witness where he got his faith from and, if he told you, it wouldn't be convincing, and as Flying Saucers seemed to me to be very much a matter of faith, I decided to let him get on with it.

'Sightings of UFOs have always suggested a definite pattern.' Harborough seemed to have little difficulty in picking up what I was thinking, so perhaps there was more to this extra-terrestrial lark than I had suspected. 'We log all sightings, of course, and we know the patterns that have been established before previous encounters. In fact, we have reason to believe that the sighting pattern is an intentional means of communication, although of course we can't be sure.'

'Have you ever personally ever met an—alien?' I tried to make it sound a reasonable question.

He looked understandably regretful. 'No. I had hoped that I might on this occasion, but I must have made a miscalculation. In fact, I know I did. Fletcher must have realized that the encounter was to take place on the eighth, whereas I was a day late.'

I remembered the eighth, the drinks party at the Club. It had hardly been the kind of night any sensible alien would have chosen to descend on a golf club. How would a Flying Saucer have made it down to the sixth fairway without being spotted? How would it have got away again?

'Mr Harborough,' I said, 'Keith Fletcher went to witness a UFO landing a day earlier than you expected, so you didn't have a chance to see the encounter yourself.'

'That is correct.'

'But you did visit the course the following night and found nothing there.'

Harborough was making a good job of hiding a growing impatience. 'Fletcher's calculations had been right and mine wrong, so naturally there was nothing to see.'

'But Fletcher was dead by that time,' I reminded him. 'So how do you *know* he was killed by an alien?'

He looked at me for what seemed a long time. Perhaps he was wondering why he hadn't thought of that for himself, but he could equally well have been congratulating himself on the fact that he knew something more than I did.

'I can't prove Keith Fletcher was killed that way, Inspector,' he said at last. 'I just know.'

'I suppose,' I said rather more caustically than was strictly necessary, 'there weren't any witnesses besides Fletcher when this alien arrived?'

'There was one.' Harborough looked as though he was surprised that I hadn't asked before. 'But second-hand accounts are a poor substitute for the real thing. I'd much rather you question him yourself.'

'Him?'

'A schoolfriend of my son, young Jeremy Thurston. His father's Secretary at the West Wessex Golf Club, I believe.'

I drove back to the Club in a chastened frame of mind. If I had been on duty I'd probably never even have considered visiting Harborough, and now I had all this on my plate. There was something curiously convincing about the man, I had to admit. I tried to analyse it but couldn't and in the

126

end decided that a certain plausibility was an essential part of the true eccentric, and I even felt vaguely amused about the whole thing. Jeremy Thurston's involvement seemed more natural, because schoolboys and flying saucers very properly went together in my estimation. But I'd have to speak to him, just the same.

Held up in the High Street by a lady exercising half-a-dozen Yorkshire terriers, I glanced sideways into a radio dealer's window and my eye was caught by the screen of a demonstration television. Someone in check trews and a blue cap was marching intently across a golf green. It had to be the Tamworth Classic—it was the only golf scheduled for that day, but weren't the camera crews on strike? Obviously they were not, though it was news to me. Had the Union thrown in the towel, I wondered, or had the company simply paid up?

At the West Wessex my instinct was to ask Ambrose but that was hardly going to be on since he would be up to his neck in the commentary. I parked my car in the main entrance under the reproachful eye of a young WPC and wandered along the edge of the tented village. By and large, the place seemed to be doing a roaring trade, with people round every stall in sight. Mind you, the portable televisions on every counter probably had a good deal to do with it, but with a captive audience on their hands it would be their fault if they didn't make a killing.

I looked up at the huge leader board facing the stand by the eighteenth green. Shroeder was leading by three strokes from Bill Sadiq and a South African called Washbrook, Kawasaki was another stroke behind them and then there were five and six all tying for next place. Well, it was early days yet and the tension doesn't really begin to build up until the later rounds, but there seemed to be good crowds. The stand at the eighteenth wasn't full, which was understandable at this early stage in the tournament, but the car parks looked pretty full and, from what I could see on the TV screens, the gallery was tight packed on the holes where they were covering the action. One could hear the applause at intervals and the sympathetic groans when a putt didn't go down, although it was impossible to tell whether one was hearing the real thing or the loudspeakers of God knows how many televisions. But it had that indefinable air of an occasion, and with any luck the West Wessex was going to end up well in the black.

I found Alan Thurston surrounded by marshals asking him for this and that, and he caught my eye and nodded to the tent that housed the Committee bar. I took the hint and bought myself a sandwich to go with a beer, grateful for the fact that the place was surprisingly empty.

'Ghastly business about the Appleby girl.' Thurston had got rid of his marshals and looked in need of a drink. I fetched him one and he swallowed it with the air of a man who'd just parked a camel. 'Kempton told me. He's pretty shaken and I don't blame him. Pretty bizarre kind of accident, when you come to think of it.'

I said, 'I suppose if it had been a twelve-bore, nobody would pay that much notice. It's just the archaic business of bows and arrows that gets one.'

'I suppose it *was* an accident?' Thurston swirled what was left of his gin round the bottom of his glass.

'That's up to the Coroner to decide.'

He nodded hastily. 'Yes, of course, I appreciate that. But as you were there—'

'I can assure you I didn't do it.'

'Well—yes.' He changed horses firmly. 'You've heard that the TV trouble's cleared up?'

'Yes,' I said, 'who gave in?'

'That's the funny thing. Nobody.'

'Then why no strike?'

Thurston finished his drink in a hurry and waved for a couple more. 'Well, you remember that the camera operators wanted a special daily bonus to cover this, that and the other?'

'Tamworth wouldn't play,' I said. 'And I can't say I blame them.'

Thurston nodded. 'I know—it was sheer bloody blackmail. I thought we'd had it because Crawford—the TV union man—is one of those bolshie sods who'd wreck a golf broadcast on principle anyway, just because he reckons it's not a game for the masses. God knows who he thinks is playing on all those municipal courses, but that's beside the point.'

'It is,' I agreed. 'Tell me what happened.'

'Some anonymous benefactor coughed up the money and saved the day.'

'Tamworth paying up out of the petty cash just to save face?' I guessed. It wasn't totally unknown in the circumstances.

'I suppose so.' Thurston was wagging his hand at the barman again—it must have been some sizeable desert he'd been in. I shook my head over my own glass.

I said, 'Odd, though. I thought there was almost a blood feud between Tamworth and the Union over something that happened last time. I gather Kempton was doing his "over my dead body" bit and meaning it.'

'None of them mean it when it gets down to the nitty-gritty.' Thurston looked moodily into his glass. 'And this only amounted to about seven grand. Like you said, Tamworth would have paid it out of petty cash.'

'I suppose so.' Indeed they could have done. But in view of the fact that everyone would naturally take it for granted that they'd turned chicken at the last moment, it would have been odd if they had. 'When did all this happen?' I asked.

'Earlier this morning.'

'And how did the money arrive?'

Thurston shrugged his shoulders. 'I never asked. But I gather it was in cash.'

'Well, anonymous donors don't normally sign cheques,' I agreed. 'Not unless they're after knighthoods.'

'No,' Thurston agreed. 'I suppose not.' He nodded out through the open entrance to the marquee. 'Going to have a look?'

'Maybe later.' I left him ordering another drink and hesitated by the yellow-painted mobile TV centre. I could go and see Crawford but there didn't seem much point in being insulted by some surly scion of the Trade Union mafia who presumably had no more idea of where the pay-off had come from than I had. Or, if he did, I had no means of forcing him to tell me. Why worry about who'd paid it, anyway, I thought. It could have been any one of a number of firms who had a vested interest in seeing the tournament a financial success—for that matter, it could have been some stalwart union-basher who was well-heeled enough to spend a little of his disposable income on backing Tamworth's stand. But I didn't really believe it was as easy as that. Odd how bloody-minded one can get.

I'd have liked to have watched the golf for a while but the thing was niggling at me so I drove to Harlington instead. Dick Tracey and I played golf together occasionally and he was manager of the biggest branch of Caymans for some miles around. I dislike the idea of making use of one's friends for official purposes, although God knows, in most businesses one uses them for little else, so I sat on my finer feelings, no more than an occupational risk when all is said and done.

Dick was as usual, stripe-suited behind half an acre of desk. Affable and wary, not too wary, though, because I wasn't a customer so there wasn't going to be any unpleasantness over an overdraft.

'Angus, it's good to see you!' This after I'd jumped his appointments queue by flashing warrant cards at his busty secretary. He could have demanded, with some justification, to know what the hell this was all about, but that's not the way you get to be managers of the larger branches.

Well, no messing about. I said, 'Dicky, I'm looking for someone who drew seven thousand quid yesterday.'

Dicky blinked. It takes a good deal to make a bank manager blink, but I'd done it. Not with the question. Dicky didn't wear a good old school tie for nothing, it was the chap who had asked the question. Embarrassing when one finds that the chaps you play golf with are shits after all. He said reproachfully, 'Come off it, Angus! Even if I knew I couldn't tell you that.'

'Not necessarily from this branch. Maybe some other

branch hereabouts.' I smiled benignly. 'I thought I'd start with you because you're the biggest.'

Dicky let a little professional ice into his voice. 'Well, speaking for this branch, I simply don't know if anyone withdrew that amount of money yesterday. And if they did, the matter would be totally confidential.'

'You can prod that computer gadget on your desk,' I told him, 'and find out in a matter of moments. And nothing is confidential in this worker's paradise, least of all bank accounts.'

He said huffily, 'There are procedures—'

'It's like a search warrant,' I told him. 'You can chuck me out if I haven't got one, but I'll get it in the end, as well you know.' I let him think it over for a bit. 'Look,' I said, 'it's important. It's even more important to save time.'

'What happens if nobody withdrew that amount yesterday?'

I said, 'Then I go through all this with the Midland, Lloyds, and if I draw a blank there, with the Natwest, and then the Trustee Savings Bank and Barclays—'

'I can't say I like it.' Dicky was a lad on his way up the banking ladder and I could see him thinking that breaches of confidence were not the sort of thing he wanted to see featured in his record when the next step forward came along.

'I don't like it either,' I confessed, 'but it's just one of those things. But if you do happen to come up with an answer, I promise you that whoever is concerned will never know I've even got the information, let alone where it came from.'

He said doggedly, 'If a customer opens an account here, he's a right to expect it to be inviolate. *You* do, for a start.'

'That's a lot of balls,' I told him. 'You know as well as I do that you'll open your books for any snivelling little bastard of a tax inspector who flashes his card at you.' I was having a bad time with my friendly neighbourhood Inland Revenue man and was in no mood for charity.

'But that's different.'

'It's two different aspects of the same establishment,' I

131

reminded him. 'I'm sorry, Dicky, but you know as well as I do that it comes to the same thing in the long run, and at the moment I'm in a hurry.'

'I get your point.' There was just enough chill in the words to inform me that, should I be fostering ambitions to become a member of any club that numbered Richard Tracey among its committee, I could look forward to at least one autographed black ball. He prodded the keys of his computer with the air of a man who thought he might catch something off them, then stared at the screen and prodded again. If you don't know about the electronic miracle, there's something daunting about the business, like watching someone in direct contact with God.

'It looks as though you may have hit it first shot.' Dicky looked faintly put out. 'There's a client here who got an unsecured loan on his credit card yesterday to make a total of £7,400 available. Would that make any difference to you?'

'Not so long as he withdrew the money yesterday,' I said.

'Oh, he did that all right.' Dicky frowned. For a moment I thought he was actually going to say my man's name but at the last moment his courage failed him. Instead he picked up the sort of slip counter clerks write your balance on if you're rash enough to ask what it is. He scribbled and pushed it over.

I read it and rolled the paper up into a small ball and dropped it into Dicky's wastepaper basket.

Alan Thurston.

CHAPTER 11

Before leaving a bunker, a player should carefully fill up
and smooth over all holes and footprints made by him.
                                                    Etiquette

My mind wasn't on the job as I drove home. Admittedly there was no reason why Alan Thurston should not have paid the strikers off if he felt that way about it. In fact, hardly a month passes without the newspapers reporting that some unknown wellwisher has paid the fine of some bloody-minded OAP who has dug in his heels regardless of the consequences.

Refusing to pay a ten-pound fine at Marylebone Magistrates Court today for not wearing a crash helmet, 76-year-old motor-cyclist John Bloggs said, 'I am prepared to go to gaol. A cloth cap was good enough for my father and it is good enough for me.'

Maybe Alan was just another wellwisher, righting the wrongs of the unjust society. Only one couldn't help wondering why. Obviously he wanted the tournament to go on, but surely not to the extent of seven thousand quid of his own money? He had never given me the impression that he was a rich man, and in my experience rich men get to be that way because they are nobody's fools. Logically, if anyone was going to keep the tournament going, it had to be Tamworth, even if they couldn't very well make a public climbdown after the 'no surrender' line that they'd made such a song and dance about. They could have got Thurston to square the Union for them, I supposed, as a convenient and discreet go-between, but in that case why hadn't they given him the necessary money to do the job?

I tried to think of some other convincing reason why Alan should have handed over seven grand just to keep the TV cameras turning, and failed totally. Should I ask him? I imagined that had he wanted me to know he'd have told me, which meant that he'd either lie or clam up entirely. An elderly gent in an ancient Marina flashed his right-hand indicator at me and immediately turned left, while a demented blackbird, deep in a game of last across, sped perilously in front of my radiator. All the world, it seemed, was full of instant decisions except me.

The Thurstons lived in a pleasant Edwardian villa on the edge of town, a substantial building set in a largish garden, well cared for and shaded by large old trees. I parked at the bottom of the shingled driveway and banged the brass lion knocker on the door. A good-looking girl of about eighteen opened it. She was in jeans and a checked shirt, with flour

133

on her hands, and the controlled look of a woman who had been disturbed getting dinner.

She said, 'Hi! Daddy's not back yet. I'm his daughter, Sue. Anything I can do?' She was a bright girl, on top of her job. I liked her.

'My name's Straun.' I produced my warrant card, beamed to show I wasn't on that sort of duty. 'I'm here because I gather your brother Jeremy's deeply into flying saucers.'

Alan's daughter grinned. 'You could say that.'

'It sounds daft, but that's what I'd very much like to have a word with him about.'

She blinked. 'You mean believing in flying saucers is a *crime*?'

'Good heavens, no!' I said hastily. 'Nothing like that. It's just something that's come up.'

A voice said, 'Who was it, Sue?' and Jeremy appeared in person. He was a comic artist's idea of a thirteen-year-old boy, shaggy and freckled. I supposed Sam would be like him eventually, if he was lucky, which at the moment he wasn't.

Sue said, 'This is Inspector Straun, who wants to have a word with you.'

'Oh.' No particular welcome for Inspector Straun. No signs of distress, but distinct embarrassment.

His sister eyed him with something like alarm. 'Jeremy, you little creep—you've been doing something!'

I said hastily, 'No, he hasn't. At least, if he has I don't know about it.' But all this was a bit dodgy by the book. Dodgy anyway. I addressed Sue Thurston before she set about her brother in earnest. 'Look, I know your father quite well through golf. As a matter of fact, I thought he might be in. I'd very much like a word with Jeremy and I assure you he isn't accused of anything, but strictly speaking it's not done to talk to someone of his age without a parent being present. Is your mother around, by any chance?'

Sue Thurston shook her head. 'No, she's away visiting her brother in Bristol.'

'Then I'd better come back.'

134

'I shouldn't worry about that.' She was a competent young woman, pleased to take responsibility. 'If you want to speak to Jeremy, I'm sure Dad wouldn't mind. Why don't you come in?'

She took me into a room that Alan apparently used as his own private patch, more an office than a study, with a vast, old-fashioned partner's desk and a lot of crowded and rather badly put up bookshelves.

'You'd better let me get you a drink,' Sue Thurston said. Stopped and remembered all those TV films. 'Oh, I suppose if—'

I didn't particularly want a drink but I didn't want her to go all formal on me either, so I let her get me one. While she was gone I nosed round Alan's books and admired the already fading photograph of him and Melanie on the verandah of some colonial bungalow. There were carved heads on the windowsills and a polo stick in one corner. Somehow I hadn't pictured Alan playing polo, but then it was hard to imagine the former life of ex-administrators anyway, though probably no stranger than being secretary to a golf club was to them.

Sue brought the drink. I thanked her and said, 'How long do you have to stand in for your mother?' She was still covered in flour, rather endearing. An older woman would have wiped it off but I think she was not unproud of it.

'I don't know. Until Uncle James is better, I suppose.' She added without enthusiasm, 'He's Vicar of a tiny place called North Haddon, down Bristol way. He's never married and Mummy never hears from him from one year to the next. Now, just because he's had a stroke or something, he expects her to come running.' She shook her head. 'Forget it. You wanted to speak to Jeremy—'

Jeremy had gone. She got him back, a good mother substitute, and sat him down. 'You want to see him alone?'

'Good Lord, no!' I shook my head. 'Stick around and make sure everything's above board.' Jeremy was looking distinctly sheepish, which was odd, because there's nothing illegal about being keen on flying saucers. I went on casually, 'I understand you know Mr Harborough.'

Jeremy nodded. 'Yes, he's sort of president of our local UFO society. And then there's Tom—Mr Harborough's son. He's a friend of mine.'

'Mr Harborough,' I said, 'tells me you actually saw an Unidentified Flying Object the other night. Did you?'

Jeremy's sister said rather sharply, 'You saw a *what?*'

'A UFO. An unidentified flying object. A flying saucer.' Jeremy had the patient look of an expert explaining something basic to a layman.

'Well, answer the Inspector's question. Did you see one?'

'Yes.' Jeremy considered for a moment. 'Well, yes, I think so.'

He was uncommonly composed, taken all round, the kind of witness that impresses juries, and at the moment he was impressing me. I said, 'Whereabouts did this—sighting—take place?' I was beginning to pick up the jargon.

'On the golf course.'

'The West Wessex?'

'Yes, sir.' He was a well-brought-up lad, kind to adults and, so far, anxious to help.

'Whereabouts on the golf course?' I tried to adopt an air of someone who was perfectly prepared to believe in flying saucers but just happened to have an academic interest in where they came down. 'Which hole, I mean.'

'The sixth, I think. I've only played there once or twice.'

Well, it was reasonable enough that the son of a golfer should play a little himself. Probably if I pressed him it would turn out that he played to scratch. 'About what time did this happen?' I asked.

Jeremy thought that one over. I wouldn't have been all that surprised if he'd given me the time to the second but apparently he'd slipped up on that. Possibly he felt the same because he looked slightly embarrassed when he said, 'I'm not absolutely sure, sir. Round about ten, I think. Perhaps ten-fifteen.'

'On the night of the eighth?'

He nodded. 'That's right.'

'Don't be ridiculous!' Sue dismissed the statement briskly. 'Honestly, Jeremy, you're impossible. You know perfectly

136

well that on Tuesday you were home and in bed before that.'

'I went to bed, but I went out again.' Young Jeremy stared at his sister rather defiantly, and I got the impression that Sue had been possibly a bit over-emphatic as a mother substitute.

His sister blinked and reverted a few years. 'You little beast! How? I never saw you.'

'I went out through the window,' Jeremy told her cheerfully. And then, before she could ask the next question, 'I've got a rope.'

'When Mother hears about this she's going to just about slay you.' Not Dad, I noticed. I wondered if this was because Alan was assessed as an easygoing father or possibly the kind of man who might sympathize. If he'd been a French boy, Jeremy would almost certainly have shrugged, but none the less he managed to express the same feeling without actually moving. He said, 'Mum's not here.'

'Look,' I said, 'with any luck we can smooth over the getting out at night bit. But do you think you could manage to tell me what made you so sure that there was going to be a space invasion on that particular night?'

'Well, I can't say that I was absolutely sure. Tom knows more about that sort of thing than I do.' An air of caution, a wariness, which was odd because he seemed a nice enough lad.

I said, 'Mr Harborough seems to think that you were the one who had the better—experience.'

There was an undeniable flicker of amusement in his eyes at that, which was interesting. I wished I'd had more to do with juveniles, only that would have been with delinquents and, so far as I could tell, that wasn't Jeremy. But he was no ordinary small boy. 'If you went to the golf course together,' I said, 'how come you didn't both see the same thing—whatever it was?' And then when he didn't answer, 'I suppose you *were* together?'

Jeremy said, 'Well, yes, sir. Well, for some of the time, at least.'

Pause for the thought that when Sam grew up a bit, I'd

be doing this sort of thing all the time. Always providing that I got to see Sam that much, which was becoming increasingly doubtful. 'You mean,' I said, 'you split up when you got there?'

'Yes, sir.' That was definite enough, at any rate.

'Why?'

'Oh!' A penny seemed to have dropped with Sue, although as yet it hadn't with me. Was I being particularly thick?

I said amiably, 'Look, suppose we stop mucking about or we shall be here all day.' I tried to give the impression that I knew exactly what it was he wasn't telling me and simply wanted it confirmed. A poor kind of bluff it was, and any self-respecting villain would have laughed till the tears ran down his face, but this lad was unused to such ploys.

Jeremy sighed. 'Well, sir, there were a couple of girls—'

'You randy little reptile!' Sue Thurston said. 'Which couple of girls?'

'I don't see that matters.' Jeremy had read somewhere that it was up to a gentleman to safeguard the reputation of a lady, but apparently his sister hadn't come across the same book.

'Mary Dennison and Sarah Mancroft, I suppose.' Sue Thurston sniffed disapproval in a way that would have done credit to a much older woman. 'Which one was yours?'

Jeremy said meekly, 'Sarah.'

'Little trollop,' his sister observed. 'Dad will be charmed to hear about her.'

'Well, he won't hear unless you tell him,' Jeremy told her with some return of spirit. 'I don't see what it's got to do with you anyway.'

'If you spent a bit more time on your maths instead of trying to—'

I caught her eye. 'Suppose we calm down a bit?' I suggested. 'Jeremy's being very helpful and I don't suppose any harm's been done.'

'Well, no,' Sue conceded. 'By all accounts Sarah Mancroft's been obliging all and sundry since she was about twelve. Now—'

'This is the age of the permissive society,' I reminded her, 'and speaking personally, I don't care all that much about your brother's sex life. He can take his A-levels in it for all I'm concerned, but in the meantime there are some questions I'd like to ask and we're not going to get very far if you carry on like this. You're here to protect your young brother from me, not the other way round.'

'All right,' she conceded, 'but really—'

'Right, Jeremy,' I said, 'let's get to the nitty-gritty of all this. Which came first, the flying saucers or the girls?'

He had the grace to grin. All in all he was a rather engaging young rogue and one who would go far. 'Well, as a matter of fact, sir,' he said, 'I'm not all that up in UFOs —they're more Tom's cup of tea than mine. Mind you, I don't think *he* believes in them all that much, but his father's absolutely sold on them.'

'So?'

'Well, Tom heard that there was some kind of sighting expected over the next few days, so we dared the girls to have a look with us.'

Well, it was a new line at least. Come up and see flying saucers with me. 'If the sightings were supposed to be on Friday or Saturday, why did you go and look for them on Tuesday?' I asked.

'Well, that was the only day the girls could manage, so we put the date back a bit,' Jeremy added practically, 'I mean, we didn't reckon anything was going to happen on Friday, so it might just as well not happen on Tuesday, if you see what I mean.'

'Oh, I do!' I assured him. 'So you and Tom invited these girls to view flying saucers over the West Wessex golf course on Tuesday night. You climbed over the fence on to the ground?'

'There's a right of way, actually.'

'So there is. And once there, you and Sarah went one way and Tom and whatever-her-name-is went another, in order to explore the heavens in privacy.'

Jeremy nodded. 'Well, yes. Sort of.'

'But you personally didn't expect to see any extra-terrestrial phenomena?'

139

He grinned. 'No, sir. Not really.'

'And did you?'

He stopped grinning. 'I don't know.'

'But you saw something?'

'Yes, as a matter of fact, I did. At least, I thought I did.' He regarded me doubtfully. 'It's pretty difficult to say, you know.'

'No,' I said, 'I'm afraid I don't know. That's why I'm asking you all this. I want you to describe to me what it was you *thought* you saw.'

He frowned in concentration. 'Well, I suppose it was sort of like anyone would imagine a flying saucer.'

I tried to call up the various promotion pictures I'd seen of science fiction films and found it unexpectedly difficult. Odd that I could imagine something that happened six hundred years ago without difficulty but get completely lost when it came to things that were supposed to be happening today. I said, 'Like a jelly on a plate, puffing out smoke?'

Jeremy looked a bit startled. 'Oh no, it didn't look like *that*! I mean, it wasn't landing or anything.'

'Well, what exactly was it doing?'

'Sort of going across the sky. Quite low down, as though it was *going* to land.'

'Well, what shape was it?' Maybe in his place I'd have proved a better witness, maybe not. It was remarkably hard to tell.

'Oh, it was circular—saucer-shaped.'

'Did it make any noise?'

Jeremy thought for a moment, then shook his head. 'I don't think so.' Then, 'There was quite a din going on at the time from the clubhouse, and the automatic sprinkler on the sixth green had come on, so it was rather like being out in a heavy rain.'

'But if the flying saucer or whatever it was didn't make any noise, how did you notice it?' I asked.

He looked a bit embarrassed. 'I—we—happened to be looking up at the time.'

His sister made a noise that wasn't totally unlike a snort. 'You mean you were rolling around on the grass with—'

'It doesn't matter,' I said hastily. I was beginning to feel sorry for Jeremy, who seemed a nice enough lad and hardly unique in having adolescent urges. 'Just go on about how it looked.'

He frowned in concentration. 'Well, it happened quickly. It just sort of shot across the sky, then swerved and got bigger still and then it vanished behind the trees—you know, the sort of wood on the other side of the fairway.'

'You mean it landed?'

'I don't know, I just didn't see it any more. I suppose it could have zoomed off again, sort of low down.' The boy was obviously doing his best. He said, 'It sort of glowed.'

'Any particular colour?'

'Well—you know. Heat colour. Sort of yellow, I suppose.'

'What about Sarah?' I asked. 'What colour did she think it was?'

Jeremy looked surprised and shook his head. 'But she didn't see it. She didn't see it at all.'

'Although you were both looking up at the sky?'

'I don't think she could have been at the time. You know—' Jeremy looked a bit hunted. He went on hurriedly, 'Anyway, it was jolly easy to miss, even if you were looking that way. Just a matter of a few seconds. I suppose that's why I'm a bit vague about what I saw myself. You see something, then it's gone, and although you think you saw it quite clearly at the time, you can't help wondering whether you saw it or not.'

'I know.' He was a good witness and a good deal brighter than most. I went on, 'And Tom didn't see anything either?'

'No.' Jeremy grinned and reverted to a a small boy again. 'A bit hard on him, really. I mean, he knew a lot more about UFOs and things. He'd really have *liked* to have seen one.'

I had another go at him just as a routine precaution but he didn't shift from his story. He'd seen something that at least answered the popular descriptions of a flying saucer. He alone had seen it. Neither he nor his friends had noticed Keith Fletcher or anyone else. True, their attention may have been elsewhere, but presumably if something out of the ordinary had happened they would have registered at least *something*.

I thanked them for their help and took myself back to the car. 'I hope you get your mother back soon. Have you heard how she's getting on?'

Sue Thurston shook her head. 'No. I expect she'll ring up any day now.'

'Well, good luck with the cooking.'

I drove back home. It had been a nice day but now a wind was getting up and stirring the bracken in the hedges. Here and there one could already pick out a touch of brown, and the trees were throwing darker shadows than they had a few weeks back. Summer almost gone.

Laurie's car was in front of the flat when I got back to Staples Cross and she was sitting in the driver's seat reading a thick manuscript that she had propped on the steering-wheel. She was wearing a leather jacket and below it a red, crew-necked sweater, and as usual her glasses had fallen down her nose.

'How long have you been here?' I suppose I could have made it rather more welcoming but I hadn't expected her and I had other things on my mind.

'About an hour.' She opened the door and eased herself out of the car. 'I rang up earlier but you weren't in. Hatcher's say if they don't get that revise by tomorrow they'll have to put publication back till the spring. And if they do that, it puts paid to the American contract because that stipulates that the British and American come out together and New York certainly aren't going to hold things up because of us.'

'For God's sake!' I exploded. 'Have they gone raving mad? The deadline's not until the end of October!'

'I know.' Laurie made a 'it's just one of those things' gesture. 'There's been some kind of editorial crisis. They're full of apologies but they're also pretty adamant that this is the only way out. So, can you do it?'

'I suppose so.' I wasn't sure whether I could or not, but it was a challenge and I was reluctant to say I couldn't cope. 'It'll mean working all night.'

Laurie regarded me dispassionately. 'Well, I honestly think you'd better. Hatcher's are being thoroughly unreasonable but they're damn good publishers and it's worth leaning over backwards now and then to keep them friendly. I'd have said all this over the phone if I'd been able to get you, but in any case—'

'You'd prefer to stand over me to make sure the job gets done,' I finished for her.

'As there didn't seem any other way—yes.'

I led the way into the flat, none too pleased. 'Look,' I said, 'you know bloody well that I've got enough on my plate at the moment without this.'

'I know you have, and I'm sorry.' She looked marginally regretful but not enough to come up with any helpful suggestions. 'I'd have put them off if there'd been the slightest chance, but there wasn't, so what else do you suggest I do? I'm your agent and this is what you pay me for.'

'You'd better have a drink,' I said.

She waited till I'd poured one and then asked, 'How are the flying saucers?'

'Apparently they exist.' I told her about Harborough and Jeremy.

Laurie looked at me curiously. 'Do you believe him?'

'So far as it goes, I believe what he told me was true.' I thought about it. Yes, I did. I said, 'But it's probably like most accounts of sightings—the people concerned are genuine enough. They see something and they think it's a flying saucer. Whether it is or not is anyone's guess.'

'But at least we've got a reason for Fletcher being where he was that night.'

I liked the 'we' but on present showing she was certainly entitled. 'It's a reason,' I admitted, 'but unless he really did meet some very aggressive little green man, it still doesn't tell us who broke his neck.'

'So you've stopped thinking it was an accident.' Laurie was looking at me with her eyebrows raised. 'You think—'

'It doesn't make sense that it was an accident,' I said. 'But if it comes to that, people don't commit murder without a reason and so far the most doubtful thing we've managed

143

to dig up about Keith Fletcher is what we thought was a rather childish belief in flying saucers. Only now it seems there are as many UFO nuts as there are Freemasons. Frankly, I'm prepared to believe anything.'

'So what are you going to do about it?'

'Presumably nothing, until I've done the revise.' I looked at my watch and saw that it wasn't much after six, which meant a long night ahead. 'Look,' I said resignedly, 'this isn't going to take ten minutes. What are you going to do while you're waiting?'

'Stay here,' Laurie told me promptly. 'You know as well as I do that you'll be gone the moment I turn my back on you.'

'It's going to look pretty scruffy,' I warned. 'It'll take most of the night as it is, and there certainly won't be time to clean it up.'

'Oh, for God's sake, Angus, get on with it!' Laurie stood up and went into the kitchen and I could hear her fiddling around with the coffee-maker. She said through the open door, 'And don't worry about what your stuff looks like—I can always get an agency girl to knock it into shape. They'll be glad to get it any way it comes.'

I have a fixed objection to rehashing anything I write, not through any feeling that it can't be improved but simply because once I manage to get something down on paper, I tend to lose interest in it. There's an element of the bar-room bore about telling the same story over again, except that I imagine that so far as the drunk is concerned the story gets better each time. But on this occasion I had the story in front of me to correct, which at least gave me a comforting feeling that I was editing rather than rewriting. It was something of an effort to switch myself mentally from flying saucers to the fourteenth century but, once accomplished, the older world gathered itself around me readily enough and the fact that I had an urgent deadline removed once and for all the temptation to leave the job for tomorrow. I think that there remains enough race memory within most of us to conjure up the past without too much difficulty— easier by far, it always seems, than it must be for science fiction writers to evoke a totally unknown future, even though they manage to get it right with almost boring consistency. I stared at the pages in front of me and felt my mind lock on to them. I was aware of the first cup of coffee that Laurie put beside me, but after that my surroundings faded into the background as my characters began to move around on their own. I picked them up rather satisfactorily like old friends and I didn't consciously have to translate the way they talked or interpret the way they thought. My revision called for the action of the story to shift from Avignon in France to the fortress of Chinon and back again instead of remaining, as it had done in my original draft, located at the old capital of the Popes, and I'd put the job off for so long that it had assumed difficulties of enormous proportions. Now, having finally got down to it, I found it easy enough to account for the moves, and the job didn't seem so difficult after all. Some new action I wrote straight on to the typewriter, other shifts of scene I cobbled together on the long, shiny proof slips, constructing the curious pattern of erasures and repositionings that I'm told printers used to work from without complaint but which send today's electronic typesetters climbing up the wall.

At some time during the evening I ate sandwiches that were placed beside me, and that was all I wanted because I was too far along to break off for anything else. I knew it was long dark but I had no idea of time. Writing is much like anything else, in that if it goes well you can get an adrenalin-boosted lift to compensate for the black despair of when it goes badly. It's exciting while it lasts but unfortunately it doesn't last for ever. After a while I felt my feet getting cold and the first waves of weariness begin to wash over me. There wasn't much more to go and I knew from experience that at this point a single large whisky would see me through the last lap.

I got up stiffly and measured the drink carefully, because too little wouldn't do the trick and too much would simply send me to sleep. According to the clock it was getting on for three and I remembered Laurie. Where the devil was she!

'Laurie?'

There was no answer and for a moment I wondered if I'd dreamed her up, but her handbag was on the table, so she'd been around all right. Eventually I discovered her fast asleep on top of my bed, minus shoes and glasses but otherwise fully dressed. It was none too warm at that hour of the morning, so I pulled the duvet over her and went back to work.

The whisky lasted. It was four in the morning by the time I'd clipped the galleys and extra pages together and stacked them up in the middle of my desk but I knew without going through it again that it would read all right. I went back to have a look at Laurie but she hadn't moved, so I followed her example and got under the covers, too.

'This is getting to be a habit,' I said aloud, but I could have saved myself the trouble because she never moved. The light was still on over my desk and enough of it came through the open door to see her lying there. Either she was very tired or she was made differently to most people because she never moved, not even when the phone beside me started its trendy warbling.

'Straun,' I said, 'who is it?'

He said it was the duty sergeant at Harlington, sir, and he'd been trying to get me most of the night but the line had been engaged. 'I thought maybe you'd taken the receiver off, because you didn't want to be disturbed.'

'Well, it wasn't off,' I said, 'so you must have been getting another number. Did you check with the operator?'

'No, sir.'

'For God's sake,' I said, 'it could have been important!' Could have been? I hadn't even asked. 'All right,' I said, 'what did you want me for, anyway?'

'Mr Hawkins left a message for you, sir, before he went off duty. Regarding the Vicar of North Haddon and Mrs Thurston. The gentleman has been attending a convention in Brussels for the past two weeks, something to do with Missions to the Third World. He is said to be in good health and nobody down there knows anything about a Mrs Thurston.'

146

'No,' I said, 'I didn't think they would. But thanks for trying.'

I put the phone down to find that Laurie's eyes were open. She didn't look as though she was exactly asking what that had all been about, but I told her anyway. 'The desk sergeant says that this phone's been off the hook all night.'

'I know. I took it off.'

Well, that made sense, but she shouldn't have done it all the same. 'Don't you think that was a little presumptuous?' I asked.

'I thought it was rather practical.' I half expected her to reinforce her case by putting her glasses on but she didn't. Instead she said, 'You know perfectly well that if I hadn't, you wouldn't have got any work done.' She paused. 'It *is* finished?'

'Yes.'

'Well, that's all right then. Who was it wanted you?'

I said, 'Alan Thurston's wife isn't at home because she's supposed to be visiting her brother near Bristol. I got the station to check it out. Apparently she isn't.'

'She's probably engaged in a little harmless adultery.'

I said, 'A wife who wants to spend a week with her lover would hardly tell her husband she was staying with her brother, for God's sake! Alan might have rung up.'

Laurie frowned. 'Maybe her brother could have covered for her.'

'He's a parson,' I told her. 'And anyway, he's out of the country.'

I found myself remembering Sue Thurston, the pat way she'd delivered her bit about Melanie and her brother. Did she know? How did she *not* know?

Outside the window I thought I saw a streak of grey in the sky. 'It'll be dawn soon,' I said, and pulled my half of the duvet back on top of me. Laurie's leg touched mine, comfortingly warm.

'Like bundling,' I remarked.

'Bundling?'

I was surprised. For a literary agent she seemed unexpect-

edly ill-informed. I'd thought everyone knew about bundling.

I said, 'It's an old country courting custom. The couple
court in bed with their clothes on.'

Laurie's eyes opened wide. 'What on earth for?'

'Something to do with saving fuel and at the same time
observing the proprieties, I believe.'

'You don't mean to say that's how you were brought up?'

'No,' I said, 'it's a custom that's been discarded these
many years.' Her scent was faint but now it seemed to fill
the room.

'You feeling cold?'

'No.'

'So how about trying bundling with our clothes off?'

CHAPTER 12

*A player is not necessarily entitled to see his ball when
playing a stroke.*

Rule 12–1

Over breakfast Laurie said she wanted to watch the Tamworth. 'I haven't seen a proper game for ages. Not even on
the box.'

She meant since her father died, understandable perhaps.

'What round is it today?'

I buttered toast. Post-coital euphoria is enhanced by food
and we had eaten what bacon and eggs I had been able to
find and were starting in on the marmalade. Last night may
well just have been a momentary impulse on both sides but
I wasn't all that sure, because Laurie's presence on the other
side of the table was remarkably pleasant, even allowing for
the circumstances. I caught her eye and we smiled at each
other. She was wearing one of my dressing-gowns and she
looked clean and scrubbed and about eighteen.

She said, 'I wish you'd stop looking smug and answer my
question.'

'Second round.'

'I like second rounds.'

At that particular moment I was prepared to like just about anything she suggested, but in fact there is a lot to be said for the second round of a golf tournament. The first may not exactly sort the men out from the boys, but at least it demonstrates who is on form and who isn't. Pressures get tense later on, so that a lot of otherwise very good golfers are apt to do some very silly things, but with luck the second rounds show most competitors at their best.

'Fine,' I said, 'we'll go.'

Laurie's face did a double take. 'I must be out of my mind. There are your galleys to be sent back.'

'Post them.' I'd forgotten about the galleys.

She said impatiently, 'Don't be a fool, there isn't time. They've got to be at Hatcher's today.'

'They'll be there tomorrow. For that matter, you can take them yourself tomorrow. It's only another twenty-four hours,' I said.

'If one more day wasn't too much, I shouldn't have come down here myself in the first place.'

The sky had a clean, rain-washed look about it that almost certainly meant we were going to have a decent day. I wanted to watch golf and in particular I wanted to watch it with Laurie at my side and it seemed ridiculous to be thwarted by a pile of printed paper.

'Look,' I said, 'if the bloody galleys get to your office, I presume there's someone who can get things cleaned up and delivered without you being there yourself?'

'Oh yes—no problem.'

'Well, there's a car going to Met headquarters this morning. Stick everything in an envelope and I'll give it to the driver to deliver.' It was sheer luck that I happened to know that young Phillips was due in London for an interview and planning to go by car. If there had been no convenient Phillips, I suppose I'd have hired one.

'There really *is* a car going?' Apparently Laurie was a young woman of some perception, to whom thought-reading came easy.

'I'm not authorizing a car specially for the job, if that's what you mean.'

Laurie nodded. 'Okay. I'll ring my secretary as soon as she gets in and tell her to expect it.' She put her toast down as a thought struck her. 'I suppose I can trust you to call in at your police station without getting involved? I mean, you'll come *out* again?'

'Scout's honour.' She was not a lady who took chances, and I was rather surprised to discover that I meant what I said. I was on leave and today it was going to stay that way.

Laurie was studying me the way women do when they've convinced themselves that they've made a bad bargain. 'You'll regret that, but never mind.'

'What makes you so sure?' I asked.

'Because I think I'm almost as hooked on this thing as you.' She poured more coffee for me and then herself. Odd how, for lovers, even everyday actions take on a kind of special intimacy.

'But there isn't anything,' I told her. 'All we've got is a run of disconnected happenings. Some cranks dig up a golf green and a bar steward demands money with menaces. A jokester starts spreading exploding golf balls around and someone kills my cat. A PRO gets a crossbow arrow through the heart and an agronomist breaks his neck in a golf bunker after getting over-excited about the prospect of seeing a flying saucer. And just for good measure, a schoolboy apparently *has* seen things from outer space.'

'So?'

'I just want to know what the connection is between a dead cat and a flying saucer.'

'Does there have to be one?' Laurie could be tiresomely undramatic at times. 'Be realistic, Angus. It could be coincidence.'

'All that lot?' I protested. 'This isn't Brixton. Nothing's happened at the West Wessex that's remotely unlawful since some kids pinched a car to go joy-riding three years ago.'

'Then perhaps this is adjusting the balance.' Laurie reached out and touched my hand. 'Look, darling, if you're going to be in a state about this, there's not much point in going to watch golf—you might as well go into your office and get on with the job.'

'Unlikely though it may sound,' I said, 'I am officially supposed to be on leave.'

'Then don't you think it would be a good idea to get on with it? I mean, when are you due back at work, anyway?'

'Next Monday.' I had to think before I answered, the holiday, up till now, not having been very easily identifiable.

'Then maybe you could hold the whole thing over till then?'

'All right,' I agreed. 'I'll just ring the nick to make sure we can get that stuff off.'

I'd half expected someone to make a jump for me as soon as I opened my mouth but it was all right. Phillips was still going by car; no, he wouldn't leave till I got there. We finished breakfast amiably, dressed with the odd diversion and made our way to the course. The early cloud had cleared and the sky had that pale, washed-out look that one gets in early autumn and the odd, over-anxious tree was already taking on that slightly deep-shadowed look that comes before green gives way to brown. We were unchatty but pleased with ourselves, the quiet euphoria that follows a successful encounter that trails no unpleasant spin-offs in its wake. Sexual encounters, close encounters. Were there such things as flying saucers? People like Keith Fletcher weren't noticeably potty, but he'd believed in them, and when one thought about it, there was a certain plausibility about the whole thing. But even if flying saucers did exist, I still couldn't see why they should be interested in the Tamworth Trophy, unless little green men were deeply into golf.

I dropped the envelope with my night's work into the station and briefed Phillips as to where it had to go and the urgency with which it had to get there.

'Yes, sir,' Phillips said. 'Most urgent. What security category will it be?'

'It's too important to have a category,' I told him. 'It's my Will in there, Phillips, and my birth certificate and my marriage lines. If you lose them I shall be deported as an undesirable alien and if it comes to that I shall take you with me, so keep an eye on that envelope all the time.'

Phillips said, 'Yes, sir,' looking worried, but he was a conscientious youth so I knew all would be well.

There were no little green men at the West Wessex when we got there but an exceptionally large number of blue ones, mostly unknown, and there was a good deal of warrant-card waving before we got into a car park that wasn't a mile away from where we wanted to be. We walked over to the tented village, which wasn't all that busy, ten o'clock in the morning being a bit early for the bars even at a golf classic, and a lot of people without grandstand seats were out on the course trying to get themselves a decent pitch.

I went into the Press tent to find Ambrose uncharacteristically silent with a sheaf of TV shooting schedules on a clipboard before him, making notes with a concentration that was notably different from the bar-room chat approach that seemed so natural when one saw it in action. He looked up and waved a pencil.

'Good morning, gentles, been here long?'

I made noises like we'd just arrived.

'Time I stretched my legs, and I don't have to do anything till after lunch, thank God.' He was wearing a pale pink cashmere sweater and pearl grey slacks, duo-toned shoes and Argyll checked socks. He must have seen my eyes widen because he said, 'They make you wear bright colours—they come out better on the box.'

'And how are our television friends?' I said. 'Getting ready for another strike?'

'So far as I know the sons of bitches haven't spent their last load of blood money yet.' Ambrose led the way out of the tent with his usual air of a ship's captain starting his morning round of inspection. 'You saw how they finished overnight?'

Overnight I hadn't exactly been glued to the television and said so, but there was a scoreboard high above the grandstand at the eighteenth green and I read off the red-lettered leaders.

Shroeder was in front at the end of the first day's play with a round of 70, two under par for the course, Bill Sadiq and an Irishman named John Bond were second at one under, Omi Kawasaki, the South African, John Van de Blet, and a total unknown from Spain called Ramón Ferago were sharing third spot at a level 72. At the moment another total unknown, unimaginatively named Smith, seemed to be causing a certain amount of excitement by having birdied the first two holes, eagled the third, parred the next two and somehow managed a hole in one at the sixth, all of which had him running at six under for six holes, which was no mean achievement for what the biography sheet described as a twenty-two-year-old assistant professional at a small club in Sussex.

I made surprised noises but Ambrose was not impressed. 'He was six *over* yesterday, so he's still only level for the tournament. Something will go wrong sooner or later and he'll come down off that high he's on with a bump. If I was a betting man, which I'm not, I'd give you five to one he'll blow it by the turn.'

In fairness, Ambrose was no gambler, probably because at some time in his life he'd worked out the percentages and found them not to be in his favour. Nevertheless I had few doubts that the five to one odds could have been checked out on the spot by your friendly neighbourhood bookmaker and would have proved to be dead right.

I said, 'Let's take a look at him.'

'Why not, dear boy. Easy enough to get to the seventh.'

At least it was easy with Ambrose, because he simply walked across the fairways with the magnificently proprietorial air that came automatically to him and which would probably have allowed him to cross unrebuked even if he hadn't been something of a national institution. But it was a good way to spend the morning. The crowds lining the more interesting parts of the course were large and would be a good deal larger as the day wore on, and on some out of sight greens one could hear the distant 'ohs' and 'ahs' and occasional scattered applause as some competitor either did or didn't do whatever it was he was attempting. On the final round there would be a general surge up the course as people followed the leaders, leaving the also-rans to complete their last round in virtual solitude, but early on this second day there was a general air about the place of people who had settled for the morning and were proposing, come lunch-time, to eat a sandwich where they stood.

I asked Ambrose if he thought Don Shroeder would still be up with the leaders by the end of the afternoon.

'For my money he'll *be* the leader.' As he never risked that money, Ambrose was fond of speaking as though he did.

'You don't think Sadiq will catch him?' It was early days yet to forecast who was going to do anything and Ambrose was never one for nailing his colours to the mast if there was a chance he might be wrong.

He sniffed. Ambrose's sniff was a successful affectation that was universally recognized as an expression of intense disapproval. He said, 'That young man was seen dining at the Griffin's Arms last night. Did you know that?'

Compared with the Griffin's Arms, all other hotels in the area could be said to provide their services free. I said, 'No, I didn't. But apart from the fact that his dinner will have cost him the best part of any prize money he hopes to get, why not? The man's got to eat somewhere.'

Laurie said unexpectedly, 'Don't tell me, he wasn't dining alone.'

'No, he wasn't.' Ambrose looked slightly put out. 'He was dining with a rather spectacular black lady, and he certainly didn't bring her with him.'

I said, 'No, he didn't. He met her down here.'

'Did he now?' Ambrose opened his eyes wide. '*Did* he now? Who is she?'

'Her name's Selina de Cruz and she either picked him up or the other way round,' I said. 'But if Sadiq buys her dinner, it's hardly likely to spoil his game.'

'He bought her breakfast, too.' There were times when Ambrose could very easily drop into the role of a disapproving dowager, and this was one of them.

'Since when has sex been bad for golf?' I asked him. It

was one of the cherished beliefs of the game that it actually improved one's eye for a ball. I added, 'Every other player here has got his wife or at least an equivalent with him, and they don't sit up all night playing bridge. Who saw this happy couple?'

'I did.' Ambrose looked virtuous. 'I happened to be staying at the Griffin myself.'

'Alone, of course.'

'Yes, I bloody well am.' For a moment Ambrose looked put out, and I realized for the first time that there really was a slightly puritan streak in him that was part of his charm.

'Well, let's not worry about the sex life of the stars,' I said hurriedly. 'Who do we see on the seventh?'

'Kawasaki and Smith,' Ambrose said. 'It's early for Omi but the cameras should be able to use him by the time he gets to the eighteenth. Besides, if you get all the leaders bunched together in the afternoon, it's hell doing the commentary.'

'I thought individual players' start times were drawn for,' I said. I didn't think, because I knew they were.

Ambrose grinned. 'Bless you, old friend, for your touching faith, but the draw's weighted a bit today.'

'You mean it's fixed?'

'If you insist. But there really isn't much alternative when you've got the TV people insisting that the big names come on during viewing time. Doesn't matter on the last day because mostly it's being shown in four-hour chunks.' Ambrose's puritan side stopped short when it got in the way of work, but I let that one go, because we were in effect his guests, after all.

There was a stand at the seventh but Ambrose marched on to where the officials were standing just below the big bunker that guarded the left side of the green. The green itself was on the small side, a two-level affair backed on the high side by six-inch rough. It looked flat enough but, in fact, the whole thing was set at a slight angle, like a raft at sea, so that if you landed up short you not only had to hit your putt hard enough to climb the rise to the upper level

155

but you had to compensate for borrow as well. I'd played the hole more times than I could remember but only about one time in three did I get it right.

'This looks like Kawasaki's ball coming now,' Ambrose said.

The Japanese was out of sight behind a bulge of spectators lining the fairway but I watched his ball against the blue of the sky as it seemed to hang there for an appreciable time before it arced down and thumped on the close-cut grass ten feet short of the green. Ten feet short was ten feet short, but as I knew Kawasaki couldn't even see the green from where he was, it was a pretty impressive performance, although since he had made his stroke first, Smith was presumably nearer to the green. I awaited his shot with some interest, because if the man could get himself six under par in six holes I wanted to see how he did it.

Smith wasn't difficult to find; thanks presumably to the TV people, he was wearing a shirt of rather aggressive blue and white stripes so that, all things considered, he didn't look unlike a zebra lurking in the shade of the trees a hundred or so yards away on the right-hand side. I saw the chrome shaft of the club flash as he made his stroke, the ball climbed in a leisurely fashion and thudded down on the edge of the green. It was better than Kawasaki's but not that much. Probably scared of running past the pin and into the rough, but it still left him at the bottom of the hill.

'One club under,' Ambrose said.

Personally I doubted that, but one doesn't argue with one's betters on these matters. The players tramped up, Kawasaki looking his part as the inscrutable oriental, Smith young and somehow rather brashly confident. Omi, as the back marker, went first with what looked like a sand iron. The ball went high, dropped about six inches beyond that God-awful cliff in the middle of the green, rolled on obediently and ended up a couple of feet from the pin for what would undoubtedly prove to be a birdie three. Flawless and impressive.

'Cocky little bugger,' Ambrose said. I thought for a moment he was talking about Kawasaki and that it couldn't be less true, but he was, in fact, looking at Smith, putting from the edge of the green. A birdie here would make him seven under. Even the regulation two putts would still leave him six under for seven holes.

'He'll be short,' Laurie said to no one in particular.

Would he? I very much doubted it, because over-confidence makes you hit too hard, if anything. Smith was prowling round the green, presumably hoping for inspiration because the whole thing was one big borrow. Finally he settled himself down over the ball and gave it a pat. It looked good, running fast, which it needed to climb the rise, but not so fast that it was going to vanish into the distant rough. As it turned out, it came to a full stop about six inches short of the top of the rise, stayed there for a moment and then ran back, picking up enough speed on the way to carry it back virtually to where it started from.

'Well, that's one stroke gone,' Ambrose said.

Smith tried again. I had expected that he would hit harder —a lot too much harder—this time, but he'd apparently worked this one out for himself and it all went the other way, with the ball a full foot from the top of the rise. Unexpectedly it managed to get the same velocity on the way back and arrived obediently at his feet once more.

Ambrose said cheerfully, 'Two!'

The wretched Smith's third attempt was a mirror image of his first, and his fourth was the resounding clout that one had half expected him to give it all along. The ball shot up the rise, rocketed across the back half of the green and ended up ten feet in the rough on the other side.

'He's blown it,' Ambrose said with ill-concealed satisfaction. 'Lucky if he gets down in seven.'

In the end the poor bastard was lucky to get down in eight, which left him one over instead of seven under, a depressing lesson to everyone except Ambrose who, so far as I could see, had willed the whole thing to happen from the start.

Laurie said, 'I think you should be ashamed of yourself. He'll be useless for the rest of the round now.'

'He was useless before,' Ambrose told her complacently.

'Everyone has freak runs of good luck now and then—nothing to do with the way you play. You could get a chimpanzee to do a hole in one if you let him try long enough.' Smith's disaster seemed to have restored his good humour, although I had no idea what he'd got against the man. 'Come along, children. We'll see what kind of mess he makes of the next hole.'

We started back across the ropes, and at the same moment Angela came out of the crowd.

She'd never been a great one for golf and it had never occurred to me that she might be watching the Tamworth. Equally, I suppose she could have worked out that the odds were pretty well on that I was going to be there. Perhaps she reckoned that in a crowd of some twenty thousand or whatever there was little chance of her actually running into me, or then again, perhaps she simply didn't care.

'Hello, Angus,' she said.

She was wearing a light tweed suit with her pearls and some rather nice country shoes I hadn't seen before. Her brown hair was pulled back severely, but because she had a silk scarf tied loosely over it, the effect was studiedly casual. She was a trifle paler than usual but it could have been her make-up, but for whatever reason, her dark eyes looked huge and defenceless in that small face.

'Hello.' There was a man with her, tall and thin and rather army, the conventional long-skirted jacket and cavalry twill slacks that you see in every third-rate pub but they looked all right on him because he'd got the right tailor. Angela introduced us but his name was gone the moment she said it. Apparently he was a major.

'You're looking in fine form,' Ambrose said.

Angela smiled brightly back. 'So are you, Ambrose. Putting on weight?'

'No, dear, it's my sweater. Thin as a wraith underneath.' Typical Ambrose banter. Had he known she was going to be here? I dismissed the idea as uncharitable. Ambrose wouldn't have set this up and, in any case, I couldn't imagine that Angela was wild about having run into me.

We got through telling each other who was who and I got

158

back to wondering who the soldier was. To the best of my knowledge, he had not been on the scene at the time of the break-up. In those days Angela's main attention had been on someone called Castleton who was deeply into office furniture. Should I ask about Castleton? For a moment I was tempted but my nicer nature told me it wasn't on. She said, 'Does all this make you want to play again, Angus?'

'Don't we all want to play the games we were so fond of when we were young?' I said. Behind us there was a round of polite clapping but we didn't turn our heads to see what it was all about.

'I saw Alan Thurston a few minutes ago.' She sounded casual but I'd lived with her too long not to pick up the slight over-brightness in her voice. She was as ill at ease as I was, so the meeting had been chance after all. But why risk it in the first place? She went on, 'I asked him about Melanie. He said she was fine.'

'It's a long time since I've seen her,' I said. I could feel Laurie looking at me and I wondered what she was thinking. Introducing one-time husbands to new lovers, ex-wives to new bedmates, is all the stuff of good French farce, like boyfriends hidden under the bed or stuffed into wardrobes. Why were these complications supposed to be funny? Maybe because men have always laughed at each other's misfortunes—thank you, Lord, that it hasn't happened to me.

'Come into the hot box,' Ambrose said unexpectedly.

Come into the hot box, Maud, for the black bat night hath flown. What was a hot box anyway? Presumably the thing like a Victorian bathing hut on wheels, sprouting cables, a TV company's logo on its side, part of Ambrose's stock in trade. The door was open and we could see someone in shirtsleeves sitting in the middle of the usual electronic gadgetry, monitoring a bank of screens. Presumably the different pictures were accounted for by the different cameras. Ambrose said, 'Hello, Harry, all right if we come in?'

'Sure, why not?' Harry was a young Indian who spoke with an American accent, as comfortably at home in this world as the next, multi-lingual, multi-cultured. He asked Ambrose, 'You recording yet?'

'Later. How did that crowd stuff look?'

'Not bad. You want to see?'

'If it's no trouble.' Ambrose at his most affable? Probably Ambrose just doing his usual thing. He included us in the proceedings, 'I have a wench who is laughably called my assistant who put in half an hour chatting up a few of the spectators while this round was getting going. They're an interesting cross-section. Very knowledgeable, most of them, very well-mannered. You get the odd lad who's had a skinful and won't keep his mouth shut while someone's putting, but by and large they're a league ahead of the galleries you get anywhere else. May use it this evening, may not.'

Harry fiddled with this and that. Ambrose appeared on one of the screens looking friendly with a bunch of spectators grouped around him. A middle-aged man in a checked shirt was saying something with a fair amount of animation, but as there wasn't any sound, it was impossible to tell what it was. Ambrose supplied the missing dialogue. 'Chap came all the way from Newcastle. Never played golf in his life but he's completely hooked on watching it, rather like football, I suppose, God help us all.'

The screen shifted to a youngish couple, two teenagers and someone in his seventies. 'Still plays to four,' Ambrose commented. Then the scene switched to views of the course, trees, odd people wandering about.

'It's getting so that some of them even sleep out,' Ambrose said. 'The Lord knows why no one picks them up, but they do. I tell you, this game is going to be the biggest sporting growth industry since squash. It wasn't so long ago that virtually every spectator was also a player. Now television's changed all that—after all, you see it a damn sight better on the box than you're ever likely to from the side of the fairway. Mind you, for folk like us there's nothing like being on the spot—it's the atmosphere that counts.' He paused to draw breath, eyes still on the screen. 'Now here's a good-looking kid coming up. Could we have the sound to go with it, Harry?'

160

Selina de Cruz might give me the creeps but she was a striking-looking girl and, from the evidence before us, exceptionally photogenic. The TV camera had taken her sitting beneath a background of trees, with something that looked like a sleeping-bag beneath her. The camera zoomed in on her face, and for a moment her eyes were huge and hostile until suddenly they became no more than wary as she smiled and the sound came on and the interviewer was saying, 'Now here's someone who seems to have got here early to avoid the rush. Now you're—'

It always surprises me that, when faced with that question, more people don't stand up for themselves and say that their name is their own business, but this one could have been facing impertinent reporters for years.

'My name's Selina de Cruz.' Lots of flashing smile. 'And I'm from Kariba in Africa.'

'My, that's a long way to come for a golf match.' I felt Ambrose wince, but then the girl had to learn some time.

A cheerful smile. 'Well, I suppose it would have been, but I was over here anyway.'

A shot of Ambrose's assistant clutching her stick microphone and doing her best to look as though she was in charge of the situation. 'I see you've got your sleeping-bag with you. Does that mean you camped out last night?'

The lens worked its way back to Selina, prodding the thing underneath her, which seemed to be a king-sized sleeping-bag. She said, 'Well, yes. I suppose they'd have thrown me out if they'd found me, but it was a nice night.'

A nice night indeed, but how had she managed to be tucked up under the trees on the West Wessex if, according to Ambrose, she'd been having it off at the Griffin's Arms with Bill Sadiq?

'Do you get to a lot of tournaments?'

'As many as I can.' I'd have laid good money that this was the first golf course she'd ever set foot on, but she sounded convincing enough. She even threw in, 'I think it's a wonderful game,' for good measure.

'And who are you backing to win?'

Selina laughed. She seemed to be getting into her stride,

any moment now she'd qualify as TV interviewee of the year. 'Well, Bill Sadiq, I guess. Who else?'

'Who else indeed! You'd have thought the silly bitch would have done that much homework!' Ambrose seemed to have lost his customary calm and one could hardly blame him. In his own way he was a perfectionist and even I could see that his assistant had a lot to learn. Unlike Ambrose, I felt a certain sympathy for the wretched girl, who at this moment was all too obviously racking her brains for something to say other than, 'Oh, of course, he's black, too!' For a moment I thought she might actually say just that, and she might well have done if Selina hadn't unexpectedly taken pity on her.

'He's from Kariba, like me.'

Ambrose groaned. 'Thanks, Harry, that'll be enough. Like the man says, if you've got a job to do, do it yourself. Maybe I should have got Alan Thurston to do it. Old African hand. Might have the right touch.'

'Good idea,' Angela said unexpectedly. 'He was in somewhere called Harate, so far as I remember.'

I said, 'No, he wasn't, it was Zambia.' Old habits die hard. It didn't matter a damn where he'd lived but it was depressing the speed with which I still came out fighting. If she'd said there were seven days in a week I'd still have had to contradict her.

Angela didn't seem to notice. 'I know,' she said. 'But he did a couple of years in Harate, too, when he was working for that mining firm. Melanie had a miscarriage there.'

'Oh, I didn't know.' I withdrew gracefully. A miscarriage was possibly an odd thing by which to locate a place but women have their yardsticks and Angela and Melanie had always been pretty close.

Ambrose was saying something about getting stuck in and doing the interviews over again.

Some people have extraordinarily consistent trains of thought. 'Ambrose,' I protested, 'can't you forget about your public for just a minute? Didn't you say that girl spent last night in a hotel?'

'What—the useless Kay? No idea, old boy. Her love-life is something I've been mercifully spared.'

'Not the interviewer. Selina de Cruz. The black girl. You said she spent the night at the Griffin's Arms with Bill Sadiq.'

Ambrose blinked. There were times when one realized that beneath the carefully cultivated appearance of cheerful urbanity there lurked a dedication that sprang from the fear that someone might take his cars away. Outside his work it was largely a matter of luck if Ambrose noticed anything that was happening in the world around him. But he made the necessary adjustment and the penny dropped. 'Of course! I thought I'd seen her before.'

'You're absolutely sure it's the same girl?'

'Quite sure. I'd have spotted her right away if I hadn't been listening to that Godawful wench they've foisted on me.' Ambrose frowned. 'But why make out she spent the night on the course? She'd even got a sleeping-bag to prove it.'

Had she? I'd thought at the time it was an odd bit of equipment, but what else could it have been? 'Look,' I said, 'do you think we might have that film run through again?'

'Why not?' Ambrose turned back to the technician. 'Could you oblige, Harry? And when we get to the bag bit, stop the frame?'

'Sure. Sleeping-bag coming up.'

The screen blurred against a background of high-speed voices jabbering, jerked suddenly into focus.

I see you've got your sleeping-bag with you. Does that mean you camped out last night?

It's curious the things one's eye picks up unexpectedly. The first time I'd seen that particular bit of film I hadn't been expecting to see Selina and she'd jumped out of the screen at me. Now that I was expecting her it didn't work that way at all, and I found myself taking in a pair of trousered legs that were close up to the girl, a disembodied hand that reached down out of top frame and was resting on her shoulder. The hand let go, the legs moved, and at that moment the camera-man had pulled back his zoom in order to bring in an atmosphere shot of the general scene, and suddenly I could see the owner of the pair of legs making his way back into the crowd.

He didn't waste any time about it either, but one gets used to picking up one's shots where one can. He was turning slightly, his head coming round to camera.

I said, 'On a couple of frames.'

The screen flickered and the face was centre and clear. It was a face I knew all right, but I had to think twice before I could place it. A restaurant table. The Gate House, and the man with Polly Appleby had been Clive Whitton.

Clive Whitton. There must be something quite exceptional about Selina de Cruz, the way she pulled the most unlikely men. I amended that. Bill Sadiq was her countryman—therefore reasonably predictable—but what in God's name had Selina got in common with the Council's trendy leftie?

I ran Clive Whitton to earth in the Tamworth hospitality tent, drinking the bosses' champagne for free, and with no visible signs of distress. He was pretending to watch the progress of the players on one of the televisions provided and, when he looked up and saw me, he managed to show no more surprise than I did, which was something of an achievement because he had no means of knowing I was coming, whereas I'd known all the time.

'I want a few words with you,' I told him. 'There's a lonely-looking table over there. Suppose we go and sit at it.'

Whitton frowned at his champagne, as though he'd seen a fly in it. 'Perhaps some other time? I'm rather enjoying a day off from business.'

The barman hovered, so I got myself a glass of Tamworth's champagne too. 'No,' I said, 'not some other time. Now.'

'What's the trouble? My car parked in the wrong place or something?'

It was pretty well judged as the sort of remark he might have been expected to make in the circumstances, so he got eight out of ten for trying. 'Any more jolly japes like that,' I told him, 'and I'll call in some of my fellow fascist capitalist lackeys to commit an outrage on you.'

He blinked at that. 'Come off it, Inspector, I've no idea what you're talking about.'

'Well, for one, I'm talking about Selina de Cruz,' I said. 'Shall we sit?'

We sat. Possibly I was still in some kind of shock because I dislike the idea of bullying policemen, but at that moment I was prepared to forget my manners. I'm not sure why a sudden lack of restraint should make me want to take it out on Clive Whitton, apart from the fact that I loathed everything he stood for, from his neo-Trotsky politics to the classic hypocrisy of his soaring personal expense account living to the fact that the snivelling little bastard dared to stand there drinking free champagne at a golf club from which by rights he should have long ago been shown the door. I was well aware that I was so prejudiced against Councillor Whitton that by rights I should never have been allowed within spitting distance of him, and the fact that I alone knew this cheered me up no end.

'Look,' he said, 'I do think you're making a big mistake. I don't even know a Selina de Cruz.'

I said, 'Yes, you do. You also knew Polly Appleby, and she knew the de Cruz girl, too. I'm interested in finding out what the three of you had in common.'

If Whitton had had any sense he'd have called my bluff and walked away, but he didn't. Instead he said carefully, 'I didn't know Miss Appleby any better than anyone else in the Club. I'd never set eyes on her till Tamworth sent her down here as their PRO.'

'Listen,' I told him, 'I don't intend fooling around playing patsy with you over this. A month or so before Appleby came here for the first time you'd been sharing a platform with her in Liverpool at a fund-raising meeting for something called the Marxist African Front.'

To give him his due, he never even blinked. 'Someone has been pulling your leg,' he said.

'I have witnesses who'll swear to it.' Which I hadn't. 'I've also got a remarkably good photograph,' which, courtesy of *Socialist World*, I had.

Whitton thought that one over. 'It isn't actually illegal to go to a political meeting in this country,' he ventured at last. 'With anyone.'

'No,' I agreed, 'but it does happen to be an offence to withhold information from the police.'

'I've already said that I don't know Miss de Cruz.'

'You also said you didn't know Appleby,' I pointed out. 'I know you're also acquainted with Miss de Cruz and again I have the evidence to prove it. As de Cruz is African, I suppose the link between the three of you is political. But why this cosy meeting at a golf tournament?'

'No comment.'

'I'm not joking about the obstruction charge, you know.' I remembered something on the spur of the moment. 'The council elections are due in a fortnight, and it shouldn't be difficult to keep the charge hanging around until just before polling day. We could release a good deal about your connection with the African Marxist stuff, too. You've done all right as a pinkish liberal but you're hardly living in a city ghetto—some lurid revelations about you and the urban guerrilla movement ought to scare the pants off the local voters.'

For the first time I thought I detected a certain wariness in Whitton's pale eyes. 'Where do you propose finding the lurid revelations, as you call them?'

'I haven't the faintest idea,' I confessed. 'But it shouldn't be too hard. If it is, I'll make them up—I can always withdraw them later with apologies. After the elections, of course.'

'You wouldn't dare.'

'No,' I said, '*you* wouldn't. It's an article of faith with you that the police in this country only exist to harass the workers.'

Whitton looked impatient. 'The whole system's corrupt —' he began.

'All right,' I said. 'So I'm corrupt. In which case, I shouldn't have any qualms about a little perjury if it's going to make your life difficult. And I agree that *nothing* that happens to you is going to give me any sleepless nights.'

There was a longish pause. Behind me I could hear the comforting drone from the TV and the sound of distant clapping as someone or other made his putt and I thought

166

that however commercial the enterprise, golf was still the most civilized of sports.

Clive Whitton sighed. 'Very well then, if you're going to be bloody-minded about it, Polly and I knew the de Cruz girl through the African Marxist movement. Head Office wanted us to give the girl a hand if she needed it.'

'A hand doing what?' I asked.

'Some sort of protest. But she didn't seem to want our help, or anybody's. Played things very close to her chest.'

'You mean,' I said, 'that she wasn't part of the African Marxist movement?'

Whitton said impatiently, 'No, of course not! Up to now the Kariba faction have always kept clear of any affiliation and they seem to be sticking to that line. The KFP are pretty set on doing things on their own as far as I can see —at least, they seem pretty sure of themselves.'

'I'm not a student of African politics,' I said. 'Who are the KFP?'

'The Kariban Fundamentalists.'

I tried to remember what little I'd read of Kariba, and came up with very little more than that it was a pint-sized ex-Portuguese dependency sandwiched somewhere between Namibia and Angola. By all accounts it was pro Western and reasonably run by a Western-educated president whose name I'd either forgotten or never known. Apparently it was a place with a taste for sport because I'd read that Bill Sadiq was a kind of national hero, which was some kind of record for a country that didn't own a single golf course. And that was about that. 'The Fundamentalists are the opposition party?' I asked. With a name like that they'd have to be.

'They're all for strict Islam, same like the Middle East. But of course, Amhari's a Marxist.' He added for my benefit, 'Bodo Amhari is the KFP's top man.'

'*Ex Africa semper aliquid novi,*' I said.

'Come again?'

'There's always something new out of Africa,' I translated. Not only new but nasty with it, but I supposed it was par for the course that only people like Whitton had even heard of Bodo Amhari. Considering that we had ourselves so much trouble from that part of the world, it was a pity we didn't know a bit more about it. I tried again. 'What you're saying is that Bill Sadiq isn't in with the Fundamentalists because he's a sort of popular Western hero.'

Whitton hesitated. I think that for a moment he was on the verge of saying that Sadiq was a race traitor and that his proper place was in a Fundamentalist homeland, but he changed his mind and said, 'Yes.'

'So what sort of demo are they putting on?' I asked.

'I don't know.'

Which was nothing out of ten for an answer because the bastard would know all right. Or would he? It wasn't hard to imagine the in-fighting that would go on in the political lunatic fringe, but I suspected Whitton lacked the hard core he'd need to come out on top. Even so it was hard to believe he'd been kept completely out in the cold.

'Well, one hardly imagines they're going to unfurl a banner,' I said, 'so what's it to be? Cutting up another green?'

'Perhaps.'

'Is the girl still here?'

'No.' Whitton shook his head. 'She said she was going back home.'

'Did she speak to anyone while you were with her?'

'No. Except we happened to run into Alan Thurston and she had a few words with him.'

'I didn't even know they knew each other,' I said. 'What did they say?'

'God knows.' Whitton had got back enough confidence to give one of his little patronizing smiles. 'You know what the old Africa hands are like—never turn down a chance of showing off their grasp of native languages.'

I was so startled I said the first thing that came into my head. 'What the hell does Thurston know about Kariba? He worked in Harate.'

I'd given Clive Whitton a chance to look patronizing again. 'You're not very well up in modern Africa, are you, Inspector? Kariba's the new name for what used to be called Portuguese Harate.'

168

CHAPTER 13

*In making a stroke a player shall not accept physical
assistance or protection from the elements.*

Rule 14–2

When I drew up in the yard, Epsilon House looked very
much as though it was still Rose Cottage, and if anything
had rubbed off from its occupants, it certainly didn't show.
The last of the year's roses still twined themselves round
the door and the pantiles glowed orange in the September
sun. The swifts had not yet gone and a flight of them swung
screaming in tight formation round the eaves, seeming to
be the only living things around. No other car, no face at
the window, just one example of the kind of cottage estate
agents long to get on their books.

I got out of the car with my usual guilty feeling about
having just driven ten miles a lot faster than I'd enjoy
justifying in Court, and what was I doing here anyway?
There was no reason why Selina de Cruz should not have
pretended she'd spent the night in one place when in fact
she'd been somewhere else, but equally there was no reason
why she should. Supposing such a frightening girl actually
had a mother, it was unlikely that she was living in these
parts, and even if she was I couldn't see her having much
say in her daughter's sex life. I stared at the house and tried
to work out how the girl had managed to sleep in two places
at once. Or what was more to the point, why she should
want to *appear* to do so.

Behind me, Laurie said, 'Well, you could always ask.'

I hadn't realized I'd been talking. Come to that, I'd
forgotten she was even there, but I could hardly say that as
I walked over to the door and pushed the bell. But I was
glad I'd remembered to pick her up, just the same. I could
hear the bell ringing inside but that remained the only sound
except the screaming of the swifts. I rang again, knowing

169

quite well that it was no more than a gesture while the birds mocked me. Unless they happen to have a search warrant, policemen have no more right to break into other people's homes than anyone else and I was certainly not in possession of a warrant. Training dies hard, and I stood back and looked at the door.

'I've got a credit card.' Laurie. Helpful as ever in an emergency and full of useful ideas picked up on the box.

I said, 'You can't use a credit card on a deadlock.' A slip of plastic was fine if all you had to do was push the tongue back on a Yale, but April Tonge had got her private castle bolted and barred with an unexpected efficiency that even American Express wasn't going to shift in a month of Sundays.

'What do you do, then?'

'Try somewhere else.' I walked round the back to see if there was a handy window, the first time I'd seen more of Rose Cottage than the front door. There was more ground than I'd expected, an orchard, some rather well-kept rose-beds and a somewhat less maintained greenhouse, set against the brick wall of an ancient kitchen garden. It looked comfortable and safe, like something one might find in a country vicarage, but I was beginning to have doubts about things that looked cosy. Or perhaps I was getting cold feet about burglary—one can think up half a dozen reasons for doing the things one does, or not doing them if it comes to that. But I was beginning to get ideas about Rose Cottage, so I walked down the path and looked in the greenhouse just to make sure.

It was singularly undramatic. The door was open and it took only a brief glance to see that it hadn't been used for at least a couple of years. There were a few empty seed boxes on the stagings, the odd flowerpot here and there, and a loop of rafia hung from a nail.

'It's just a greenhouse,' Laurie said.

She was right, but I was getting used to that. 'Yes,' I said, 'that's what I thought it was, too.' I shut the door behind me and we walked round the angle of the wall. There was about a quarter of an acre of rough ground there, the

170

remains of what had probably been a kitchen garden, and in one corner a caravan.

It was the kind of thing you see on holiday sites, twenty-five foot or so of mobile home that can quite easily double up as a kind of guest wing if you've got more relations than bedrooms. Rose Cottage was a fair size, but I could imagine that if April Tonge was in the habit of running feminist seminars it was conceivable that she'd be pushed for space and a big caravan seemed a logical way to cope with the overflow. I said as much and Laurie looked unconvinced.

'Why didn't she put it nearer the house?' she asked.

'Perhaps she didn't like the look of the thing,' I said. 'Maybe she couldn't get planning permission.'

Laurie frowned. 'With this much land, you're entitled to four caravans.' She thought a moment and added, 'So long as they're more than forty yards from the highway.'

'And out of sight.' I'd read the same book. I went over and looked in the big window that stretched across the front of the vehicle, and saw much what I expected—the usual bench seats with thick cushions that converted into beds, a folding table and a gas fire, with sink and cooker in the background. Someone had been using the room but more as an office than somewhere to live, because the table had a typewriter, a pile of newspapers, half-a-dozen books and a variety of scattered papers.

I went round the back. From memory there were usually a couple of bedrooms rear of the door but in this case the curtains were drawn. Everyone wonders what goes on behind drawn curtains and I was no exception. Neither apparently was Laurie, who was fiddling with the aluminium door.

'What do you do about this?'

I inspected the lock. Mr Chubb had had no hand in it, nor Mr Yale either, so I felt the time had come for a more robust approach. At some time in the distant past someone had used ex-army picket posts for fencing and there were still a few about, so I picked up three foot or so of rusting angle iron and shoved the jagged end of it in the gap between the door and the frame. The aluminium bent and the door sprang open. It wasn't particularly advanced housebreaking technique, but we were in.

Most mobile homes follow the same ground plan—a largish double bedroom backed by a smaller one that usually dispenses with a bed in favour of a couple of bunks, and this one was no exception. The small bedroom was empty apart from the bunks and a terse label on the wall that announced *Mattresses by Dunlopillo*. The second door was locked but it gave in response to a smart kick.

'Hello, Melanie,' I said.

Melanie Thurston didn't answer. She was sitting up in the family-sized Dunlopillo-mattressed bed with the sheets thrown back so that I could see that she was wearing a navy blue turtle-necked sweater, a tweed skirt and rather fancy navy tights and no shoes. Her hair was a mess and her high cheekboned, rather patrician face looked grey and old. She was staring at me but her eyes showed no sign of recognition.

I started to say 'Melanie' again but then I realized that there wasn't any point, because when I went up to her, her eyes didn't change. I touched her arm. The flash was warm and slightly damp and when I looked into her eyes I saw that the pupils were tiny, like those of someone who had been staring into the sun. She was breathing slowly and heavily and there was a curious, sour smell in the air that reminded me of rugger club changing rooms. I thought abstractedly that poor Melanie, who was a nice creature, would have been distressed to have reminded someone of a load of old socks. I pulled up the sleeve of her sweater and there were small, red pinpricks up the smooth, hairless arm.

'Melanie,' I said, 'wake up!'

Her blank eyes stared through me, lost in some place I would never see. 'For God's sake,' Laurie whispered, 'what's the matter with her?' For the first time, her voice was less than steady.

'She's been drugged,' I said, 'but don't ask me what with. You'd better stay with her and I'll go up to the house and phone for someone to come down and have a look at her.'

'The police?'

'Of course the police,' I said. 'Who else?'

'I just wondered,' Laurie said. 'Up till now I've had the distinct impression that your friends didn't want to know.'

I said, 'They'll want to know about this all right.' She had a point. But there were limits to even a Chief Constable's discretion. I was no expert on drugs and I had no idea what had been pumped into Melanie to keep her in that frightening state of vegetable-like inertia, but this time there wasn't going to be any passing of the buck in my direction. Melanie Thurston was going into hospital, and as kidnapping and the forcible administration of drugs was against the law of the land, the case was going on the books, to say nothing of the various spin-offs that were likely to go with it.

I went on back to the house and knocked the glass out of one of the small glass panels in the back door so that I could reach the catch inside and let myself in. The kitchen was much as I'd expected April's would be, with lots of copper and pine and flowers in pots, but the pile of unwashed dishes wouldn't have pleased her. There was a smell in the air that reminded me of the local Indian takeaway but there's no law against curry so I went on through to the living-room beyond. There was a doll sitting in the window with a wire coming out of the bottom of her knitted crinoline, and sure enough, when I lifted her up there was the telephone underneath. Very much April. I could imagine her having much the same kind of thing over a spare loo roll. I picked up the handset and waited for the dialling tone, but there wasn't any. There wasn't any even when I jiggled the chrome buttons and swore down the microphone.

Behind me a voice said, 'It's no good trying. It doesn't work.'

Delphine had never been my dream girl but, as I put the phone down and turned to look at her, she struck me as being even more desperate than she had before. The poor kid seemed to have been born with a kind of pink and white blotched complexion that made her look as though she had a streaming cold. Now in addition she had a wildness in her eyes that made me wonder if perhaps the wretched girl was demented, after all.

'Listen,' I said, 'out there in the garden someone's been keeping a woman prisoner in a caravan. What do you know about it?'

'She was going to tell the police about us cutting up the golf course,' Delphine said. For a moment there was a touch of the old feminist worker about her but the defiance fizzled out, died, and she became just a scared and silly girl again, staring at me with that peculiarly helpless look that some women have that makes you want to shake them.

'Listen, Delphine,' I said, 'don't you think it might be a good idea to tell me what's going on?' I tried to sound reasonable because for two pins she'd have run for her life. It's hard to exude an aura of confidence but I tried. 'Whatever it is, I'm sure we can sort something out.'

'There's nothing to sort out.'

Not much there wasn't. 'Suppose,' I said, 'you tell me where your friend April has got to.'

For a moment I thought that she was simply going to go blank on me again but I was wrong, because she said in a matter-of-fact voice, 'She's in the barn.'

'The barn by the side of the house?' I remembered the metal Alcan building where the cultivator had been kept.

She nodded like an obedient child. 'Yes, I'll show you if you like.'

I wondered what it was that was wrong with this disaster of a girl, with her switches from sullen antagonism to a kind of hopeless acceptance of whatever happened to come along. I guessed that she was stewing away on one drug or another but I found it hard to guess exactly what because she seemed to be on a permanent down. How did one get hooked in the first place to something that never gave you an up?

'All right, Delphine,' I said in my most secure voice, 'you show me.'

She stood up at once and led the way back to the kitchen and a door I hadn't noticed, because it was painted cream to match the rest of the walls. It was the solid type of fireproof door that most councils demand when there's a connection between a dwelling and somewhere that stores petrol. Normally it's there to seal off a garage but there was

174

usually a tractor in the barn so I imagined that the same precautions applied.

'She's through here,' Delphine said.

Had she stood aside to let me through, I might possibly have smelt a rat but she didn't, she simply led the way into the barn and I followed. It was dark in there, because the big metal doors were shut and the only light was through the six-inch-deep ventilation slots at the base and top of the walls.

'I'll put the light on,' Delphine said.

She went back and snapped the switch. I had my back to her and she had opened the door and was through it while I was still admiring the feeble glow thrown by the single hundred-watt bulb suspended from the false ceiling. I heard the slam and the snap of the lock, followed almost at once by the sound of the key turning. It was just about the oldest trick in the book and I'd fallen for it.

It took a certain amount of restraint not to kick the door and shout 'Let me out!' but she was hardly going to do that after she'd gone to all that trouble to lock me in, and as the door was clearly made of sheet metal, kicking it was going to be just a waste of time. Laurie was too far away to hear me, and in any case, I'd told her to stay with Melanie. I went over to the door, which was a waste of time because it was locked on the outside. I could actually see the padlock through the inch-wide gap between the two doors, but seeing was hardly enough, so I went back and inspected the rest of my prison. It's not easy to escape from a modern barn, because you can't very well prise off the odd plank when the walls that keep you in are made of corrugated metal.

I looked about me to see if there was anything that I could use to break down the door but my first glance wasn't all that reassuring, because apart from high-stacked bales of straw, a bicycle, half a dozen plastic bags of fertilizer and a king-sized freezer, the place was empty. Delphine, you silly little bitch, what exactly are you playing at?

The stacked bales were piled one on top of another, like so many building bricks, and the topmost one was only three or four feet from the plank-slatted ceiling that someone must have put up in order to provide extra storage space. There was a break in the planking that formed the ceiling that must normally have been reached by a ladder. I took another inventory but there was no ladder in sight, which wasn't surprising because I remembered seeing it propped up against the outside wall, its top rungs just below the small window that lit the hayloft. So there was a way out, after all. All I had to do was reach the hayloft.

I looked at the pile of straw bales that were piled like giant's building bricks almost up to the loft opening. The whole thing looked rather like the lower slopes of the Great Pyramid but I went up it with not much more difficulty than I'd have had with a flight of pretty steep stairs. At the top I was still six or seven feet from the opening, so I tipped the top bale on end. I was still going to be short. A bale of straw is about three feet long and I could see that with two working arms I'd have been able to pull myself up on to the ledge, but with only one that could cope with heavy work, it just wasn't on. I looked down at the nearest bale, reconciled to further building. Compressed straw is a good deal heavier than it looks and I wondered what my chances were of lifting it above head level with one hand. I looked up again to judge the distance and gave up worrying about lifting straw bales, because Selina was looking down at me from the loft like a cat eyeing the cream and the twelve-bore she was holding was aimed straight at my head.

My last encounter with a shotgun had left me sensitive to being at the wrong end of them. I don't often have nightmares but when I do they tend to feature nameless figures behind double-barrels and a pretty total recall of the sensation as a load of number six shots blew my shoulder apart. Fortunately there are plus things to be said for fear, one being that it cuts reaction time to a remarkable degree. With the gun out of reach and above me, there wasn't a hope in hell of grappling with it and if I couldn't go forward, then it was as well not to waste any time going back. It's not a difficult thing to do with gravity on your side, and I went backwards down the pile of bales at a speed that surprised even me.

The gun went off, first one barrel, followed almost immediately by the other. She meant it all right. The air was full of flying chaff and the sharp smell of cordite, but I landed on the floor with the air knocked out of me but gratifyingly in one piece.

I looked up the way I'd come, half expecting to see the crazy bitch staring down at me while she pushed another pair of cartridges up the spout, but I needn't have worried because the hill of stacked straw was between us. A load of shotgun pellets makes a ragged hole in the side of a straw bale but that's about all, and so long as I kept a few of them between myself and the opening in the ceiling I was safe enough. I wondered fleetingly whether Selina would jump down and try to stalk me but I decided that was highly unlikely because anyone down on the ground could simply watch her coming down and collar her at will.

Sitting with my back against the straw, I listened to the sound of footsteps moving above me. Where was she off to now? The boards that made up the ceiling creaked, but not much. Did Selina actually want to kill me or was she just interested in keeping my head down? There was an obvious way to find out but I was reluctant to try it, not sure how good she might be at snapshooting but knowing very well how much a charge of shot spreads, so I contented myself by admiring a lubrication diagram for a Fordson tractor that someone had hung on the wall. They hadn't been able to nail the thing into metal, so they'd hammered it on to a length of two by two and suspended that from a bolt head with a loop of baling cord, which seemed to have been a practical way of going about things. Upstairs, the footsteps had padded back to their original position, followed by a steady splashing sound and a moment later the reek of petrol.

The smell of the stuff very nearly got me on my feet and running round like a hamster who's lost his wheel, although wherever the petrol was going, it wasn't reaching me. The splashing seemed to be going on for ever and I could imagine a four-gallon jerrican or similar container being upended. What kind of person was this Selina? I wondered. Stark

177

raving mad or was there some kind of plan behind it all? Stuck there under the shadow of the straw bales, I didn't know and didn't particularly care just so long as I didn't get any petrol on me. I waited for the sound that I knew would come, and when the match scraped I ran.

Behind me there was a flash of light and a *whoof*. Flat up against the locked doors of the barn I turned round and had a look, then rather wished I hadn't because the high column of straw bales was one great spouting geyser of fire. The petrol must have reached pretty well down to the bottom of the pile and its effect on dry, highly combustible straw was spectacular. I remembered having once seen an economically minded farmer using a straw-burning furnace to heat his home and had been impressed by the sight of the burning bales glowing to an almost white heat. Now, as the first searing blast caught me, I appreciated just how efficient a heat from straw was.

It was the first breath from an open furnace door that shocked me into the realization of just what kind of trouble I was in. To call my prison a barn was to give it ideas grossly above its station—it was a toy barn, little more than a garage, and the space inside it distinctly limited. What with my proximity to the flames and the radiation from the metal walls, the heat from the burning straw was rapidly becoming overpowering. Presumably Selina had left the loft window open because the smoke was being drawn straight up, which at least saved me from asphyxiation, although the door I was pressed against was already uncomfortably hot on my back.

There weren't many tools in the barn but there was a spade, so I grabbed that and slid it between the two doors. It came up short on the padlocked bolt and when I tried to make a lever of it the spade handle simply snapped in two.

Aloud, I said, 'Bloody thing—' trying to push back the panic that was rising inside me. I couldn't remember picking it up but a moment later I found myself hammering futilely on the metal doors with a club hammer, only to throw it aside with the realization that I might just as well be kicking at the metal with my foot. Already my eyes were streaming

178

and the roar of the flames was beginning to beat into my brain. Some trick of draught flicked a blast of blistering heat in my direction and I heard my hair singe at the instant that the side of my face felt as though it had been splashed with boiling water. For the first time the fact got through to me that I was going to be burned alive and I looked round for something—anything—that might give me even a few moments' protection. There is something very fundamental about fear of fire and, given sufficient threat, it requires a major effort not to lose one's head. Standing in that damn barn with hot smoke searing my nostrils, I had to use more willpower than I thought I possessed before I could force myself to look about steadily for some kind of refuge. At first it seemed there was none and that the barn was completely empty, but then I spotted something white against the far wall. For a moment it didn't make sense, and then I recognized it for what it was. April Tonge's king-size freezer.

I reached the thing in a few desperate strides and pulled at the lid. Apparently the electric supply was still working because the motor was throbbing like a mad thing as it tried to cope with the rise in temperature that was already blistering the casing's white paint. A quick tug told me the lid was locked, but I was too far gone to be stopped by that. Clouds of vapour rose from the frosted depths as I demolished the lock with a couple of blows of the club hammer, swung one leg over the side and dropped in among April's hoarded fish fingers.

I suppose if one is hot enough one does become at least slightly demented. Objectively there is something ludicrous in the very idea of a man trying to cool himself down by diving into a freezer, but when your hair is crisping on your head, rational thinking isn't one's strong point. If it had been, I would probably have anticipated the agony of my scorched flesh as it came in contact with a contents chilled to $-10°$ Centigrade. As it was, the cold burned with more savagery than the flame. The back of a tortured hand fell against something that seared agonizingly and, as I tore it away, I felt the skin go with it. I heard someone scream and wondered who it might be as I struggled to pull myself out of the searing hell into which I'd dropped my unsuspecting body. I got one arm round the edge of the freezer and pulled myself upright until I was kneeling in the thing, and then without warning, the front of the barn seemed to explode behind me.

I don't know what I imagined it was at the time, because by then I was beyond anything that could be called rational thought. I remember seeing daylight where the door had been, and a draught of blessedly fresh air at the same time as there were hands gripping my shoulders, dragging me towards it. Then I was kneeling in the open air coughing my heart out, forgetting the pain of my scorched skin, the primæval terror of being burnt alive—forgetting everything in the sheer wonder of having pure cold air to breathe.

Behind me a woman—Laurie—was saying something about getting me to a doctor.

'I'm all right.' I'd stopped coughing, so it seemed likely that was true. I sat back on my heels and tried to look up at her but that wasn't really on because my eyes were streaming. I said, 'Was it you who got me out?'

'Yes.' And then, 'I heard shots and so I came to see what was happening. Only, of course, I couldn't get in.'

A lot of people wouldn't have felt compelled to ride to the sound of the guns quite so promptly, but then she may just have been inquisitive by nature. 'Well, tell me,' I said, 'how *did* you get in? There was a hell of a bang. Thought someone had blown the door down.'

'I rammed it with your car.'

'Did you now?' It was really difficult to think of anything suitable to say when faced with a statement like that.

'I'm sorry.' Laurie really sounded very contrite.

I wondered what the front of the Maserati looked like and decided that perhaps after all it was just as well I couldn't see. There are some things it is better not to know about.

'Are bits awfully expensive?' She was kneeling beside me now, mopping at my eyes. I don't imagine that she was all that concerned but had decided that talking about cars would take the lad's mind off other things.

I said rather ungratefully, 'I know a front bumper costs about seven hundred quid.'

'Well,' she told me cheerfully, 'that's the insurance company's worry, isn't it?'

'Providing they accept the claim. I'm not sure how they react to people driving cars intentionally through barn doors,' I said.

'I don't understand what you were doing in the barn, anyway.' She knew when it was time to change the subject. 'You were supposed to be looking for a phone.'

I said, 'I met Delphine. She told me that April was in the barn so I went to have a look.'

'Oh my God!' I felt Laurie straighten and I guessed she was looking towards the burning building. 'You don't mean she's still inside—'

'Yes, but I shouldn't let it worry you.' I tried to think of a way of making it less bizarre but I couldn't, so I went on, 'I found her when I tried to get into the freezer. She was there already, you see.' I remembered the brief glimpse I'd had through the swirling vapour as the heat hit the cold air, the frosted features of April Tonge's white face. I ended lamely, 'She must have been there quite some time.'

CHAPTER 14

A player who has incurred a penalty shall inform his opponent as soon as practicable.

Rule 9–2

Melanie and I ended up at the local hospital at about the same time, she in an ambulance, Laurie and I in a station car following on behind. Someone must have thought to call Alan Thurston because he was there in the entrance hall when we arrived. I'd have spoken to him but it didn't seem quite fair at that moment and anyway, casualty were starting to pluck at me.

A rather pretty black nurse pushed me gently into a chair while a young doctor made 'you've been very lucky' noises and sprayed my face and hands with something cool and mercifully colourless which was a relief because, for some reason, I was expecting to come out bright blue.

'Not any more,' the doctor said when I asked him about it. 'Not even in my time, as a matter of fact. I think they used some stuff called Gentian Violet during the war. Long time ago, that.'

Yes, I told him, it was, wasn't it?

'You're going to look as if you've been out in the sun too long, but that's about all.' He was looking over his shoulder because they were bringing in a road accident. 'Don't shave for a day or so. All right?'

'Yes,' I said, 'all right, and thanks.'

'Any time.'

Laurie was sitting where I'd left her in the hall, drinking machine coffee out of a paper cup. She looked up and smiled. 'No problems?'

'Nothing to it.' I sounded like a small boy who had had sticky plaster on his knee, which was about the mark anyway. 'I suppose I'd better have a quiet word with Thurston before somebody else does.'

'Why you, darling? You're not the only policeman in the world. Why don't you let it all go through the usual channels or whatever you call them?'

'I don't know. I probably shall.' The truth was that I didn't know. At that moment I was sure of very little apart from the fact that I was glad to be alive and that if possible I didn't want to have a cosy chat about things I didn't understand.

We sat there, not saying anything, not looking at each other. I'd like to have talked but for some reason my mind had gone blank.

'Look,' Laurie said suddenly, 'I'm sorry but I really must get back to London.'

'Yes, of course you must.' Was she just a perceptive girl who knew when to make herself scarce or did she really have to go? 'Thanks for coming down.' It wasn't what I'd wanted to say, but it was all that came out. I should have said, 'Thank you for saving my life,' too.

'Are you sure you'll be all right?'

I actually managed to squeeze her hand. 'Absolutely sure.'

I watched her walk away down the long hospital corridor, till eventually she got muddled up with a gaggle of nurses going on shift and I couldn't see her any more. Why hadn't I gone with her? I think I was on the point of going after her, but Alan Thurston came out of a door, a constable at his side, and the moment was past.

I told his escort to hop it and took Alan by the arm. As I towed him towards a lift I said, 'You're going to have to talk to someone pretty soon, and the way things have been going, I think it had better be me.'

He didn't say anything right away but he got into the lift with me and we went downstairs and out through the main entrance. Harlington is one of the newer hospitals, five miles out of town in what used to be some local dignitary's park. Now it's landscaped and a bit over-organized but good to walk in if you're trying to take your mind off something. Or get it on to something, come to that. Alan followed me silently as I headed off across the grass through the first of the year's crop of brown leaves.

'How's Melanie?' I asked. As a matter of fact, I knew already, because they'd told me but it seemed to be an introduction.

'They're not sure what kind of drug it is, but they seem pretty confident she'll be all right in a day or two.' He thought that over, as though he wasn't absolutely sure whether he believed it or not. 'Chap I was talking to— specialist in that sort of thing. Seemed genuinely interested, so I don't think he was having me on.'

'That was Culper,' I told him. 'He's supposed to be one of the best men in the country on narcotics.'

Alan said, 'Yes.'

Christ, I thought, it was like being a reporter with one foot in the door. *Tell me, luv, how did it feel when they told you they'd dropped a hundred tons of coal on your husband?* But this

183

was what I was paid for. 'You always knew Melanie had been kidnapped,' I said. 'Knew all along?'

'Oh yes.' He sounded surprised that I'd asked. 'From the first day.'

'And your kids?'

He shook his head. 'No. I made up some story that she was visiting their uncle. They believed it all right.'

'Like hell they did,' I told him. 'You'd better tell them that was a load of old cobblers first chance you get, because my impression was they thought Mum had run off with another man.'

You'd have thought that in the circumstances he'd have laughed that one off, but families are funny things. 'They'll understand all right when I've explained.'

'Yes,' I agreed, 'I suppose they will. Could have been easier still if you'd told them about the kidnapping in the first place.'

He kicked at a leaf reflectively, kicked it again, then used his heel to screw it into the ground. 'I couldn't have done that—they very definitely told me not to.'

'They?'

'Whoever it was on the phone.'

'So what did you have to do to get Melanie back?' I asked.

Alan looked at me for the first time—probably with surprise that it was a question I still had to ask. 'I didn't have to do anything much except keep my mouth shut.' He picked up the empty case of a chestnut, gutted by conker-hunting children. 'I didn't like it much, but what do you do when it's your wife's life that's at stake?'

There's always an impulse to justify, but he had a point. 'Look,' I said, 'why don't you just tell me what happened?'

For a moment I thought he hadn't heard me, because he just stood there staring at the bit of horse chestnut in his hand. 'You don't know Africa, do you, Angus?'

A question or a statement? 'No,' I said.

'Odd place. Some of it's as good as anywhere on earth. Melanie and I enjoyed ourselves there, specially towards the end, when I put in a couple of years in Kariba. They're in for trouble now, but it was pretty good then.'

184

'You mean the Fundamentalist business,' I said.

He started walking forward again. 'You know about that, then?'

'A rough idea.'

'I'd heard rumours—and a bit here and there from Bill Sadiq.'

'I didn't think he had any politics,' I said.

'He hasn't.' Alan smiled faintly. 'As a matter of fact, I very much doubt if he's got a thought in his head outside golf. Golf and the odd pretty face now and then.'

'So?'

'Well, that's what started it, I suppose. You remember Sadiq didn't come over here specially for the Tamworth— he was here already, playing in a couple of Pro Ams?' I nodded, and Thurston went on, 'He'd got some time on his hands so he came down here a week early so as to have an early look at the course. There was a good-looking African girl who took to following him around. They got to talking, which I suppose was natural enough—particularly as it turned out she also came from Kariba and, as I said, Sadiq likes women. Eventually he took her for a drink at that pub on the river—I can never remember its name.'

'The Wheatsheaf,' I said.

'Yes, that's right.' Thurston nodded. 'It's got a garden that goes down to the water with tables and things. Sadiq and this girl were sitting talking and, as it happened, I was there with Melanie.'

'Did they see you?'

'No, I was sitting with my back to them, but I could hear every word they said—which wasn't difficult because the girl was speaking quite loudly in Yosa, which I suppose she imagined was pretty secure. I mean, there must be still quite a lot of people in this country who speak the common African languages, like Kiswahili and Bantu, but Yosa's a kind of one-off dialect that's only found in a few parts of the south-west. It's a barbarous bloody tongue—'

'But you happen to speak it,' I said.

Thurston looked at me with what looked almost like appeal in his eyes. Appeal—guilt probably, although it didn't seem to me to be his fault. He said, 'Yes, I speak it. It's used in one or two of the little ex-Portuguese protectorates because the Yosas usually work the mines.'

'All right,' I said, 'so you understood them. What were they talking about?'

'The girl—'

'De Cruz?'

'Yes. She was telling Sadiq that he was heading for trouble playing golf—that any time now the country would be going back to strict tribal and religious rule. The pro-Western government was going to be thrown out and the KFP would sweep into power. When that happened, nobody was going to love a son of Kariba who thought only of a decadent Western game and so on.'

I could imagine her doing it, too. 'Listen,' I said, 'did the girl speak as though she was one of the KFP or was she just telling him about them?'

'She seemed to be just warning him.'

'And Sadiq's reaction to all this?'

Thurston shrugged his shoulders. 'He said in effect that the KFP could get stuffed and, so far as he was concerned, he was going to carry on playing golf, and what did she imagine a few bloody revolutionaries could do about it.'

I could imagine Sadiq saying just that, not what one might call diplomatic but pretty well to the point. 'As a matter of interest,' I said, 'what *did* she say to that?'

'Oh, she had an answer ready all right,' Thurston assured me. 'She told him that he was being a fool and that if he didn't give up golf and return home right away the Fundamentalists intended making an example of him.'

I said, 'I was told there was going to be some kind of demonstration.'

'Demonstration!' Thurston made a noise that was more like a bark than a laugh. 'For God's sake, Angus, they're not planning to wave banners and shout slogans. They're going to kill him!'

We reached the large oak tree to which we'd been heading, walked round it and started back the way we'd come. We were facing the hospital now and it looked big and white

186

and out of place in the old park, like a pile of building bricks dropped down in the middle of the drawing-room floor.

'Did she tell him that?' I asked.

Thurston shook his head. 'No, I found that out later. Sadiq said they could do what they liked but he was carrying on playing golf, and they got up and left. Which was when I put my foot in it, because they walked right past us and naturally Sadiq recognized me. He waved and said "Greetings, Great Chief!" in Yosa.'

'He knew you spoke it?'

'Oh Lord, yes!' Thurston said. 'Kind of a joke between us—saying things like that. Only the trouble was I said something like "Hail, mighty elephant!" in the same language. Bill just laughed but I saw the girl's eyes open like saucers.'

'I bet they did,' I said. 'She must have realized you'd heard every word she said. So what happened after that?'

Thurston said slowly, 'It was a couple of days after that that Melanie disappeared—she'd gone out shopping and simply didn't come back. Then I got a phone call—'

'Man or woman?'

'A woman—youngish voice and English, I should say. Certainly it wasn't de Cruz.'

'What did she say?'

'That my wife was being held hostage to ensure my good behaviour. That Bill Sadiq was to be executed as a warning to all Karibans that the love-affair with the West was over, and that if I tried to warn him or tell the police, Melanie would be killed immediately.'

I wondered whose voice it would have been over the phone? Poor dotty Delphine probably—it wouldn't have been hard to bulldoze her into anything. 'Did you believe all this?' I asked.

'Oh, I believed it all right.' Alan said. 'What's more, I know enough about the KFP to know that it's important that Bill Sadiq does get executed according to plan. The man's a sort of folk hero—the only Kariban who's actually become a household word in the world outside. He's actually *better* at something than almost any Westerner. Can you

187

imagine what that means back in that Godforsaken little hole? It doesn't matter that only one Kariban in a hundred thousand would recognize a golf course if he saw one, they still reckon Sadiq is terrific.'

'And so the KFP is going to knock him off,' I said.

Alan nodded. 'I suppose it makes a kind of lunatic sense. Bill's the arch traitor in their eyes—the man who made it in the West. He's got to die as a warning and as a sign that even a folk hero can't survive against the Fundamentalist law, and if I get my guess right, it's the killing of Sadiq that's to be the signal for the takeover.' He hesitated. 'Do you believe all this, by any chance?'

'Yes, I believe it,' I told him. I did, too. 'You don't happen to know when and where?'

He shook his head. 'No, I do not. And up till an hour or so ago I wouldn't have told you if I did. Not while they had Melanie. I tell you, Angus, you don't have to spend long in Africa to learn that life is cheap there—really cheap. Almost any young yob would cut her throat for the price of a beer so you can be pretty sure things are even rougher where politics are concerned.'

'That's all right,' I told him. 'If I'd been in your place I don't imagine I'd have done much for Bill Sadiq either.'

Alan frowned. 'Well, I did what I could. I—'

'You did what?' For a moment I thought he was going to say that he'd actually gone to the police and that my so-called informal involvement wasn't informal after all. But I needn't have worried.

Alan had stopped and was staring at me defiantly. Finally he managed to come out with it. 'Well, I tried to stop that damned tournament.'

It made sense. It had always made sense. It had just taken a long time to get around to it, that was all.

'How the devil did you go about that?' I asked. And then, as the penny dropped: 'I suppose you're going to tell me that you put April Tonge up to chopping up the green?'

'No, of course I didn't!' I suppose he was understandably annoyed, because, faced with a choice between their wives or their greens, most club secretaries would opt for the greens every time. 'But I wrote the threatening letter—the first one, that is.'

I stared at him. 'You mean it wasn't Raikes?'

'It may have been the second time, but not the first.'

I remembered that Raikes himself had said something very like that. 'You didn't really think they'd put the Tamworth off just because someone sent a threatening letter, did you?' I said.

'It was a long shot, but it gave me the feeling that I was doing *something*. Like the weedkiller and those bloody exploding golf balls.'

'That was you too?'

'Oh yes.' Alan started walking again towards the hospital, walking faster than before, with small, quick steps. Do we all try to run away from ourselves? I lengthened my stride to keep up with him as he was saying, 'I suppose it was absurd, but I was in the hell of a state and it just seemed that if enough things went wrong, they might just get fed up with it and cancel the whole thing.'

'I suppose they might have done in the end,' I said. 'But how did you fix those golf balls?'

Thurston relaxed enough to allow himself a grin. 'You must admit, old boy, that wasn't bad!'

'It was the event of the evening, old boy,' I said. 'But I'm still wondering how you did it.'

'It wasn't hard.' Thurston came back from the world of jolly japes. 'Kawasaki was fooling around in the clubhouse with some joke balls from Kobe.'

'Why Kobe?' I was curious.

Thurston shrugged. 'It's always been that sort of place. Before the war it wasn't just another port, it was world famous for sex shops that specialized in naughty gadgetry. Blow-up women and things like that. Used to call them "Joy Boxes". Now sex is a bit too common, so they make mechanical jokes instead. Good ones, too.'

'So?' It was hard to imagine Thurston with a Joy Box.

'So these joke golf balls seemed useful for my purpose, and it struck me that they could be cheered up a bit by someone who knew what he was doing, which I did. I pinched a box or so and tried my luck.'

'Wasn't that a bit risky?' I asked.

He looked surprised. 'No, not really. I've spent most of my working life around mines, and explosives have always been part of the job. It's surprising how small a charge you need to make a noise like a grenade.'

'You didn't—' I stopped because there are some things one was reluctant to link even to an acquaintance, and Alan Thurston was more than that.

He looked at me curiously. 'I didn't what?'

'I'm sorry,' I said, 'it was just a train of thought, but somebody killed my cat.'

'Well, it wasn't me. Bloody hell, Angus—'

I said, 'All right, I said I was sorry.' Policemen shouldn't apologize but I don't really know why not.

'I didn't break Keith Fletcher's neck and dump him in a bunker, either.' Alan was doing a very reasonable impersonation of an empire builder whose credit was being questioned. 'I didn't even know you *had* a cat. Someone run it over or something?'

I said, 'No, someone broke into my flat and cut its head off.'

'Did they? *Did* they?' Alan's expression changed. One moment he'd been everything people laughed at about the carriers of the white man's burden, then all at once you didn't laugh. Alan had been a mining engineer in foreign parts but I saw now that he could equally well have been a District Commissioner or a Judge. He said, 'I wish you'd told me before.'

'Why the hell should I? It was nothing to do with you if some maniac goes about killing cats.'

'No, I suppose not. But in the circumstances it's not particularly nice. In Kariba, if you mean to do someone in, you normally kill one of his animals first. Over there it's usually a cow or a goat or whatever. Once the animal's been chopped, its owner is supposed to die within a week.'

We looked at each other. 'It could be coincidence,' I said.

'Don't talk balls,' Alan said. 'How many people do you know who've had their cats beheaded?'

'Not many,' I admitted. 'Mind you, I'm still alive.'

Alan grinned. 'Don't lose hope, the week's not up yet.'

'Or maybe Polly Appleby bought it instead of me.' She'd been wearing my coat, I remembered. In the half light she would have looked as much like me as made no difference. I changed the subject. 'But I still don't see why you paid off the TV technicians. That you tried to stop the tournament makes sense, but if the strike had gone ahead it would probably have put paid to the Tamworth, anyway. So why did you use your own money to smooth the trouble out?'

Alan stared at me. 'How the devil did you check up on that?'

I said, 'Never mind how. Why?'

'Because whoever it was rang me up about Melanie got on to me again and said that was what I had to do.'

'Just like that?'

'Just like that.' He went on: 'Maybe it's none of my business, but what happens now?'

I said slowly, 'I honestly don't know.' Which was the truth, I didn't. I'd already asked Hawkins if they'd got the de Cruz girl but she seemed to have vanished without trace. Delphine was in custody pending interrogation, which for one of life's losers was probably about par for the course and wasn't going to get anybody anywhere. 'Stop the tournament this evening would be one way,' I guessed. 'Award the prizes on the placings at the end of the third round? You'll have nothing to worry about—there'll be a round-the-clock guard on Melanie. And on you and the kids too, come to that.'

'The sponsors will have a fit.'

'That's just too bloody bad.' I was not prepared to shed tears for Tamworth if they had to lose a day of the show, but I wondered how much influence they had in higher circles. It wasn't an encouraging thought but there was nothing much I could do about it, apart from waiting to find out.

*

I got the call within the hour, Mr Hawkins, Wilmott of CID and various other odds and sods to the Chief Constable's office rather quicker than now. There was a certain amount of cautious going-over of my physical appearance and encouraging noises of brotherly solidarity and general support. Good old Angus had been worth a good laugh as the Force's unofficial golfing correspondent, but now I was at least a talking point. Even the Chief, in uniform, was amiably concerned.

'Feeling all right, Angus?'

I made appropriate noises and, all in all, it was quite true because there wasn't a thing wrong with me apart from a certain shortage of hair and a sunburnt appearance that smarted a bit but it could all have been a great deal worse.

'In that case, I suggest we deal with first things first.' Linforth was standing with his back to his desk with the faraway look in his eyes that I'd always imagined meant he was back in the army. *Situation. Intention. Method*—

'Gentlemen, tomorrow there will be a golf match taking place within a few miles of this room and we know it is possible that an attempt may well be made on one of the competitors.' *Situation.* 'Clearly we must thwart any such attempt.' *Intention.* The Chief Constable hesitated. Perhaps he was thinking about what he himself wanted to say as opposed to what it was going to be expedient for him to hand out. All in all, there must be times when being a Chief Constable can be excessively tiresome, but you'd never have guessed it from his face as he droned on. 'Whatever method we use, we must ensure that it secures the intended victim at all times. It will take Mr Sadiq approximately three to three-and-a-half hours to complete the course—'

I stood up, feeling rather like a small boy who wants to leave the room. 'Sir—'

'Yes, Angus?'

'Isn't allowing him to play at all something of a needless risk? Can't we get Tamworth to agree to award the championship on the first three rounds instead of the full four? Then we could smuggle Sadiq off the course and maybe to the nearest airfield without anyone having the chance for a crack at him.'

'That's not on, I'm afraid.' He waited, presumably in case I said 'Why not?', and when I didn't he went on as though nothing had happened. 'I have received certain guidelines from Whitehall which we ignore at our peril. Politically, the match goes ahead because the Kariban government have made it clear that any cancellation of the last round would be regarded as a moral victory for the Fundamentalists. The present rulers want Sadiq to win— he's good for their pro-Western policy. So the match goes on and he is to be protected at all costs.'

We thought that one over until Hawkins said, 'They wouldn't like us to *fix* the match while we're at it?'

Linforth allowed himself one of his more wintry smiles, which indicated that he perceived the jest but was not amused by it.

'I'm sure they'd like that, but even in Kariba they probably understand that would be asking too much.'

I said, 'It doesn't seem any more unreasonable than expecting us to safeguard Sadiq when he's surrounded by at least twenty thousand people. We don't know how the KFP mean to go about nailing him. Suppose some maniac opens up with a sub-machine-gun and mows down about fifty spectators? Who's going to carry the can then?'

'Oh, we shall, naturally.'

'But surely, sir, Whitehall can see the dangers?' Hawkins sounded as though he couldn't believe what he was hearing. 'I mean, they wouldn't risk God knows how many lives just to please some dog's dinner of an African state?'

Linforth bared his teeth. 'Of course they would. You wouldn't want our government to label themselves racist, would you, Hawkins?'

Hawkins said, 'Frankly, sir, I don't give a damn what they're called, but this is bloody silly.'

'Of course it is.' The Chief Constable's voice rose sharply. 'Really, Hawkins, do you think I don't know that? Do you honestly think I *agree* with those grovelling little bastards we call our masters? Of course I don't! But I can't do anything about it, short of resigning and don't imagine they wouldn't accept it because they'd jump at the chance.' I watched him pause, and could imagine him considering whether to carry on. Presumably his time as a soldier had taught him how far was far enough, because he went on reasonably, 'Well, it's neither here nor there because, according to orders, the show goes on and nobody gets shot. Ours not to reason why, so supposing the whole thing isn't a gigantic bluff, any suggestions as to how they're going to do it?'

Somebody asked, 'Considering the fact that he's the one who's going to get chopped, has anyone asked this chap Sadiq how he feels about carrying on?'

'Yes,' Linforth said, 'I have. My impression was that he's too involved with the business of winning tomorrow to think of much else. Suggested that if we got on with our job, he'd look after his. Likeable chap.' His eyes looked us over as though deciding which of us was to go over the top. 'I asked for suggestions as to method. Angus?'

I said, 'If it's all planned as a kind of PR exercise, I don't imagine they're going to knock him off somewhere out of the way. If Sadiq's death is meant to be a lesson to the unfaithful, then they'll want it to be in front of the TV cameras so it'll get maximum coverage.

'In fact,' I went on, 'we *know* that's what they want, because when there was a chance that the TV crews might go on strike, Thurston was blackmailed into paying the technicians the money they demanded. So whatever it is that's going to happen to Sadiq seems to be scheduled to be on camera.'

'Go on.' The CC was trying to look as though he'd known all that before.

I hadn't got much more to offer. 'If he wins—*if* he wins—I suppose the most effective moment to take Sadiq out would be as he sank the winning putt.'

'Or accepted the cup,' Linforth suggested. 'The moment of triumph—that kind of thing.'

'I'd have said the moment of triumph was when you made the winning stroke,' I suggested. 'The ball drops, you throw

194

your putter into the air and bang! you get it straight between the eyes.'

The CC beamed. 'You grow lyrical, Angus! So you assume Sadiq will be shot?'

I thought of the crowds round the eighteenth green, the high-banked spectator stands flanking two sides of the square. Literally a sitting duck for anyone who could make the shot in peace and quiet, but enthusiasts don't normally carry a rifle with a telescopic sight with them to their seat.

'Yes,' I said, 'he'll be shot all right, but God knows where from. A good marksman with a decent rifle could get him from half a mile away, given enough height.'

The colonel sniffed. 'And there is enough height, if you count the trees backing to the clubhouse. Fine, we can cover that. Anything else?'

We sat back and thought it over. Hawkins said, 'What happens if he doesn't win?'

'They kill him anyway. But I'm not sure when.' Linforth kicked that one around for a few moments. 'Logically, they'd do it at the moment when they were satisfied that he wasn't going to make it. Yes?'

'Yes,' I said. 'Only they'd need someone who knew something about the game to decide when that was. How many Kariban assassins are that much up in golf?'

Linforth looked disapproving. He didn't like anyone to upset his theories, so he said briskly, 'We don't know anything about the expertise of these jokers. For all we know, the chief killer in the KFP plays to scratch, but the problems remain the same. Sadiq may or may not win tomorrow, but at least we know he'll be in the first four. If they don't shoot him, what the devil *do* they do?'

'Someone could mount a kind of Kamikaze raid on him with a knife,' I said. I thought of the prize awards I'd seen, the cheerful chaos of golfers, officials and photographers, with no one having eyes for anything other than the man who'd won. Under such conditions a dedicated killer could do anything he wanted.

The CC frowned. 'Really, Angus.'

'Look,' I said, 'at the final moment in any competition

195

the crowd are looking at one man—not at each other. Everyone's shouting their heads off and waving their arms —there isn't a soul who's looking sideways to see what his neighbour is up to.'

Nobody said anything, and in the silence we sat and looked at each other.

'All right,' the CC said. 'So what you're saying is that towards the end of the round we've got to be prepared for an attempt to be made on Sadiq's life at any time.'

'I suppose so,' I said. 'But we can't very well have someone going round with him while he's playing.'

The Chief Constable smiled. 'I don't see why not. You know about golf, Angus.'

I didn't say anything because the penny was beginning to drop.

'His caddie stays with him all the time, doesn't he?'

'Yes,' I said. It had dropped.

'Right, then. You'd better get organized while there's still time.'

CHAPTER 15

A 'caddie' is one who carries or handles a player's clubs during play and otherwise assists him in accordance with the Rules.

Definition

It was a long time since I'd been a caddie. Time was you could take your pick at the back of the pro's shop for half-a-crown a round and it would cost you ten quid today supposing you could find one, which is astonishingly difficult. The caddies on the tournament circuit are a Porsche-driving race apart, enormously knowledgeable advisers and confidants who receive, as of right, their share of any prize money and who make the lugging of the regulation fourteen clubs plus this and that look like something anyone could do if he tried.

196

Well, for me it had been a long time, particularly as my experience of the craft had never extended much beyond carrying a modest half set for my father at the tender age of fourteen. I looked at the bright red Jetdrive bag that was mine for the final round and hoped that at least I'd be able to lift it on to my shoulder. Maybe I could be the first tour caddie to use a trolley?

'You got balls there. Pegs, pitch fork, yardage notes alongside. Okay?' Joe White, Sadiq's real caddie, slapped appropriate pockets on the bag. With his money and bonuses guaranteed, he'd no objection to me doing his work for him but he was a conscientious chap.

'Yes,' I said. 'Okay.'

'Sweater and rain gear under the zip. Spare socks in case he has to play out of water. Spare shoe laces. Towel.'

I nodded. It was no wonder the bags were big.

Joe prodded a smaller pocket. 'Elastoplast, Codeine, antiseptic and all that crap. Remember, he don't take nothing without checking with an official, because you don't want your man disqualified for popping pills for the sake of a headache. Right?'

'Right.'

'He'll take his own clubs out so you don't have to guess what he'll want.' White pushed the bag towards me. 'We're carrying all the irons except 4 and 6, putter, wedge and sand iron. Woods, 1, 2, 3 and 5. Count them.'

I counted, and it came to fourteen, but I counted again to make sure. Fourteen clubs was all that was allowed and there had been all too many players who'd found themselves disqualified through overlooking an extra iron. I picked the bag up and hung it over my shoulder. I was wearing a yellow golf jacket with SADIQ emblazoned in big letters on the back, pale blue slacks and a matching baseball cap, all of which was considered to come out well on colour TV.

Linforth asked, 'All right?'

It was nice to know that the Chief Constable cared but I suppose he must have done or he wouldn't have come along.

'Yes,' I said. 'Fine.' In fact, my load didn't feel as bad as

I'd expected, now that it was balanced properly.

'You've got everything?'

By everything he meant the .38 Smith and Wesson Magnum which was under the zip, on top of Bill Sadiq's waterproofs. Big hand guns are difficult to conceal under cotton sports clothes and presumably Tamworth wouldn't have wanted it to get around that their caddies were armed to the teeth. I said, 'It's in the bag.'

'Well, for God's sake remember to keep it there, if you can.'

I didn't answer that, because I hadn't the slightest intention of flourishing a gun at anyone who wasn't doing the same thing at me, quite apart from the fact that the Royal and Ancient were bound to have rules somewhere about shooting people in the course of play. Would a .38 Magnum slug be a movable obstruction or just rub of the green? I concentrated on the job in hand and picked out Bill Sadiq's long-legged lope as he came out of the clubhouse towards me, and felt that he was coping with the whole thing rather well. He knew why I was caddying for him and presumably he knew the politics of his own country well enough to accept the fact that nobody was just playing games, but to look at him one would never have guessed it. Because he was very black, either he or the TV company had decided that it would be nice and eye-catching if he wore white, so at first glance he could have been due to play cricket rather than golf.

He came abreast of me and flashed white teeth amiably.

'You all fixed, man?'

I told him I was. There seemed to be a general concern as to my welfare that I found rather discouraging, but perhaps I was being unduly sensitive. And anyway, it was as good a day as one could have wished, a light breeze from the west, but nothing that was likely to cause anyone any trouble, clear skies and enough overnight dew for the greens to hold the ball. The stands round the eighteenth were already full and beyond it you could see a solid bank of spectators flanking the tee and the first hundred yards of the opening hole. I looked up at the red names of figures of the tournament leaders on the giant scoreboard facing the stands.

D. SHROEDER	70	68	138
W. SADIQ	71	68	139
O. KAWASAKI	71	70	141
R. LINDT	71	71	143

I imagined Don Shroeder had seen himself as being more than a single stroke ahead at the start of the final day's play, particularly as the third round was to be played in the morning, with the final following immediately the same afternoon. From what little I'd seen of the earlier games, this had been due more to the fact that the Australian hadn't been playing on top form rather than that the others had been particularly brilliant, though 6 under par over two rounds was still pretty incredible golf. Even the fourth man, Lindt, was 2 under, which I knew perfectly well I could never equal at my very best, so who was I to judge?

Sadiq asked, 'How long to nine-thirty?'

'Ten minutes. We'd best be getting there,' I told him. Nine-thirty was the time he'd drawn and in a tournament you're at the tee in time or else.

He nodded. 'Okay. Let's go.'

I looked round to have a look at my backing team but Linforth had his back to me as he spoke to some woman. The half-dozen from CID had drifted off and for all I knew were ducking off to get a late breakfast and I thought that for once it would be a nice change to work with people who over-reacted instead of displaying their celebrated British phlegm. If nobody believed Sadiq was in danger, why was I playing at being a caddie with a gun in my golf-bag pocket? And if they did, why in hell wasn't something more being done about it?

Beside me, Sadiq's dark brown voice picked up my thoughts consolingly. 'First thing first, man. We got a game of golf to play.'

And he was the one due to be shot at.

We were the fourth pair off that morning—a good time to hit a ball on the last day, with the light low and behind you and the greens still hard and true round the fresh cut hole. Not so good if the strong contenders are coming up behind because then it means a long, nerve-twisting wait in the clubhouse with your score up on the board for everyone to aim at. I looked over at Don Shroeder and Matt Walsh who'd carried his bag for years. They knew who I was and why I was there but their nods were the same as they'd have given to Joe White.

An official addressed the four-deep crush round the back of the tee. 'Attention, please. We do ask for complete quiet when a player makes his stroke. And particularly, no cameras. They're very noisy and very distracting.'

Cameras. I watched the TV gantry shifting slightly way up above me, a couple of the hand-held brigade settling themselves in front of the crowd. Shroeder and Sadiq were standing together with their hands in their pockets chatting, whatever tension they felt neither of them showed it, but all around there was the general air of heightened anticipation one gets on occasions such as this one, when the two leading players had been paired together. In tournaments, the players go round the course in twos and threes as a matter of convenience, but they are playing against the course rather than each other, each man striving to complete four rounds in less strokes than anyone else. The pairings are chosen at random, and it is quite possible for the tournament leader to play with someone who lags umpteen strokes behind. But today, with the two top men paired, the game promised instant drama, with every shift of fortune immediately apparent.

The hands of the big official clock pointed to nine-thirty, someone held up a board with *Quiet* printed on it and the starter cleared his throat. 'On the tee, Don Shroeder of Australia, 138 strokes over 36 holes. Bill Sadiq, Kariba, 139 strokes. Shroeder to play first.'

The first hole at the West Wessex is three hundred and seventy yards from the back markers, a dog-leg to the right and a couple of well-placed bunkers waiting for anyone overshooting the mark. Shroeder took a 3 wood and addressed the ball. For once there really was silence, because I suppose there wasn't anyone there who didn't want to watch that awe-inspiring swing that the years never touched. I'd seen it often enough but it still got to me, the sheer beauty of something that managed to be natural and still copy-book perfect at the same time. This morning wasn't any different. Shroeder just looked at the ball, wound his long, wiry body up and just let it go. The chrome on the club shaft blurred, the tee peg flew back and the ball was on its way, climbing in a great arc, dead straight down the centre of the fairway. We watched it for what seemed like minutes till it dropped, bounced on and stopped exactly at the point of the dog-leg, ten yards short of the nearest bunker.

He deserved his round of applause. If I hadn't been caddying for the other side I'd have given him a clap, too.

The starter said, 'Bill Sadiq.'

I held the bag out and he took a 2 iron, which wasn't what I'd expected, but he obviously knew what he was doing. He had small bones, and when he swung it didn't seem as though he'd have the strength to control the metal club. But he had the strength all right—you could virtually see the shaft bend with the sheer force of his straightening wrists and the ball whirred on its way, ending roughly level with Shroeder's and half-a-dozen paces to one side.

We went after the balls. The crowd didn't follow, because there were still a dozen pairs due to start, but we could see fresh blocks of spectators ahead, lining the fairway on both sides. I'd forgotten what it was like. The single occasion when I'd played in the Open was now ancient history, but when we reached the turn and the noise level from the watchers dropped as though it had been turned off with a tap, the feel of the thing began to come back. I remembered once asking Ambrose about the crowds and the readiness of his answer.

'They're different, you see. Nobody who watches football actually *plays* it any more—half the oafs on the terraces

201

don't even know the rules. But the British golf crowd is the most knowledgeable in the world. You play on a tour with thirty thousand people watching you—and every one of them plays the game, too.'

It may have worried Ambrose and it had certainly worried me, but from what I could see, it made little difference to either Shroeder or Sadiq. They somehow managed to exchange remarks and even jokes yet still maintain a concentration that was never anything less than total, and such was their magic that I had to keep reminding myself that I was there with a job to do and wasn't just standing in the middle of it all as a privileged spectator.

They halved the first hole with two par fours and did the same at the second. At the third Bill Sadiq hooked his drive into the trees, and although his lie was a reasonably good one, it still cost him a stroke, and although he made par, Shroeder was down for a birdie and that put his lead up to two.

It might have been the moment when he got away, but Sadiq clawed the next hole back by sinking an incredible forty-foot putt and then repeated the performance line for line on the fifth, except that this time he was down for an eagle two, which meant that it was he and not the Australian who was two ahead. I trudged after the two of them, forgetting the weight of the bag on my shoulder although sweat was beginning to trickle down my back. One glance at my man, in time to catch the ball he tossed to me. Clean it. I rubbed it with the towel, inspected the case for nicks, handed it back. Over Sadiq's shoulder I saw a black face in the crowd and my hand went to the zip of my golf bag. Whoever it was was bending down, lifting something—I jerked the zip down and then pulled it back again as the man straightened himself and lifted a laughing small child on to his shoulders. I relaxed but it wasn't easy because I was taking on some of Sadiq's concentration. I was there to keep an eye on him, to act fast if I spotted anyone in the crowd acting suspiciously, but I knew that as the game went on the crowd was becoming less and less important.

A scatter of applause, and the official's voice.

'Sadiq wins the seventh hole by one stroke.'

Three up. I put the putter back in the bag and headed for the eighth, telling myself that if anyone was going to shoot him, it would be on the eighteenth, where most of the cameras were.

Sadiq didn't stay three up. On the back nine he played well but Shroeder seemed to have hit one of those patches where it didn't seem to make very much difference how he hit the ball because it would somehow manage to end up in the right place anyway. He pushed one shot hopelessly into the woods but the ball hit a tree and bounced back on the fairway again. On the sixteenth he drove into a bunker but holed out for an unbelievable two. By the time they'd finished the first eighteen they were level-pegging at 271 strokes for the three rounds and the time was twelve-thirty and so far nobody had shot anybody.

The lunch break was scheduled for an hour and a half, and I eased the heavy bag off my shoulder gratefully. There was a lot of milling around, with the crowds coming off the stands and heading for the bars and refreshment tents, but there were enough police and stewards to keep them off the players.

'Look,' I said to Sadiq, 'just get inside the clubhouse and stay there till it's time for the final round. I'd feel happier if I knew you weren't walking about outside.'

He nodded. 'I'll do that. File my card, then keep out of the way.'

I guessed that now he could let up on the concentration, the other thing was beginning to get to him, and about time. There'd been a suggestion that I should have stuck with him at lunch too, but caddies don't go into the clubhouse and there wasn't any point in inviting comment. Linforth had detailed off some other keeper for the job, for all I knew dressed up as a bar steward.

I said, 'See you after lunch, then,' and pushed my way towards the caddies' quarters. Hawkins came out of the crowd, looking not quite himself in a very horsey check.

'See anything?'

'No.' There were several people in front of me showing

no inclination to move and, for some reason, staring at the sky. I glanced round and discovered that most of the crowd were doing the same thing. I said to Hawkins, 'What the hell are they all looking at?'

'The Red Devils, I imagine.' He must have caught some kind of blankness in my face because he added, 'The Army skydiving show, you know. Somebody said they're due to land on the practice ground.'

I looked up, too. Quite high up a bulky prop-driven aircraft droned above a patch of light cloud, and below it tiny dots were falling against the blue of the sky. They seemed to fall for ever and then suddenly patches of coloured silk blossomed above them and the parachutists began to form a pattern as they swung down towards their dropping ground.

I must have stared at the falling figures for a long time because Hawkins said, 'Anyone would think you'd never seen a parachute before.'

'Oh yes, I have.' The jumpers were out of sight now, dropping below the level of the marquees. There was a certain amount of applause, so presumably they must have landed on whatever it was they'd been aiming for. If I'd had any sense of gratitude I'd have given them a clap too, because now I knew what it was Selina had been hugging when the TV camera had come across her. No wonder it had looked big for a sleeping-bag. Come to that, it was no wonder she hadn't been exactly overjoyed at the prospect of being interviewed. What she'd been lying on hadn't been a sleeping-bag at all—it had been a rolled-up parachute.

'Listen,' I told Hawkins, 'I've got to get over to the Tonge woman's cottage. You'd better tell the CC.'

Hawkins blinked. 'Don't be a bloody fool, Angus—the golf starts again at two.'

'Well, get them to extend the lunch break or something.' But even as I spoke I knew that wasn't on, because if they cut down the playing time it would mean some of the late starters would still be out there by the time it got dark.

A thought struck me. 'Is there anyone looking after the cottage?'

'Permanent surveillance *this* week?' Hawkins looked hurt. 'Haven't got the men, and there's not much point now, in any case. The girl's hardly going to be such a fool as to go back there, is she?'

'No,' I said, 'I suppose not.'

Wind stirred the canvas behind us and the sun vanished behind the rising bank of cloud. Magnificently on cue, it suddenly began to rain.

CHAPTER 16

If a player plays out of turn, no penalty shall be incurred and the ball shall be played as it lies.

Rule 10–2

Most of us regulate our lives by hunches, however much we may kid ourselves that our decisions are made on balanced judgement. Or maybe hunches are the result of some kind of subconscious assessment that one doesn't even know what is going on, but as I headed the car towards Langham I hadn't any doubts as to just why and how I'd gone wrong. No wonder, I thought, that kids had been seeing things drifting about the night sky. So maybe it had been a coincidence that the UFO fraternity had been expecting little green men at the same time as the KFP had dropped its hit man by parachute, but as the flying saucer boys were always expecting something pretty exciting to happen, the coincidences weren't exactly freakish. He'd come down in the dark and where there should only have been his fellow party member, Selina de Cruz, to welcome him, there had been a middle-aged agronomist rabbiting on about visitors from outer space. Small wonder whoever it was had broken Fletcher's neck and dumped him in a bunker before going to ground himself at Rose Cottage.

Yes? No? It seemed to hold water, but I wished the killer had tried to hide the body, which would have been the obvious and instinctive thing to do. Just leaving it in the open to be found and written off as accidental was rather more intelligent than I liked.

I drove my rented Anglia in at Rose Cottage and went up to the front door, half expecting to find Delphine behind it somewhere, even though we were holding her for questioning. I wondered for how long. With that accent it seemed likely there were a couple of well-heeled parents in the background, and even with a daughter like Delphine there might still be an urge to call in the family solicitor on her behalf. Still, that was Hawkins's problem, not mine.

As a matter of form I rang the bell and was suitably relieved when nobody answered. As there seemed no point in drawing attention to myself at the front door, I walked round the blackened remains of the barn towards the kitchen. I was pleased to see that someone had taken poor April's freezer away and I felt rather more light-hearted as I repeated my breaking-in trick and let myself in by way of the back door. It was all very quiet. A quick look round the downstairs rooms yielded nothing of interest, but I wished I'd brought the hand gun just the same.

I called out, 'Is there anyone in?'

It wasn't as daft as it sounds because I'd already made a fair amount of noise and I didn't particularly want to advertise myself as a policeman. Nobody answered and nobody took a shot at me, so I went upstairs. One bedroom was large and bright and rather frilly, with—of all things—a small fourposter bed. April's. One of the others was rather a mess, which I put down as Delphine's, and another that was less of a mess but had an indefinable alien air about it, which I imagined must be Selina's. A fourth bedroom looked like something out of an East End squat, from the unmade bed to the odd bits of furniture that had apparently been kicked out of the way from time to time. There was a certain amount of uneaten food around, a half-empty bottle of Coke, a pair of men's socks. I had a closer look at the food, and judged the sandwich to have been made of cheese, which might or might not have meant something. A fundamentalist Muslim would not be allowed alcohol or any meat that had not been ritually slaughtered, so a soft drink and cheese would fit. Which appeared to be the lot, because the cupboard proved to be empty, and there was nothing under the bed. Against the wall was some crumpled brown wrapping paper and on the bedside table some pieces of cardboard and what could have been bits of string. I looked again and put them in my pocket, feeling suddenly faintly sick.

Why in God's name hadn't we been able to spare a bloody constable? I went downstairs at the run, looking for the phone. It was in the kitchen, one of those wall affairs and not much good because someone had dragged the wires out and smashed the handset into the bargain. Beside it, on the stainless steel draining-board my eye caught something white. I picked it up and saw it was the card I'd given Delphine so she'd have my number if she needed me. How had it got there? *When* had it got there? It wasn't difficult to imagine how, because obviously the girl had been around. Which meant either that someone had decided there were no grounds for holding her or that some solicitor had been making his presence felt. The latter, probably.

I stared unseeingly out of the kitchen window, trying to picture exactly what had happened. From the evidence it seemed that Delphine had been trying to get me on the phone and someone had caught her at it, the someone presumably being the unknown parachutist or Selina. It seemed unlikely that Delphine would have stood a cat in hell's chance with a KFP strong-arm man, and as there weren't any signs of her splattered over the walls, that came back to Ms de Cruz. Presumably without a gun.

Where would Delphine have gone, supposing she had managed to get away, I asked myself? And all at once my eyes focused on the mile-distant copse that hid Staples Cross. She'd tried to ring me until somebody stopped her, so probably she'd never discovered that I wasn't at home. But I'd told her how to get to my flat, hadn't I? Suddenly I knew beyond any doubt what had happened. Delphine had headed for Staples Cross and the dubious safety of my home.

I went back to the car. It seemed to be getting darker every minute and the rain was bouncing off the bonnet, which struck me as the one good thing that had happened to the day. Golfers get used to playing in bad weather and there's a general reluctance to halt proceedings simply because the players are getting wet. On the other hand, really hard rain stops everything dead because the greens simply can't drain it away in time, and with any luck that was what was going to happen this afternoon. I turned the car round and, disregarding the streaming roads, drove flat out for Staples Cross.

She was there all right. I saw her as I swung into the drive, a lumpy figure in a sodden floral print standing helplessly in the entrance with the air of someone who had found nobody at home and didn't know what to do next. I suppose she didn't recognize the car, because she was staring at it in a kind of helplessly terrified way like a hare trapped in the headlights until I got out and went over to her.

'I thought I'd never find you,' she said. Her plain, spotty face crumpled up and she began to cry. I put my arms round her and took her indoors, just in case someone might see her. She really wasn't very self-sufficient and April Tonge would have had a fit, but it does everyone good to be a father figure now and again.

'You'd better have a drink,' I said. Delphine nodded and sniffed. Tears made her even more unattractive than she had been before and I was glad of the chance to leave her momentarily uncomforted. It was dark and close in the flat and I opened a window on to the balcony and for a moment watched the rain coming down. Already there was a bright line of light on the horizon, enough to suggest that it was going to clear quite soon, but I could guess what the torrential downpour was doing to the course.

I went into the kitchen and poured the girl a stiffish brandy, catching a glimpse of my reflection in the glass-fronted cupboard as I did so. I'd forgotten I was wearing my photogenic caddie clothes—no wonder Delphine had wondered who was coming for her. I gave her the drink and suggested she sit down, but she wouldn't, although she swallowed the brandy and it seemed to steady her.

I said, 'What happened?' I didn't ask her how she came to be out of custody because it didn't seem important.

She looked at me helplessly. 'How was I to know?' she asked me. 'I mean, nobody *told* me.'

'Told you what, Delphine?' I tried to sound reassuring and she was so pathetic that it wasn't all that hard.

'About the man. That horrible man.'

'The one who came down in a parachute?'

She looked blank. 'Did he? I didn't know that. They said he was a freedom fighter and his name was Fred.'

'It doesn't sound a very likely name,' I said. 'Did he look like a Fred?'

Delphine shook her head. 'No, Selina said he was her cousin from Kariba but I don't think that was true either. Selina's beautiful and—well—Fred was ever so ugly. Besides, if he'd really been Selina's cousin, they'd both have spoken whatever it is they speak out there, wouldn't they?'

'Yes,' I said, 'I'm sure they would. And didn't they?'

'No. They spoke English.'

Well, it made sense. The two bits of cardboard and plastic I'd found on Fred's bedside table had been bubble packs for four torch batteries, scattered around them the clipped-off snippets of insulated wire. It wasn't the kind of thing a rifleman needs, but just the kind of thing for a bomb, even though—from what I'd heard of the place—it wasn't one where sophisticated explosives men came two a penny. That meant the KFP would have had to hire someone knowledgeable from outside, and since Alan Thurston seemed to be just about the only non-Kariban who actually spoke their Godforsaken language, Fred and Selina would have had no alternative but to use something common to both of them. Like English.

I said, 'It's all right, Delphine, you've got nothing to worry about. Just tell me what you overheard.'

'They killed Miss Tonge.' Delphine's eyes filled with tears again. Perhaps she'd been fond of April, I thought. Perhaps she just cried easily. She said it again, in a kind of strangled whisper as though she still couldn't believe it. 'They—they actually *killed* her!'

'Yes,' I said, 'I know. Did they happen to say why?'

Delphine nodded again. 'I heard them from the room next door. They said that if people found that another green had been chopped up and that April had disappeared, they'd take it for granted that she'd done it.'

'But why did they want to dig up the green, anyway?' I asked her. 'I don't imagine Fred's very worried about women's rights, is he?'

Delphine said seriously, 'Oh no, I don't suppose so. But they had to dig the green up, because that's where they buried the bomb.'

I stared at her. The rain was pouring off the balcony in a steady stream because the gutter was blocked with an old bird's nest that for months I'd been telling myself I ought to clear out, but the worst of the storm was over and the kitchen was beginning to fill with an odd yellow light as the first of the sun fought its way through. Rather as though it belonged to someone else, I heard my own voice saying, 'You mean the groundsmen actually covered the bomb up when they patched the green?'

'Yes,' Delphine said. 'And when the Kariban player stands on it, Fred's going to set the bomb off by radio.'

Dear God, I thought, and it would work, too. I tried to imagine Bill Sadiq holing his last putt with the TV cameras sending the picture out to god knows how much of the world. I could see the ball dropping in the cup and Sadiq taking it out and holding it up in the instant before the centre of the green blew apart. Well, it would certainly make one hell of a picture.

'Listen, Delphine,' I said. 'Where's Fred now?'

'I don't know.' She shook her head as though resigned to her own dimness. 'I meant to find out. I *tried* to find out, only I'm an awful fool and I let the cat out of the bag and Selina—I—knew she meant to kill me. I tried to telephone you but she pulled the wires out, so I hit her with something, a milk bottle I think it was—and ran.'

'Just as well,' I said. 'It probably saved your life.'

'Please,' Delphine whispered, 'please—'

But I never did find out what it was she wanted to ask me, because at that moment a crossbow dart sang through the open window and buried itself in her chest. It must have hit her with the force of a heavy bullet because in the moment before I caught her, she rocked back on her heels. She stared at me in that curiously bewildered way that one sees with the desperately injured, and then she coughed and bright blood splashed down the front of her rain-sodden dress.

I should have left her then, because there was nothing I could do and I could have used the time. With hindsight I knew it was then that I should have made a rush for Delphine's attacker, because loading and cocking even a modern crossbow is a longish business. But then, how does one develop reflexes for coping with that sort of thing? I eased the girl down on the floor with some idea of making her comfortable, but of course it was a waste of time because by the time I got her there she was already dead.

Poor silly little bitch, I thought. I don't know why her death moved me so much, except perhaps the futility of it and the fact that the absurd creature had died before she'd grown up enough to know what it was all about. I suppose Delphine dying like that wasn't any more tragic than God knows how many girls of her age killing themselves with drugs, but this was personal, and as I straightened up I realized I was murderously angry. Whoever was behind the crossbow must have been having a spot of bother with the draw because I could hardly have made a better target as I stood over Delphine's body looking for some kind of weapon.

As it happened, I didn't have all that far to look, because my big war bow was still propped up by my desk where I'd been carving the upper nock. I don't remember stringing the thing, but I know as I went through the door and out on to the balcony I was holding it before me with an arrow notched. Once on the balcony there were only two ways to look, and I chose the wrong one. There was nobody to my right and, in the time it took me to swing my head and body to the left, Selina had got her bow cocked and was swinging it up smoothly and swiftly like a farmer with his twelve-bore when a rabbit jumps out of the hedgerow.

Once loaded, a crossbow should be a quicker weapon for snapshooting than the six-foot stick because the power is all there, wound up, just waiting for a finger on the trigger. Had I been physically capable of drawing back the arrowhead fully, it must inevitably have given Selina the time she needed. As it was, my damaged arm restricted me to a half draw and half the time.

The gut twanged like a harpstring.

Fully drawn, an English war bow could drive an arrow through plate armour at a hundred paces. Mine was only half drawn, but then the target was no more than ten yards away and Selina was not wearing armour. The clothyard shaft hit her high up in the left shoulder, went right through and pinned her like a specimen butterfly against the nine-by-nine oak post that supported the balcony roof. She dropped the crossbow and stared at me like a cornered animal. And it wasn't until then that I realized for the first time that she was wearing a nurse's uniform. With so many black girls working at the local hospital, she could hardly have chosen a better way of making herself inconspicuous. No wonder we hadn't managed to pick her up.

I turned and went back indoors and phoned the station and told them to send someone round to pick her up. There was no way the girl could move because I knew that the arrow would be embedded up to the barb in the wood. I didn't even look at her. The rain had stopped, so I ran back to the car and drove back to the West Wessex. All I had to do now was to think of a way of stopping radio waves from exploding a bomb at the end of the final round.

Chief Constables are an unpredictable lot, pulled presumably this way and that at the whim of crime prevention and political expediency, so that one was never sure why ours said anything at any given time. Now he said, 'Do you suppose this bomb story is true?'

So presumably if some woman had come up to him in a crowded airport and said that someone had left a parcel under a seat in the restaurant and it was ticking, he'd have said, 'Madam, are you absolutely certain it's a bomb?'

'Yes,' I said, 'I'm pretty sure.' He still seemed to be waiting, so I went on. 'I don't see why that wretched girl should have made it up. And besides, it's more dramatic. If the KFP want to make a thing out of what happens to a backsliding Western Kariban, blowing him up at the moment of triumph takes some beating. Particularly if you've got world TV coverage to go with it.'

Linforth looked at me with the usual distaste he reserved for anyone who didn't agree with him. Usually it was something he tried to veil but I suspected that since my translation to caddie, he felt he didn't have to try so hard. 'So what would you suggest?'

'Scrub using the eighteenth green.' The solution seemed so obvious that I was surprised he'd presented it to me on a plate. 'If there really is a bomb buried under it, it's pretty obvious that nobody can move the damn thing, so let's just steer clear of it.'

'And finish the tournament a hole short?'

I shrugged my shoulders. 'Not necessarily—let them start again at the first. After all, it's only what they'd do if there was a play-off.'

'I wish we could.' Linforth dropped his part as the worried ass and reverted to being a worried policeman. 'But it's not on, Angus. I've been on to the Home Office just before you arrived and they're adamant that there's to be no change made. Apparently the present lot in Kariba have got wind of this and made representation to HMG that any obvious deviation from the programme would be tantamount to a propaganda victory for the Fundamentalists. The Home Secretary's made it clear off the record that there's a pretty massive contract in the air for rebuilding the Kariban railway system, and while that's up for grabs no mere policemen are going to be allowed to upset the apple cart.'

I said, 'But that's bloody criminal! It's not just going to

be one Kariban golfer who's going to be blown up—Don Shroeder will buy it for a start.'

'Probably the caddies, too.'

I wasn't deeply enough into my role as a caddie to have thought of that before, but given the hint, I caught on quickly enough. I considered whether I could risk telling the Chief Constable to simply ignore his orders and switch the final green, because with any luck the whole thing would be over and done with by the time the Home Secretary found out. Fine, except that it would cost Linforth his job and whatever it was he'd got lined up on the Honours List to coincide with his retirement. 'A man with a gun has got to be within sight of his target,' I told him, 'but presumably a simple radio transmitter could be anywhere. For all we know, our man could be sitting over a beer and sandwich, ten miles away.'

Linforth shook his head. 'We've checked that out and the radio people say it'll have to be a close range job—probably not much more than a hundred. Something to do with not having an aerial and being underground.' He added, 'They say the transmitter could be very small.'

'We know the man's a Kariban. So let's bloody search every black chap on the ground. There can't be that many,' I said.

For a moment the CC looked genuinely upset. 'Christ, man, are you blind? There are *hundreds* of blacks here today, all come to see their man win.'

'Sorry,' I apologized, 'but I haven't had much of a chance to look at the crowds. Do you want me to turn in this caddie lark and just—mingle?'

Linforth shook his head. 'No—the Home Office have told the Karibans their man has a high ranking police officer as a permanent guard, and you're it. In the meantime the HO have sent some of the local radio experts from that research place up the road. They're tucked away in a tent doing their best to jam his signal.'

I said, 'You'd better make sure it doesn't interfere with the TV transmissions or you'll risk offending them, too.' Bill Sadiq had come out of the clubhouse and was looking

214

like a man who was wondering where his caddie was, so I picked up his clubs and headed for the first tee.

'You all right, man?' Sadiq seemed obsessed with my welfare and somehow managed to give the impression that his own safety simply wasn't involved. Maybe his people had the right idea—from what I'd heard about his country, they couldn't afford to let people like him just play golf. If I'd had any say he'd have been prime minister at least.

I said, 'I'm all right, but do me a favour and keep on the fairway, will you? I don't think this is a day for going for walks in woods.'

He grinned amiably. 'Straight down the middle, man. No problem.'

Don Shroeder was there ready and waiting at the tee.

Here we went again.

The last round of the Tamworth, seen from a caddie's eye view, should have been stored in memory as something with which to bore one's grandchildren but somehow it didn't work out like that. It is difficult to caddie a player and do one's best to keep a watchful eye on everyone around him at the same time, even more difficult as the holes go by and you wonder exactly what may be waiting for you on the very last hole of all. I could remember that it was an extraordinarily close game, with rarely more than a stroke in it, with the advantage shifting from Kariba to Australia, then back again. The eighteenth arrived with the match, incredibly, all square after seventy-one holes.

The eighteenth at the West Wessex is a longish par 4, 472 yards of narrowish fairway between thick belts of trees, so that when you come out into the chipping area of the green, it's like finding the daylight again at the end of a long tunnel. The wise or cautious take a long iron, because it's the kind of hole that demands a straight drive rather than a long one. Don Shroeder had the honour and, as he certainly wasn't cautious, he took a driver and slammed the ball three hundred yards mathematically dead centre in the middle of the mown grass.

215

Sadiq said, 'That was one hell of a shot.' He wasn't saying it for the microphones, he meant it. I held the bag out to him and just for once found myself forgetting bombs and praying that he wasn't going to risk it. Sadiq hit a frighteningly long ball but his drives could get a little wayward now and again. He caught my eye, shrugged his shoulders and took out his own driver, teed up and swung apparently without even lining himself up with the ball. He pushed it a fraction but nothing to cause trouble and it landed five feet behind the Australian's ball and a little to the right.

We tramped up and it seemed a long way. Ahead of us we could see the white front of the clubhouse and the blurred mass of the crowds packing the stands. A hundred and seventy-five yards to go. Sadiq took a 7 iron and hooked it and I winced. As a shot it wasn't dramatically awful, flying a hundred yards or so before suddenly curving left and vanishing into the trees. From where we stood, it was impossible to tell about the lie. Shroeder lifted his ball to what looked like the foot of the green.

There should have been a girl waiting to mark the ball when Bill Sadiq and I came to the point of the wood where it had disappeared, but apparently it wasn't going to be as easy as that, because the undergrowth was pretty thick and the usual small crowd of spectators who like to look for balls weren't getting anywhere.

Bill took out a sand iron and we joined in and got looking, too. You're allowed only five minutes in which to find a lost ball and it was too late for Bill to start collecting penalty strokes now. I grabbed a wedge and prodded hopefully, trusting that this wasn't going to be one of the occasions that proved my personal maxim that in a match you either find a ball right away or you never find it at all. As it happened, I almost tripped over the thing within about thirty seconds, lying in a blessedly clear patch of pine needles.

'Here!' I said.

I looked up, and for a split second I thought I was looking at Bill. But no, it wasn't, because Bill was standing a couple of paces to the left of this character. Male, black, dressed in a loose grey cotton jacket and blue jeans. We looked at each other. His face had none of Bill Sadiq's latent good humour, because it seemed curiously immobile and inhuman. But that didn't make him Fred. The odds were that he was just one of the hundreds of Bill's supporters come for a day out, and from what I could see, he hardly seemed bristling with electronic equipment. He relaxed suddenly and stepped back a pace.

'Look out!' He jumped. I jumped, but it was only a girl bending down at the man's feet. She straightened, holding out something. She laughed and said, 'You nearly trod on your cassette-player.'

He looked down at the thing. It could have been a cassette-player. It was black, plastic, with knobs. It could have been anything. The man, in laboured English, 'Not mine.'

I watched the girl frown in puzzlement. 'Oh, but it is! I saw you holding it just now!'

With a quick movement he sent her sprawling. *'Not mine!'*

Fred.

His hand was in his jacket pocket and the black butt of a pistol half out before I realized that the golf bag I'd carried all that day was leaning against a tree well out of reach, with my own gun inside it. I hadn't a hope in hell of reaching it and unzipping the pocket before Fred started blowing me apart, and the wedge I was holding was no weapon against a man twenty feet away. With a kind of visual slow motion I saw the gun start to come clear of the pocket that had snagged it and then my eyes dropped and I saw a white blob at my feet that was Bill's ball. I made a grab for the shaft of the wedge with my left hand and chopped down at the ball with every ounce of strength of which my wrists were capable.

My short game had always been my best and, for a hurried chip shot, it was nothing to be ashamed of. The ball must have come off the club face at something approaching a hundred miles an hour and I heard its flight zip like a bullet. Had it been an absolutely perfect shot, I suppose it would have hit Fred in the middle of his forehead and he'd have dropped like a Goliath zapped by David's stone. As it was, all I achieved was a very near miss that just about parted Fred's hair and he ducked damn nearly to his knees. He didn't get up again because he was still crouching for dear life when Bill Sadiq's sand iron whirred in a chrome arc and caught him with appalling force just behind his right ear.

'And was there really a bomb?' Laurie asked.

It was nice of her to phone. I stretched my legs and eased the shoulder that was still aching from carrying fourteen clubs all day. It was damn good to sit down. 'Yes,' I told her. 'There was a bomb all right. The Bomb Squad dug it up after everyone had gone home. They said it would have made quite a bang. Anyone on the green would have been blown to bits.'

'Your stock must be high.'

'I suppose so,' I said. I wasn't intentionally playing it down, it was just that anyone who makes politicians happy must have gone badly adrift somewhere. I tried to enlarge. 'I'm glad Bill Sadiq didn't get the chop, but in a way I'm sorry the whole nasty business will be kept under wraps just so that, diplomatically, all can be sweetness and light.'

'You must be growing out of being a policeman. Tell me what happened to Fred.'

I said, 'Fred is in hospital and I'm not surprised. God knows what they'll do about him. I know he killed Keith Fletcher but the Foreign Office has got its teeth into that one, so my guess is that they'll quietly deport him.' Privately I didn't think it would do Fred much good, because as a known KFP activist, he'd almost certainly be due for the chop as soon as he landed.

'And that ghastly girl?'

'Selina? Oh, I don't imagine we'll be prepared to deport

her. Crossbows are becoming something of a public menace, so it's time an example was made of someone.' I tried to sound more confident than I felt.

'What about you?' Laurie was asking.

'What do you mean, "what about me"?'

Her voice said impatiently, 'Don't be a fool, Angus, you can't have forgotten someone hit you on the head! Who was it that night in Fletcher's flat?'

'That,' I said, 'was a strictly unofficial exercise so the clout on the head had better be unofficial, too.'

'I don't care whether it was unofficial or not, but who *was* it?'

'Well,' I told her, 'you saw a blue Metro outside the flat, as I remember. And I noticed a blue Metro in Alan Thurston's garage when I visited his house. He had the incentive and he was incredibly jumpy next day. It's all wildly circumstantial, so I'm just going to forget the whole thing.'

There was a pause and a rattle of rain on the window, which should have made me feel comfortably secure in my own lair, with the electric fire warming my feet and a whisky at my side. Tonight, for some reason, it didn't. Tonight the telephone seemed a poor substitute for real people. Person.

I said, 'Are you still there?'

The piece of plastic against my ear said yes, she was. 'You never told me who won the game.'

I hadn't, either. I said, 'Nobody. The Committee decided to scrap the last hole, so as Sadiq and Shroeder were level at the seventeenth there's to be a play-off tomorrow. Sudden death, starting at noon.'

'Sudden death means they simply go on playing till one of them loses a hole, doesn't it?'

'It does.' It was a lousy arrangement that had resulted in more than one title being won by a lucky fluke. I said, 'They ought by rights to play at least a whole extra round, but the TV people need a quick result.'

'I like quick results too.'

The rain seemed to have stopped as quickly as it had begun, which was just as well. I watched a last drop crawl down the windowpane and join a little puddle on the wooden sill.

'Well,' I said, 'you'd better come down and have a look.'